You're the Duke That I Want

She was a good girl, innocent and trusting.

He was a bad, dangerous rake. The kind of man that a girl like her should run from, should hide from.

Their lips touched, just a brush, the softest caress. He held still, steeling himself for what he must do. Pull away, leave her in the garden.

And then she kissed him. He should have expected her to do something impulsive. Of course she dove into this kiss, wanting to rebel against her mother's control.

She kissed him passionately, crushingly, and very, very inexpertly. He couldn't allow her to go away thinking that this was all there was to kissing, this mashing together of lips that she seemed so very intent upon.

He shifted his head back a little and wound his hand around her neck, taking control of the kiss. He was a bad, dangerous rake.

This was what he did best.

Chapter One

Splashing about in the sea is for fish, not respectable young ladies.
   —Mrs. Oliver's Rules for Young Ladies

I wish you wouldn't go out today. I have a dreadful feeling that something bad will happen if you do."

"I'll be quite safe, Mama." Sandrine Oliver adjusted the cushions behind her mother's back and gave her a reassuring smile. "I'm only going to the bookshop and then to gather some lavender for your soothing compress."

Her mother suffered from various unspecified and undiagnosed nervous ailments and rarely left their cottage except to attend church.

"The bookshop!" She pronounced the words as though Sandrine had announced she planned to visit the backroom of the Squalton Squire where the village men gathered to smoke, drink, and gamble. "Pray do not climb any of those ladders. Dangerous death traps! You'll go crashing into a crumpled heap on the floor and suffer an agonizing demise. Or be crippled for life."

"I shan't climb the ladders."

"Are your bonnet strings tied securely? Bend down, my dear, and let me see."

Sandrine bent forward and her mother undid and retied her silk bonnet strings. "There, that's secure now. I wouldn't want your strings to come untied and be caught in a carriage wheel and have you dragged to your death."

"I shall endeavor to avoid a tragic death by bonnet-string strangulation," Sandrine promised, attempting to maintain a serious expression.

Mrs. Oliver clicked her tongue. "Are you making light of my motherly concern? Reverend Pilkington wouldn't approve."

The subject of what the town vicar approved and disapproved of was dear to her mother's heart and made Sandrine want to scream. "Of course not, Mama."

"Speaking of Mr. Pilkington, if you should happen to meet that most eligible of gentlemen on your perambulation you must smile prettily and be civil and make complimentary references to his address last Sunday." Her mother was determined that her daughter would marry the vicar. Which also made Sandrine want to scream.

"I'll be sure to smile," she replied brightly. *Right before I cross the street and hurry in the opposite direction.* She was fervently hoping to avoid Mr. Ernest Pilkington and his admonishing lectures on the perils and punishments awaiting young ladies who strayed from the straight and narrow path of righteousness.

She heard more than enough about that from her mother.

Her mother's life was ruled by fear. Every day, every hour, every minute contained the potential for calamity. Sandrine had been raised on harrowing tales of young girls who were seduced by handsome strangers and led into a life of degradation and destitution. Or stories about good, honest country-bred men who contracted unspeakable diseases while visiting that most vile and immoral of cities, London.

"And don't walk too close to the sea on your way home. Remember the sudden wave that swept poor Miss Milburn to her death."

How could she forget? She was reminded almost daily of the accident that had happened a decade before she was born. Her mother had a horror of sea bathing, and Sandrine was the only girl in the village who wasn't allowed to go for a swim on a calm and sunny day such as today.

"I won't venture too close to the water."

"And keep your pelisse buttoned tightly, even if the sun grows hot. And keep your eyes modestly upon the ground if you should be approached by any man other than Mr. Pilkington. And heaven forbid you should speak with a stranger! A glimpse of unprotected throat, or an innocent smile, can transform a man into a ravening beast."

"I shan't invite any bestial ravishment," Sandrine promised solemnly. "I should leave now. I want to see if the history book that I ordered has arrived. I'll be back in an hour," she called over her shoulder, making a hasty retreat before any more dire warnings could be issued.

As she left their little cottage and walked down the stone steps toward the village square, she pondered the necessity of her mother's warnings. In Sandrine's twenty years of life experience nothing shocking, or even particularly noteworthy, had ever happened in the sleepy village of Squalton-on-Sea.

She'd been keeping a list of unpredictable and thrilling occurrences in a journal since she was a small girl. The list was laughably short.

There'd been the one journey she'd taken to Brighton with her father before his death where she'd marveled at the magnificent Royal Pavilion built by the Prince of Wales as a discreet location in which to entertain his scandalous companion, Maria Fitzherbert.

And there'd been the time that the schoolmaster had accidentally set the schoolhouse on fire attempting to demonstrate a chemical reaction.

But lately the only entries were about an escaped bull overturning a vegetable cart (unpredictable but hardly thrilling) and the harrowing tale of Mrs. Harbottle's cook attempting to retrieve a haunch of beef from cold storage only to have it fall upon her head, which everyone agreed could have proven fatal but which luckily resulted in only a small bruise and a faint ringing in her ears.

Not the stuff of which extraordinary adventures were made.

Though, there wasn't much chance of anything too thrilling happening in a town called Squalton-on-Sea. The name Brighton called to mind sunshine sparkling on blue waters, while Squalton reminded one of squalls of wind, or a baby squalling, or squalor, none of which was likely to attract fashionable seaside revelers.

But worse than the unfortunate name were the abandoned and empty buildings. She looked back at the once grandiose and now decrepit Squalton Manor, its mullioned windows dark and sightless, chimneys crumbling, and doors choked by vines.

It was as though the neglected manor house on a steep promontory overlooking the sea set the tone for the entire village. No matter how tidy people kept their homes, or how freshly painted, no matter how many colorful flowers they planted in window boxes, there was a general air of dereliction and neglect.

As secretary of the Squalton Historical Preservation and Improvement Society, Sandrine had penned countless petitions and letters to the owner of the manor, the Duke of Rydell, pleading with him to lease or bestow the manor to the historical society for renovation and use as a museum, attraction for travelers, and venue for charitable events.

She longed to see the vines trimmed and the windows sparkle. She pictured elegant assembly rooms that could be used for charitable-fundraising events. Perhaps a small tea shop serving baked goods that would also sell copies of the pamphlet she was drafting: an entertaining account of Squalton Manor's long and interesting history.

Visitors would flock to Squalton. Her museum pamphlet would be so popular that people would beg her to write an actual history of the house . . .

Take your head out of the clouds, her mother always said. *No more silly flights of fancy that will never come to pass.* The current Duke of Rydell, like generations of his ancestors, always turned a deaf ear, preferring to allow the manor house to molder in perpetuation of some long-forgotten grudge against the original owner of the property, the first Earl of Amberly, Sandrine's distant relation on her father's side.

The little bell mounted over the bookshop door rang merrily to announce her arrival. To Sandrine, the sound of that bell was one of the happiest noises in all the world. Books were one of her only escapes from her mother's carefully regulated version of her life.

"It's arrived, Miss Oliver," said Mr. Dunlop, handing her a handsome, crimson book. *"Memoirs of the Court of Queen Elizabeth*, by Miss Lucy Aikin, still crisp from the presses."

Sandrine hugged the book to her chest. "Thank you, thank you, Mr. Dunlop! I shall begin reading it immediately."

"I've never seen anyone so excited about historical tomes. It does my old heart good."

"And this one is doubly intriguing because it's by a female historian and biographer about the most illustrious of female sovereigns. It promises to be a domestic history of Queen Elizabeth's reign. I'm hoping some light will be shed on why the queen decided to gift Squalton Manor to the Earl of Amberly."

"For your pamphlet about the history of the manor house."

"Exactly. I want to have every detail perfectly correct."

"I very much look forward to reading and distributing your historical pamphlet, Miss Oliver."

She left the shop, walking along the promenade and down onto the beach, reading the introduction of the book and dreaming about life in Queen Elizabeth's court. She'd stay out in the fresh air with her new book for as long as possible before climbing the steep hillside to collect lavender from the manor's herb gardens, which had gone wild and unkempt from disuse.

The moments away from her mother's control were precious and few. Sandrine knew her mother loved her, but sometimes she felt like a fish trapped in a net of maternal anxiety, flopping this way and that and only succeeding in tightening her snare.

She followed the progress of a distant ship, tossed on the waves, dancing gaily, sails filled with wind.

She didn't want to marry Mr. Pilkington and be swallowed by the butter churn of village life, pounded into the kind of proper young lady that was pleasing to her mother and to the vicar.

She yearned for more. One or two interesting occurrences pertaining directly to her, to record in her journal.

Just one small adventure beyond the predictable story her mother had already written for her life.

Mr. Pilkington was considered pleasing by the other village ladies, being tall with a somber, long face, elegant hands, and a willowy figure. The vicarage was a handsome one, with an ample living, and she knew she could hope for no better.

She'd been raised to believe that, as a girl with no fortune, her purpose in life was to marry as well as was possible. Her mother was fast friends with Mr. Pilkington, and they shared the same beliefs, which meant that marrying him would double the lectures she received. Her mother would live with them at the vicarage, and the two of them would rule her life.

Sandrine didn't want to marry him. She didn't love him, and he didn't love her, but everyone expected him to propose any day now, and she was a dutiful daughter who'd never crossed her mother in any way, never broken any rules.

She would take comfort in the thought that she wanted a large family, and she would find joy in raising her children with kindness and love, sending them off into the world as stout branches of a flourishing family tree.

But was that enough? To walk the predictable path. To never have a glimpse of life outside of Squalton. To marry the man her mother chose for her.

She was never allowed to walk around the promontory because once she rounded the bend she would be out of sight of both the village and her mother's cottage. She half turned to walk back on the familiar path but then her feet continued walking.

It's up to me to do something out of the ordinary.

The thought seized her mind and kept her feet moving around the promontory and into a beautiful, sheltered cove. It had been used by smugglers in times past, and some said there were shipwrecks with buried treasures nearby.

The sun sparkled and danced over the waves. She selected a smooth round pebble and flung it into the sea where it skipped once and fell. What was it like to float in the sea? To be weightless, to feel the sun on your face and be supported by the gently lapping waves?

She scraped a line in the wet sand with a sharp piece of driftwood. This was the line her mother had drawn, the strict boundary she must never cross. Sandrine never disobeyed her mother's rules. What would happen if she did?

What would happen if she dipped her toes into the water? It would only be a small, harmless act of disobedience, a safe little detour from the approved path.

With the toe of her boot, she scuffed at the edge of the line she'd drawn. She was completely shielded from view. Her mother would never have to know.

Her heart pounding, she set her book and herb basket down a safe distance from the sea and began unbuttoning her pelisse. Then she unlaced her boots and removed them. Next, she unfastened her garters and slid her stockings down, folding them carefully and placing a rock on top of them to ensure they came to no harm.

She hiked up her skirts and tucked them into her sash, staring down at the line still etched into the sand. Did she dare? She took a quick, sharp breath, leaped over the line, and ran toward the water.

Cold seawater swirled around her ankles. No thunderbolts from on high arrived to smite her.

How she longed to float for a few seconds, as she'd seen other young ladies do, their bathing costumes filling with water and belling out around them. She'd heard them giggling and exclaiming about how wonderful it felt and how healthful it was for one's constitution.

She ventured ankle-deep into the water. Mud squished between her toes, and the occasional sharp rock impeded her progress. A mad idea gripped her. Why shouldn't she go out far enough to lift her feet and float for a few seconds? There was no one to see, no one to report back to her mother. No current to speak of in this sheltered cove.

If she kept walking . . . but she'd ruin her gown. Get seaweed in her hair. Her mother would discover what she'd done and chastise her most heartily.

It wasn't like Sandrine was planning to flout her mother's rules in any consequential way. She was still the dutiful daughter, devoted to caring for her mother, likely marrying the man her mother chose for her, and living the rest of her life in this sleepy little village.

It was only a small rebellion, and if she left her gown on the beach and dried her hair and chemise in the hot August sun, her mother need never know. She wouldn't go far. She'd still feel the bottom beneath her toes.

Her feet carried her to shore, and she was unbuttoning her gown before she had time to compose objections. And then she was in the water up to her calves . . . her thighs . . . wading deeper until she let herself go. Allowed herself to float. Toes level with her head. Wisps of happy clouds above, and blue-green water cradling her body.

Bobbing about in the bracing water with the sun on her face and gulls wheeling overhead. Weightless and giddy with forbidden freedom.

Delicious, unpredictable freedom.

DANE WAS PARCHED from riding his horse for hours in the hot sun. He needed a dark room and a cold pint. He scratched between the ears of his new stallion, Gladiator. "You're thirsty too, aren't you?"

Gladiator whinnied a response, which was clearly a demand for a dark stall and a pail of cold water. As he led him by the bridle through the bumpy cobblestone streets, gathering stares from the good townsfolk and frightening small children, Dane noticed that Squalton-on-Sea was hardly a prosperous seaside resort. Most of the shops were shuttered, and the ones that weren't displayed more dust than merchandise.

He hadn't inherited much when his father, the Duke of Rydell, died a year earlier. When the will had been read, he'd learned the surprising news that he'd been bequeathed the titles to several properties in Squalton that an ancestor had won in a game of cards from his foe, the Earl of Amberly.

Dane's much older brother, Roman, had inherited the title, the fortune, a vast number of properties, and all the tiresome and weighty responsibilities of the dukedom.

He was welcome to all of it.

Dane preferred to be wild and free. As the spare, he could be.

He and his disreputable friends had founded the Thunderbolt Club, a group of youngbloods who ruled the London demimonde and excelled at riding fast horses, racing jaunty carriages, and making beautiful women swoon. None of which came cheap.

Roman, a humorless and moralizing man with a cruel streak, kept a tight hold on the family purse strings. *You'll only squander it. Your very birth was a mistake. You killed our mother by being born. You caused father to grow bitter and angry. You'll never do anything but make mistakes.*

Dane was here to see whether there was some profit to be had by selling the unentailed Squalton properties to the highest bidder.

He stopped in front of the Squalton Squire, the lease of which he now held.

The building had seen better days. The wooden sign hung at a precarious angle, the whitewashed walls were coated with soot, and the roof was missing half its tiles. Still, one would hope the ale on tap would be decent, and that was all that mattered. Dale was only here for a quick pint before viewing the highlight of his inheritance, Squalton Manor, and returning to Brighton, where he'd left his carriage.

When Gladiator was settled in a stall and munching contentedly on sweet meadow hay, Dane found the taproom and approached the bar.

"Charming village you have here," he remarked to the barkeep after his pint was poured.

The man grunted. "If you say so."

"Charming, ha!" an older man with worn and patched trousers said. "It's a village that time forgot. Nothing round here but dead dreams and dross."

"More like the village the duke forgot," said another grizzled fellow.

"Dukes. Greedy, rotten scoundrels, the lot of 'em," said the first man. "Bloody blasted Duke of Rydell."

All the men in the place raised their mugs, as if this were a prearranged signal.

"Bloody blasted Duke of Rydell. May 'e damn well rot in 'ell," they all chanted in unison, lifting their mugs and glowering at a portrait hung behind the bar, which, upon closer inspection, was identical to one of the portraits hanging in the gallery at Rydell House in London.

Dane shifted lower in his seat, hoping they didn't notice the resemblance between him and the portrait. He was getting the distinct feeling that he, and all his kin, weren't very welcome here.

"What's the Duke of Rydell done to you?" he

had to ask. Probably should have kept his mouth shut, but he'd never been much good at that.

"It's not what 'e's done, it's what 'e hasn't. Left this town to rot. Don't care if the manor house falls into a pile of rubble, nor if there's rain dripping into our ale." The man with the patched pants glanced up at the ceiling through which daylight could be seen. "He's too high-and-mighty to give a damn about the likes of us."

Sounded like his father hadn't been the most solicitous of landlords.

"Poor, sweet Miss Oliver," said the barkeep. "Always writing 'im letters, and 'e never replies. The pretty little thing thinks she can melt a duke's cold, cold heart, but of course, 'e don't care about her precious historical society and all that muck about preservation and enrichment she's always going on about."

"I can't say as I understand her historical lectures, though I do love to watch her talk," said a younger man with work-roughened hands and a wind-chapped nose.

"Aye," agreed the barkeep. "She's lovely, she is. She could sell sand at the beach, and we'd all line up to buy it."

Good thing he wasn't staying overnight. If no one found out he was brother to the Duke of Rydell, and their new landlord, he might escape being chased out of town by a mob of pitchfork-wielding villagers.

The groom from the stables approached him at the bar. "Sir, I'm sorry to tell you, but your horse needs to be reshod. There's a stone lodged between the shoe and the frog."

"I didn't notice any limp."

"Just happened, most like. But he's limping now, and he'll be lame if you don't attend to it."

"Fetch a new shoe, then. I'll do it myself."

"We don't have any extra."

"You've a farrier in this town?"

"Aye. Big Harold is both smithy and farrier."

"And can he make me a new shoe?"

"Oh, aye."

"In the next few hours?"

The barkeep doubled over with laughter, slapping his hand on his thigh as if this was the funniest thing he'd ever heard.

"'Ere, Big Harold," the barkeep shouted when he was able to talk, "can you make this fellow a new horseshoe within the hour?"

A huge giant of a man who'd been snoring with his head resting on his elbows grunted and raised his head. "Wassat?"

"This fine gentleman wants a horseshoe."

The farrier rose unsteadily, propping himself up by one enormous hand on the table. "I'm not feeling well," he announced and lurched from the room.

"Don't think you'll be getting that shoe within the hour, my fine fellow." The barkeep smirked. "Maybe tomorrow."

Splendid. Stuck in Squalton overnight. "Is there a hotel around here?"

That made the barkeep laugh even harder. "A

hotel?" He wiped his eyes with his apron. "This ain't bleedin' Brighton. I let a few rooms upstairs. You can have one for the night. What's your name, then?"

Lord Dane Walker, second in line to the dukedom of Rydell and leaseholder of this grubby, ill-favored public house. That would go over swimmingly.

He tossed a few coins onto the bar. "Danny . . . Smith." He couldn't admit to being the bloody Duke of Rydell's brother, also known as the town villain. He'd be made to answer for his sins, even if those sins were not of his making.

The sight of the coins made the barkeep stand up straighter. "Right, then, Mr. Smith. We'll sober up old Harold under the pump, and you'll have your horseshoe by tomorrow morning."

Dane threw his traveling bag into a wretched little room under the eaves, inspected Gladiator's injured hoof and gave him some soothing ointment, and set off to view Squalton Manor.

One hour later, he understood why his disapproving father had bequeathed him the Squalton properties. It hadn't been a gift, it had been a curse. The manor house was a rambling, derelict eyesore that any buyer would have to tear down completely. No quick profit to be made here. Though, the view from the manor house was stunning.

He shaded his eyes with his hat brim and looked out across the bright blue sea. The house sat on a cliff overlooking a small, sheltered cove. He started down the overgrown wooden stairs to the sea, thinking to have a closer look at the boundaries of the property. He was halfway down when he saw something yellow and pink out in the water. An escaped parasol bobbing about on the waves?

Not a parasol. A girl. Knocked back and forth by a sudden wave. Flailing her arms about in distress. She was going to drown.

He raced down the rest of the stairs two at a time, flung his hat to the sand, and ripped off his coat. "Hold fast, miss. I'll save you!"

Chapter Two

The voice was low-pitched and male, bellowing something about saving her. Sandrine paddled her hands and kicked her feet until she was facing shore.

"I'm quite all right," she called to the man on the shore. "Please go away," she added, conscious that she was clad only in her shift—her bonnet, gown, and boots a heap of white and blue on the sparkling sand. So far away.

Her mother was going to murder her. She'd been caught swimming in the sea by a stranger. A tall, well-built stranger. She couldn't see his features clearly, but he looked young. And maybe he was . . . handsome?

Sandrine was absolutely forbidden from speaking to strange men. But this one appeared to believe that she needed rescuing.

He performed an awkward dance to divest himself of his boots and loped toward the sea.

"I'll save you!" he shouted again, crashing into the water.

"I don't need saving, my feet reach the bottom," she shouted back. "See?" She righted herself, walking toward him, but he paid her no heed, diving into the waves and heading straight toward her.

Goodness! The huge dark shape of him bore down upon her. Did he mean to run her right over? She scrambled about, attempting to flee the impending collision. She reached a deeper spot, and suddenly her feet had nowhere to land.

A wave splashed over her head and she sputtered, flailing her arms a little, only because she was surprised, not because she was drowning. She was nearly back to the shallower part when he was upon her in a great churning of powerful arms and a rearing of broad shoulders.

He clasped hold of her waist with one strong arm, his face looming in front of her. She could only see parts of him through the wet hair plastered to her brow and cheeks. An angular jaw. A deep cleft in the middle of his chin. Dark eyebrows over deep blue eyes.

"I've got you now, don't panic. We'll be on shore in no time," he said in a husky growl.

"I wasn't panicking at all until you—" she attempted to explain, but her words turned into gurgles as he hauled her through the water by her waist where she bobbed up and down, tucked under his arm like a piece of driftwood. She struggled to free herself but only succeeded in swallowing more seawater, which made her cough, only adding credence to his misguided belief that he was rescuing a helpless, drowning damsel.

There was no reasoning with or stopping him. Rescue her he would. She was obliged to twist out from under his arm and clamp her legs around his waist like a limpet clinging to a rock so that her head remained above water. She was finally able to draw enough breath to speak.

"I wasn't drowning," she sputtered, the erratic motion of his striding jostling her tighter against his hard body.

"Stay calm," he instructed. "We're nearly there."

He half dragged, half carried her up the beach and deposited her beside the heap of her clothing, dripping water onto her book.

He was breathing heavily, his chest heaving, the sodden fabric of his dark-colored shirt clinging to his wide chest and muscular shoulders. She could see the outlines of his body through his wet clothing. His leather riding breeches were plastered to his thick, powerful thighs, and the visible bulge between.

He loomed over her, blocking out the sun.

The sight made her feel light-headed. Or maybe it was all the seawater she'd swallowed.

And if she could see his every outline . . . she glanced down. Her shift was transparent. He could see *everything*.

She heard her mother's voice ringing in her mind. *Keep your gaze modestly lowered and your ankles crossed.* But really, was there any point in attempting modesty when one was already so thoroughly exposed? Everything about this encounter was completely forbidden. She squeezed her eyes shut, trembling a little from the breeze on her wet flesh, but mostly because of the handsome stranger still looming over her.

He dropped to his knees and wiped hair out of her eyes. "Don't die on me now." His fingers closed around her wrist, feeling for a pulse. "You're shaking, poor thing," he muttered. He rubbed her hands with his, blowing on them with hot breath. "We'll have you warm in no time. The sun is high." Gently, he rolled her over until she lay on her back. She kept her eyes squeezed shut. His fingers hovered over her mouth, his thumb brushing her lower lip.

"Still breathing," he said hoarsely. "That's a good sign."

She peeped at him from under her lashes, watching for signs that he'd been transformed into a ravening beast at the sight of her exposed flesh.

He appeared genuinely concerned about her welfare. Although, she did notice his gaze lingering on her bosom for a brief, heart-pounding moment.

He really was undeniably good-looking. Sandrine noted this while keeping her eyes mostly closed and lying still. She was attempting to catch her breath and make some sense of what had just happened. She also needed to formulate a plan whereby she obtained his solemn promise never to mention any of this to her mother.

The longer she lay still, the more agitated he became. Which was rather satisfying, given the distress he'd so recently caused her.

"You'll catch a cold," he muttered. He left for

a moment and then was back with his coat. He
lifted her by the shoulders, wrapping his coat
about her and cradling her against his chest.
"Wake up, miss."

There was a lovely scent about his jawline despite his seawater dunking, as though he'd shaved
with expensive soap scented with manly things
like cedarwood and leather. She fit perfectly
against his wide chest, enclosed in the safety of
his strong arms.

Her breathing quieted as he stroked her back
and wrapped her in warmth. His lips had a sensual fullness about them and on closer inspection the cleft in the center of his chin was a deep
dimple.

Could it be that she was the one undergoing the
beastly transformation? She did feel an unprec-
edented stirring in her bosom. Her mother was
always warning her about the danger of carnal
cravings. Perhaps this was what she meant. She
had the strangest urge to pull his head down to
her level and kiss those finely sculpted lips.

He reached around her, wrestling something
out of his coat pocket with one hand. Something cold and hard pressed against her lips,
opening them.

Molten fire burned down her throat, and her
eyes flew open as she sat up and wiped her lips.
"What was that?"

"Brandy." He screwed the lid back onto a silver flask. "Works wonders for reviving fainting
young ladies. Though, I did notice you peeping
at me from under your lashes."

"I wasn't! And I'm forbidden by my mother to taste strong spirits. Oh dear, I'm breaking so many of her rules today." The taste of it lingered on her tongue, heavy and spiced with forbidden vice.

She'd never tasted strong spirits. Or dipped so much as a toe into the sea. Never allowed her feet to leave the earth and her arms to spread wide in a cradle of water. Never worn a wet shift in front of a man. Or been clasped in a man's embrace, or felt his thumb brush her lips.

His eyes were a clear blue, and dark wet hair curled over his brow. She'd have to remember every detail. How he'd held her so solicitously. How, when he laughed at her, his lips quirked to one side and his eyes sparked with devilry.

She was up to at least six unpredictable and thrilling occurrences by now—and she'd broken so many of her mother's rules that she'd lost count.

"I should leave. We can't be seen together."

"Stay a moment and dry yourself in the sun. There's no one about. We're quite sheltered."

She twisted her hair and squeezed it until seawater dripped onto the sand. "My mother is going to be livid when I come home wet and bedraggled. 'Splashing about in the ocean is for fish, not respectable young ladies,' she always says to me. And if she knew that a man had witnessed me bathing, she would surely faint dead away. She can never, ever know about any of this."

"You were drowning, and I did the only chivalrous—"

"I wasn't drowning."

"You were in distress."

"I wasn't. I was delightfully bobbing about in complete control of everything before you descended upon me and half drowned me dragging me to shore."

"What was I supposed to think? Young ladies don't go swimming unchaperoned and without a bathing machine in which to change into their costume. At least none of my acquaintance do."

"I can assure you I don't make a habit of it! This was my first—and last—foray into the sea."

"What made you decide to bathe today?"

"I was driven to an act of disobedience by an impending marriage proposal from Mr. Pilkington, the village vicar."

He frowned. "You were attempting to drown yourself to escape marriage?"

"No, no, nothing of the sort. I only wanted . . . well, it seems silly now. I wanted to do something out of the ordinary."

"So this was an act of rebellion."

"And I was promptly punished."

"It's not so terrible to have been rescued by me." His teasing smile did something odd to her heart.

"Once again, I didn't need rescuing." She fluffed her wet hair over her shoulders in the hopes that it would dry in the sun.

"Use my coat as a towel to dry yourself."

"If you'll turn around, Mr. . . . ?"

"Smith. Of course." He helped her rise, and then he turned away, staring out to sea as she

used the fine black cotton of his coat to dry herself and take some of the water from her hair. She
noticed that it was a very well-cut coat with the
name of a London tailor stitched inside.

She drew a sharp, shuddering breath. Could
Mr. Smith be one of the remorseless and wicked
London rakes her mother was always warning
her about?

"Where have you come from, Mr. Smith?"

"Brighton."

"And where did you grow up?"

"Oh, here and there. I was raised in the countryside, mostly."

She breathed a sigh of relief. A country-bred
man, then, not a London rake roaming the streets
in packs like wolves, searching for maidens to
defile.

Not that it would matter to her mother. A
stranger was a stranger.

She slid her dress over her head and fastened it,
taking care to wrap her shawl over her shoulders
so that her damp hair wouldn't get her dress wet.

"Thank you, Mr. Smith," she said when she
was restored to a semblance of order.

"Quite all right, Miss . . . ?"

"Sandrine Oliver."

Poor, sweet Miss Sandrine Oliver who thought
she could melt a duke's cold, cold heart.

Those blighters at the pub had been dead-
on about one thing: Miss Oliver was extremely
pretty, with a heart-shaped face and aquamarine
eyes the color of a sunlit sea. When her long hair

had been tangled and spilling over her shoulders, she'd looked like a bewitching sea nymph.

And then there'd been the sight of her wet, transparent shift clinging to the soft, swooping curves of her breasts, belly, and thighs.

If he were an honorable gentleman, he would have promptly turned away from the sight. But he was a depraved rake, and so he'd looked his fill at the undeniably arousing sight.

"You have some seaweed in your hair," he said gruffly, forcing himself to look only at her face and forget about the lush body he'd glimpsed.

If she knew who he was and what he'd inherited, she'd pester him with historical lectures and outrageous demands. And if she knew of his dreadful reputation . . .

Women in spectacles wrote pamphlets warning their sex about him and his ilk. Everywhere he went, daughters were pulled inside doorways, and other men gave him envious stares.

His curricle was custom-built in France, he bedded only the most coveted of courtesans, wore only the finest leather, raced carriages and horses with his rakehell friends in the Thunderbolt Club, and generally lived a thrill-seeking life of pleasure, the scandalous details of which would send Miss Oliver running back home to her overprotective mother.

"What brings you to Squalton, Mr. Smith?"

"Just passing through your town, Miss Oliver, on my way back to Brighton." He wasn't supposed to engage in conversation with the villagers. The less they knew about him and the quicker he left, the better. "There, you're quite restored. None shall be the wiser."

"Upon that point, Mr. Smith, if you should happen to encounter my mother, Mrs. Barbara Oliver, during your stay in our little village—not that you would, for she's a very reclusive and anxious sort of mother—but if you should encounter her, I beg of you not to mention anything about our meeting."

"I shall feign complete and utter ignorance of your acquaintance, Miss Oliver."

"Thank you. You can't know what a relief that is. My mother is very opinionated about what constitutes proper conduct, and chief among her rules is that I must never speak to strange men. Not that I normally have much chance of that."

"You don't have many visitors in Squalton?"

"We do not, though I hope to change that by petitioning the Duke of Rydell to lease or gift the town manor house to our historical society for use as a museum to attract visitors. The manor has a most fascinating history. I have just collected this book about the reign of Queen Elizabeth to better understand the role she played in gifting the manor to my distant ancestor, the Earl of Amberly. He lost the house to the Duke of Rydell in a game of cards. They were bitter enemies. The duke left the manor house to rack and ruin out of pure spite."

"Bloody blasted Duke of Rydell, may he damn well rot in hell."

"I beg your pardon?"

"And I yours." He bowed. "I was repeating something I overheard in the public house."

This just got better and better. Miss Oliver was related to the Earl of Amberly. Which made him her sworn enemy, historically speaking.

Miss Oliver glanced at the sky. "Gracious, it's getting late. I promised my mother I wouldn't be gone long. She'll have invented fifty horrifying outcomes for me by now."

"Then run along home, Miss Sandrine Oliver, whom I've never met before in my life."

The hint of a smile tugged at her lips. "I do hope you enjoy your brief visit to Squalton, Mr. Smith. And if you happen to return, bring your friends to enjoy the seashore and the beautiful sights."

She collected her book and rushed away, the wind catching her bonnet ribbons, rippling them behind her as though slender threads of blue sky followed wherever she went.

He could do more exploring around Squalton, but he was quite certain that he'd already beheld the most beautiful sight on offer.

The luscious Miss Sandrine Oliver in a wet, transparent shift.

Chapter Three

Be constantly on guard against the temptation to stray from the narrow path of righteousness.
—Mrs. Oliver's Rules for Young Ladies

Had Mr. Pilkington looked directly at her as he read the ninth commandment in sepulchral tones, long face stern, one elegant finger lifted?

Miss Oliver, thou shalt not bear false witness.

Sandrine squirmed in her seat, face hot and palms itching. This was the first secret she'd ever kept from her mother. How could she have told her the truth about why her gown was damp and bedraggled about the hem and her hair tangled when she arrived home yesterday? She'd been forced to tell a lie. She'd said that she'd been splashed by sea spray because she'd stumbled and fallen.

All night long she'd tossed and turned, thinking about Mr. Smith in his wet shirt and clinging breeches looming over her. Dropping to his knees to caress her. The brush of his thumb over her lips. Thinking about it gave her palpitations and tinglings and all manner of alarming symptoms.

When she'd finally drifted off to sleep, her dreams had been filled with him. And they hadn't been tethered to reality. In her dreams, he'd laid her down on the shore and lowered his body on top of hers to keep her warm. He'd been forced to kiss her to revive her. He'd had to rip off her chemise to warm her so she didn't catch a chill.

And then . . . and then he'd sprouted horns and cloven hooves, transforming into a hulking half beast, half man, and defiled her right there on the beach! Although her sleeping mind had been rather hazy on what, precisely, constituted defilement. It had involved lots of grunting, that much she remembered. And a most agreeable melting sensation in her most secret places.

Miss Oliver, thou shalt not imagine handsome strangers transforming into beasts and doing unspeakable things to you while you sit in church!

Her breath caught. Thank heavens. She'd only imagined Mr. Pilkington speaking those words. If he knew . . . if her mother knew . . . but they didn't know. And Mr. Smith had promised not to tell anyone. He was probably already gone.

What on earth had she been thinking? To remove her gown in daylight, to go so far out from the shore? Why, she could have been swept out to sea and lost forever. Perhaps, in a way, she had been. The sinfully attractive Mr. Smith with his teasing words and admiring gaze had obviously been thrown in her path to illustrate the storms and temptations of life that her mother was always going on about.

Mr. Pilkington's brow creased, and his Adam's apple bobbed up and down as he warmed to his topic. "I know some of you are thinking, 'It's only a little lie. And I told it for good reason.' But small lies beget larger ones. Small sins become bigger ones. The Great Deceiver knows our weaknesses. He tempts us when we are most vulnerable. He lures us down a crooked path that leads to immorality. One spark can ignite the conflagration that consumes the moral integrity of our soul."

Mr. Smith had been the spark that ignited the conflagration of carnal cravings.

She inhaled deeply and rubbed her temples with her fingers, which usually made her feel more centered.

"Stop fidgeting," her mother whispered without turning her head.

She mustn't betray the turbulence of her emotions. She'd most likely never see Mr. Smith again. But then, there was the possibility that he might decide to stay longer. What would she do, what would she say, if she encountered him again? Especially after the dream version of him had debased her in such a thoroughly debauched, yet undeniably delicious, manner?

Her mother turned and stared at her. "What is the matter with you?" she whispered.

Mr. Pilkington cleared his throat, and her mother snapped back to attention.

"And thus sayeth the scripture, *Enter ye in at the strait gate: for wide is the gate, and broad is the way, that leadeth to destruction . . .*"

Sandrine only made it through the rest of the service by counting the stitches on the hem of her handkerchief. Finally, they were released into the warm sun.

She searched the churchyard for any sight of Mr. Smith, but of course he'd said he was just passing through and could be already gone.

Why on earth was that prospect so thoroughly disappointing?

LATER THAT AFTERNOON Sandrine walked to the cottage of the widowed Mrs. McGovern and her companion Miss Dodie Hodwell to read to them as she did every Sunday. Her mother allowed such outings because reading to elderly parishioners was a charitable endeavor. She had no idea how much fun Sandrine had with the ladies, who kept her in stitches with their opinionated conversation.

As she entered through the garden gate, a deep male voice sounded from the open front door. She paused, listening intently. If Mr. Pilkington was paying them a visit, she'd have to miss today's reading. But it wasn't Mr. Pilkington's voice. A maid ushered her into the parlor where Mrs. McGovern was holding court in her usual elegant fashion, with upright posture, her hair dressed in elaborate curls, a double strand of pearls about her neck, and a fresh white carnation pinned to the bodice of her gray gown.

Miss Hodwell sat next to her eating almond macaroons and sipping tea, with her unruly white hair sticking out from under her lace cap and her lace hem unraveling. Were her slippers mismatched? Dear old thing.

The man speaking with them had his back turned, but as Sandrine entered the room she froze, tempted to run back the way she came.

It couldn't be. But it was.

Mr. Smith, balancing on a spindly white chair that looked far too dainty to support his tall, muscular frame.

"Miss Oliver, there you are! We've been waiting for you," cried Miss Hodwell.

"Miss Oliver comes to read to us every Sunday afternoon," Mrs. McGovern explained. "Mr. Smith, allow me to introduce Miss Sandrine Oliver."

Mr. Smith rose and turned to face her. He was fully clothed, of course, but all Sandrine could see was a wet shirt clinging to a sculpted chest. The glimpse of dark hair disappearing into his trousers. His thumb brushing her lower lip and that trembling sensation deep within her.

"Miss Oliver," he said with a glint in his eyes that said he knew exactly what she was picturing. "Whom I have never met before and have only laid eyes on just this very moment."

Miss Hodwell quirked her head.

Sandrine willed herself not to blush, but telltale heat crept up her neck. "Mr. Smith, whom I have likewise never met. How do you do?"

He captured her hand and bowed over it, winking at her. "Such a pleasure to make your acquaintance."

Sandrine's pulse quickened. How could he destroy her composure so thoroughly with just one word? *Pleasure.* Yes, please and thank you.

The maid brought in another tea setting for Sandrine, gawking at Mr. Smith all the while. He was quite a sight. Dark hair gleaming, an almost too-handsome face, broad shoulders, narrow hips encased in tight buff-colored breeches, and shiny black leather riding boots.

Sandrine gulped her tea. "What brings you to our village, Mr. Smith?"

"I'm only passing through, Miss Oliver. Seeing the sights. Enjoying the seashore. Collecting shells and such. Sometimes the most astonishingly beautiful things wash up from the sea, do they not?" The words he spoke were innocent enough and addressed to all three ladies, but Sandrine knew they were aimed at her.

"Do you know, I was walking along the shore yesterday, and I could have sworn I saw a mermaid."

Miss Hodwell laughed. "Probably a piece of driftwood."

"Oh no, this was no driftwood. This was something shapely, curvaceous even, with hair streaming down around a heart-shaped face and—"

"You must have been out too long in the hot sun, Mr. Smith," Sandrine said curtly. He'd promised not to speak of their encounter.

"Perhaps. But I prefer to believe that mermaids are real. And this one quite stole my breath away."

"Mr. Smith is staying at the Squire while his horse is being reshod." Mrs. McGovern took a small, measured bite of a macaroon, while Miss Hodwell popped a whole one into her mouth.

"We've been extolling the healthful virtues of

life by the seashore and the beauties of Squalton," said Miss Hodwell, when she could speak
again.

THE BEAUTIES OF Squalton. Did Miss Oliver have
a sister? Dane didn't think his heart could stand
such a thing.

"I believe I have all the beauties of Squalton assembled in this parlor, Miss Hodwell."

"Scoundrel," she giggled, swatting the air with
sugar-coated fingers.

Today's Miss Oliver was a far cry from yesterday's. Every strand of hair was tucked into place,
every seed pearl buttoned on her gloves, lace
up to her throat. Wholesome and nourishing. A
bowl of healthful oatmeal with honey drizzled
over it. The very picture of propriety.

But he knew better. He knew that she had a rebellious streak that no amount of pearl buttons
and corset boning could contain. The way she'd
darted those shy glances at his chest and his
lips, and the wide eyes and rapid breathing that
had betrayed her approval of what she saw . . .
He'd thought of nothing else since.

"You have a most dashing air of mystery and,
dare I say, danger about you, Mr. Smith," said
Mrs. McGovern, a touch disapprovingly. "Do
tell us where you hail from and who your people are."

"Perhaps I prefer to leave it a mystery, Mrs. Mc-
Govern, since you find it so dashing."

"I thought you were . . . that is to say, when are
you leaving, Mr. Smith?" Miss Oliver asked.

"The village farrier must stay sober long enough to make me a new horseshoe. I'm at a loss as to what one does to pass the time here, Miss Oliver."

"You couldn't ask for a more excellent guide to our fair town than Miss Oliver. She's an expert on the town's storied history and secretary of the Squalton Historical Preservation and Improvement Society," Mrs. McGovern said proudly.

"Indeed." That would explain the historical lectures referred to by the men in the pub, who were all in love with her, for obvious reasons.

"We hope to one day convince the Duke of Rydell to give us Squalton Manor for use as a museum or other attraction for visitors," Mrs. McGovern continued.

"I viewed the manor yesterday, and it's in a dreadful state of disrepair. It should be demolished and something more modern erected in its place."

"Demolished!" Tea splashed over the edge of Miss Oliver's teacup. "You can't be serious, Mr. Smith. A building of such historical significance must never be destroyed. It must be lovingly renovated, its beauty and stories preserved for future generations to enjoy."

"Why don't you give Mr. Smith a tour of the manor, Miss Oliver?" asked Miss Hodwell. "You'll convince him far more easily that way."

"Do you have a key, Miss Oliver?" Surprising. The documents from his father's man of affairs had stated that the house was boarded up and uninhabitable and hadn't been opened in decades.

"I don't."

"Then, you broke in?"

"I did not."

"How mysterious."

"You're not the only one with secrets, Mr. Smith."

"Now I'm intrigued."

"Go on, then, Miss Oliver," urged Miss Hodwell. "You can read to us another day."

"I couldn't possibly," Miss Oliver demurred.

"I'd love to see the manor," Dane said.

Miss Oliver wavered, sensing danger, like the sunshiny, innocent thing she was. But Dane wasn't trying to get her alone in a dark house, though the thought was stimulating.

He hadn't expected the chance to enter the property without alerting anyone in town to his status as the new owner. This was a chance to view the condition of the interior with an eye to selling the property, and perhaps the furnishings and decorations, if they were in good repair.

"I'll go with you, dearie," said Miss Hodwell. "I haven't visited the manor in some time, and I shall enjoy the tour."

That decided it. With a suitable chaperone in place, the proper Miss Oliver agreed to give the tour. They all walked together toward the manor house, Miss Hodwell chattering the whole way about Miss Oliver's plans to restore the structure.

"This is the house where my mother and I live," Miss Oliver said, indicating a small stone cottage on a hill a short distance from the manor.

"Am I going to meet your mother?" Dane asked.

"Heavens, no!" Miss Oliver exclaimed, as if that would be the worst thing that could ever happen. "She'll be at the vicarage taking tea. We're only going into our garden." She led them up a flight of steep stone steps, through a wooden gate, and into a small but neatly arranged garden.

She stopped in front of the vine-covered back wall of her garden. "I discovered this secret entrance to the manor estate when I was a young girl," Miss Oliver said, brushing aside some of the ivy to reveal a circular wood door set into the wall.

"There's no clasp or knob," he observed.

"The door swivels inward when pressed in precisely the right location to release the spring mechanism." She demonstrated.

"Watch your head, Mr. Smith," she called.

He helped Miss Hodwell through the dark doorway, which opened into a walled kitchen garden, overgrown with weeds and ringing with birdsong.

"From this garden we can access the house through the servants' back entrance, which was never boarded up like the front of the manor."

Once inside, they walked through the kitchens and up the stairs to the main floor, their footfalls muted by dust, cobwebs hanging overhead.

The house was slightly more presentable inside, but he didn't see many objects of value. A suit of armor, some swords hanging over a fireplace.

"I don't know exactly when it was built," Miss Oliver said, "but I do know from the records that it was destroyed during the Norman Conquest of 1066 and rebuilt somewhere before 1085, when

King William I used it as a reward for service and gave it to a knight. I could give you a very detailed account of the history after that, as I've pored over every available record. Queen Elizabeth took possession of the manor and lands in 1567 and granted it to Sir Ralph Oliver, later Earl of Amberly."

"How are you related to the earl?" Dane asked.

"My father was distant cousin to the current earl. The Oliver family mostly left Sussex after the earl lost the manor to the Duke of Rydell in the late seventeen hundreds. My father's branch remained."

"Miss Oliver's father was a good man," said Miss Hodwell. "We all miss him."

They passed into a great hall, adorned with oil paintings and more ancient weaponry.

"The manor house once had fourteen bedchambers, five reception rooms, a ballroom, and several cottages on the grounds. Now the cottages are ruins, and one of the reception rooms has been taken over by a family of mice."

"So tragic." Miss Hodwell sniffed. "I don't understand why that hard-hearted Duke of Rydell persists in keeping it empty and ignores all of our petitions."

"Houses need love and care." Miss Oliver walked in a small circle, her arms outstretched, as if attempting to enfold the house in her embrace. "The manor doesn't know why the people stopped coming, the dancing ended, the children stopped laughing." She gave a small laugh. "I used to come here as a child and talk to the house as if it were a friend of mine. My mother didn't allow me to have actual friends, but she allowed me to come here and play in this empty house by myself."

He pictured young Miss Oliver running about the old manor house, skipping and singing and bringing laughter to the dark, dusty rooms.

"And I made friends here," Miss Oliver said, dropping her voice to a whisper. "The ghosts of two sisters who used to live here."

"I do wish you wouldn't speak of such things, Miss Oliver." Miss Hodwell shivered. "It gives me a chill feeling along my spine."

"But ghosts can be good for a house's reputation, Miss Hodwell," said Miss Oliver. "Preston Manor in Brighton has its Lady in White and her disembodied hands appearing on the bedposts. Squalton Manor has Captain Ephraim Oliver and his two daughters, Coraline and Lucidora. Captain Oliver was a very strict father who never deemed any suitors good enough for his daughters, and so they never married. I've read their diaries, and they were such bright, creative, accomplished young ladies."

"What happened to them?" Dane asked, pulled into the history of the manor by the passion sparking in Miss Oliver's eyes.

"They all perished in a fire, the damage from which you can view in the west wing. Coraline and Lucidora will feature prominently in my historical pamphlet because the tragic story of beautiful young sisters who died too young will attract visitors to the house."

"I'm afraid that the house is too far gone to become an attraction for visitors, Miss Oliver." He poked the edge of the fireplace mantel, and a huge chunk of tiles and plaster crumbled away, raising a cloud of dust.

"Don't do that!" Miss Oliver cried. "Lucidora is sure to be vexed if you destroy that mantelpiece."

Dane folded his arms. "Why are you speaking of her in the present tense as if she's standing next to me?"

Miss Hodwell shivered. "She's not standing there, is she?"

Miss Oliver bit her lower lip. "Er . . . no, of course not."

But Dane could see the truth of it. Miss Oliver believed that the two sisters still lived in the house, the only friends she'd been allowed to have as a child. She'd lived such a sheltered and restricted life. Squalton Manor was a connection with her ancestors, a living link with her past, a historical treasure trove.

To Dane, it was a fathomless pit that would burn through a fortune in renovation costs.

"This house is beyond repair, Miss Oliver. You'll have to resign yourself to the idea that it will be demolished and replaced with something more modern and serviceable at some point in the future."

"Replaced? Where would Lucidora's and Coraline's spirits dwell? Would you doom them to roam the seashore, moaning and frightening visitors away?"

"You just said they were imaginary."

"They were real women who lived and died in this house. Their legacy must be honored so that their deaths were not in vain. They must be remembered. I want to display their diaries for visitors to read."

"Perhaps you could have a display in the building in which your historical society meets."

"We only have temporary meeting rooms in the town hall. This is where we should be meeting. Squalton Manor cannot, and must not, be destroyed. It's a site of historical interest, and the house should be preserved, and the land used not for the benefit of one rich lord but for the edification and enrichment of all. My wish is to make the site a museum with a tea shop, where I will sell my historical pamphlet and donate all proceeds to the Squalton Benevolent Society."

"You'll save the manor with a pamphlet."

"I'll try," she said, her chin set at a determined angle. "I'll find more details about Lucidora and Coraline and include information about them. Everyone loves a safe thrill from ghostly apparitions. Captain Oliver will be sighted in the window with his spyglass, looking out to sea. And his two spinster daughters will enjoy having visitors to keep them company. We'll have portraits painted and hung in the gallery."

"I don't like this talk of hauntings," said Miss Hodwell. "Let's go back to my house and have more almond macaroons."

But Miss Oliver wasn't finished with her lecture yet. "Generations of Olivers have petitioned generations of Rydell nobility to return the manor house, but to no avail. I wish I could meet with the Duke of Rydell and tell him a few things."

"If the duke were here, what would you say to him?" he couldn't resist asking.

"I'd appeal to his better nature, if he has one. I'd spin him the sad tale of a village that lost its heart when Squalton Manor was shuttered. Townsfolk are out of work and down in the mouth because no visitors frequent their shops. I'd ask him to find it in his heart to heal the rift between our families with a magnanimous gesture of good-will and charity."

She clasped her hands together, her lovely face earnest and determined. "I hear the duke is a supporter of many charities in London, and I'd find a way to make him see that our cause here in Squalton-on-Sea is equally as worthy of his patronage and benevolence."

Some long unused chamber of Dane's cold, cold heart thawed a little during this impassioned speech. But no—all the passionate speeches in the world didn't change the fact that this was more a pile of rubble than a house worth saving.

Miss Hodwell clapped her hands. "Well said, Miss Oliver! Surely the feud between the dukes of Rydell and the earls of Amberly has fizzled into nothing by now. You should go to London and appeal to the duke in person. He couldn't fail to be inspired by your zeal and eloquence and moved to do the right and charitable thing."

Or he could do the expedient and profitable thing and sell this crumbling dust heap to the highest bidder to tear down and build something modern on this fine slice of seaside property.

Chapter Four

Keep your head out of the clouds, and never indulge in fanciful imaginings.
        —Mrs. Oliver's Rules for Young Ladies

Gladiator was freshly shod and eager to be on the road again. But Dane was still here after nearly a week. Why? He'd anticipated riding back to civilization as fast and furiously as Gladiator could gallop.

Yet here he remained.

Doing such uncharacteristic things as holding balls of yarn for elderly spinster knitters, listening to history lectures from learned young ladies, and even joining in with the grizzled gossips at the Squalton Squire.

Good-for-nothing bloody damned dukes, he'd cursed the other night while raising a pint to the portrait of his long-dead ancestor, which hung behind the bar, before throwing a knife dead between his eyes.

London seemed worlds away. Life here was simple and surprisingly idyllic. He woke with the sun streaming through the garret windows, and he fell asleep early because there was nothing to do late at night.

No Thunderbolt Club, gaming hells, horse

races, artists' salons, bawdy houses, or theaters. None of the decadent amusements with which he filled his nights in London.

He plunged into the sea whenever he felt like it, and the waves seemed to wash him cleaner than any bathwater had ever done.

Time was different here. Had it been a week, or a year? He wasn't drinking as much, and his dreams were clearer, more crystalline, filled with one subject over and over: Miss Sandrine Oliver.

Miss Oliver emerging from the sea wearing nothing more than clamshells strung together with twine. Miss Oliver taking him by the hand and giving him a tour of Squalton Manor that included each one of the fourteen bedchambers.

Giving Miss Oliver a ride in his new curricle. They sped down the road with the wind in their hair until one of the wheels came loose and they were forced to stay the night at a country inn. Where there was only one bed, naturally. They piled pillows in between them as a barrier. But then Miss Oliver climbed right over the flimsy wall of pillows and begged him to ravish her.

That was a good one.

And now he'd have a new dream to dream. Miss Oliver meeting him in Squalton Manor's secret garden to pick herbs, her white skirts tucked up to avoid brambles, a wicker basket over one arm. The fragrant smell of sun-warmed lavender and mint in the air as he helped her gather plants.

"How are you finding Squalton society?" she asked with a shy smile as she snapped rosemary stalks.

"Surprisingly charming."

Squalton didn't need bathing machines, assembly rooms, and souvenir shops—it had Sandrine. She was the inviting, joyful, inquisitive heart of this village. Everyone lit up when they saw her, everyone wanted to speak to her, to be the recipient of her smile or the messenger of some clever witticism that made her eyes shine.

He placed a handful of rosemary in her basket, his fingers brushing hers. "Have you never left?"

"Only one journey to Brighton with my father." Sorrow shadowed her face. "If he were still alive, I might have gone on other trips with him. My mother doesn't like to travel and won't allow me to leave Squalton. If she had her way, I would stay inside the house with her and never leave. I can't so much as cross a road without her proclaiming that I narrowly escaped being mowed down by a runaway carriage."

"I haven't met your mother, but it does sound like she issues far too many orders about how you should live your life."

"She's very anxious about matters concerning health and propriety. The day you met me I was flouting her rules by swimming. I want to feel the sun on my face, walk along the beach, listen to the gulls cry, match my breathing to the waves and . . ." a shy, little glance ". . . I want to make new friends."

"Ah, but I'm the unscrupulous rake your mother warned you about," he said, dropping his voice to a growl. "Aren't you afraid to be here alone with me, Miss Oliver?"

"For some mad reason I'm not." Her smile warmed some forgotten frozen corner of his heart. "I suppose I should be. My mother says that rakes have only one thing on their mind."

"She's right, you know." Torrid images from his dreams thundered across his mind. "I'm everything she ever warned you about."

"Are you? You strike me as honorable. We've been alone together on several occasions, and you haven't even attempted to kiss me, much less transformed into a ravening beast."

He snorted. "You have no idea the beastly paths I've traversed in my mind. And in my past."

"Really?" She looked more intrigued than repelled by his warning. "Tell me more about your past exploits."

"How about we finish picking these herbs and you go safely home to your strict mother."

"I've noticed you always change the subject when I ask you about your past. I think something bad happened to you, but I don't get the sense that you *are* bad. I see the kind way you treat Mrs. McGovern and Miss Hodwell. I trust you."

"You shouldn't trust me. I've lived a regrettable life."

"That doesn't mean you can't be more virtuous in future."

"I'm leaving Squalton very soon, you know. I should have been long gone. I've no idea why I'm still here."

Her teasing smile said she knew exactly why he was still here. "You're here because you love Miss Hodwell's macaroons. You can't leave before tasting more of those delicacies."

He couldn't leave before tasting Miss Oliver's sweet lips. That's what he really wanted. That's why he was still here. It was time to admit that, stop delaying, and leave immediately.

"And before you leave," she continued, "I'd like to show you Lucidora's and Coraline's diaries."

For a moment he was lost, and then he remembered those were the names of Squalton Manor's ghostly spinster sisters. "I'll read about them in your pamphlet," he muttered. He really should leave now. A clump of lavender came out of the soil, roots and all.

"You mustn't pull so forcefully," she chided.

He'd met enough ghosts in Squalton already. The ghost of his ancestor who'd decided to neglect the manor house and turn this beautiful woman against him. The ghost of who Dane could have been if he had been born under different circumstances—a simple, ordinary man who was free to love and build a life with this glowingly intelligent and gorgeous woman.

But he wasn't that man, and he never could be.

"There's one thing I've been meaning to say to you before I go, Miss Oliver."

"Oh?" Sunlight found gold in her hair, and her eyes were as cloudless as the summer sky.

"I honestly don't think you should be wandering about in the manor house. The condition of the structure is unstable. The floorboards could give way and send you plummeting into the cellar."

"Why, Mr. Smith, I never thought you'd sound like my mother."

"That house is a death trap."

"It's a sanctuary. *My* sanctuary. And Lucidora and Coraline are as real to me as any live persons. I made the mistake of expressing that opinion to Mr. Pilkington at dinner one evening, and he was aghast. He assured me that believing in ghosts is evil and sinister."

"Mr. Pilkington thinks drinking ale is evil and sinister. He ministered about it at the taproom yesterday. Not that anyone listened to him. You absolutely can't marry that sanctimonious man."

"I've no choice in the matter. My mother has my life all planned out for me. I'm to marry the vicar, though I don't love him and he doesn't love me. The only way I can resign myself to it is to picture a large brood of children running about this garden. I'd put them to work weeding between the rows, and soon we'd restore it to its former glory."

"You'd still be married to that sanctimonious blowhard."

Her laughter was tinged with sadness and a hint of desperation. "I know. That's the problem. He's stern and pious, but I'll have my family and my historical society and charities to manage. It will be a good, useful existence. Or at least that's what my mother assures me. Although I do wish she could marry him—they'd make such a perfect May December couple."

Dane chuckled. "Don't you have any relations in London? Mightn't you have a Season?"

"My mother was raised in London, and both her parents died there. She won't tell me the particulars, but I can only imagine it must have been something terrible because she believes London to be the most wicked, immoral, and dangerous city on earth. She won't allow me to so much as mention it without her flying into a fit of anxiety. You've been to London, and Brighton, and probably many other cities. You must find us hopelessly provincial here in Squalton."

"I find it quite charming."

"I do sometimes grow tired of the sameness, knowing what everyone will say and do, never anything new or exciting. That's why I read history books. They're filled with the noteworthy stuff of life. No one writes a history about everyday experiences or petty village gossip and squabbles, the silly feuds that everyone's forgotten the origins of."

She brushed her fingers through a clump of lavender, picking one of the stalks and waving it at Squalton Manor. "Like the feud between my ancestor and the Duke of Rydell that resulted in the Oliver family losing the manor house. I've scoured the history books and the house and asked everyone in town, but no one knows why the Duke of Rydell hated the earl enough to want to ruin him. There are several theories involving a lady of questionable virtue, a racehorse, or an insult hurled over a gaming table."

Sounded like activities an ancestor of his would

have engaged in. Dane stayed silent, afraid of saying something incriminating. Every day he remained meant more lies, more evasions. Every day he lied to her, the more she would resent him when she learned the truth.

"If the manor house had stayed in my family, I'm sure we would have tended it and cared for it and made it the glowing jewel of Squalton. The entire fate of this village rested on that feud. I wish I could travel back in history and prevent it from happening. I'd talk some sense into the both of them."

Dane could imagine her suddenly appearing at a gaming table to chastise his ancestor and hers, shaming and cajoling them into harmony with a sweet, earnest speech about the ghosts of their future.

"If you could travel back in time, where and when would you go, and what would you do?" she said.

He didn't have to even think about it. He'd wished for it so many times. "I'd go back to before I was born and inform my mother that my birth would kill her."

"You would prevent your own birth? How tragic."

"If it meant she could live a full and happy life."

"I don't like you preventing your own birth. Please pick something else."

"All right, then. I would travel back in time and attempt to prevent Napoleon from taking power so that he wouldn't start the war that claimed so many of my friends and maimed one of my best friends." His friend, Deckard Payne, Duke of Warburton, had returned from the war a changed man, with scars on the outside and even deeper wounds within.

"Preventing war and bloodshed would be an excellent use of traveling back in time. Just think of what we could do if we had the ability to travel through history. The people we could warn, the wars we could prevent. I'd like to save Anne Boleyn from having her head chopped off."

"I've visited the Tower of London to see where she was executed. They say they brought an expert swordsman from France for the occasion."

"How gruesome! Her death was so unnecessary. I've always wanted to visit the Tower where so many spine-chilling things occurred. I think it's because my mother is forever warning me about the dangers lurking around every corner, and I take a certain pleasure in reading about the times when she would have been proven right."

"My friends and I like to race our curricles. It's a dangerous pursuit."

"Why do you like it so much?"

"I live for those moments when the horses' hooves are flying and the world flashes by in a blur. Nothing else matters except riding hard, fast, and far. In those brief moments, I'm free."

"Then, you're a thrill-seeker, Mr. Smith?"

Flirtation in her voice and a sidelong glance from under long golden lashes.

"Always, Miss Oliver." Somehow, she made picking herbs as thrilling as any carriage race or gambling table. Talking with her, laughing with her, made him feel vividly alive, his body aware of even her smallest movements.

The ladies he knew would laugh at her, slight her, whisper about her work-roughened fingers, her outmoded gowns, the way she wore her hair in a simple twist at the nape of her neck. And yet she glowed with vitality, sweetness, and beauty in a way that would put any debutante glittering with diamonds to shame.

It had been a long time since a young woman had looked at him like that, with not only interest and admiration but with trust.

Don't trust me. I'm not who you think I am.

His life was as far from hers as any could be. The decadent life. The midnight life. Women's cheeks heated and flushed from wine, not sunshine. Jests and innuendo instead of innocent musings. An invitation in a fine, sparkling pair of eyes. *Follow me into the library. Press me up against the wall. Let's take our pleasure while we're young.*

But Sandrine wasn't a London lady eager for diversion. She was a country lady, a good girl. She went to church on Sunday, read novels to elderly ladies, raised funds for charities, and was being courted by the vicar.

She was completely forbidden for anything more than conversation.

They could gather herbs, walk along the beach, eat macaroons. He could admire her from a distance, but anything more would be cruel. He never toyed with the affection of innocents.

He could only hurt Miss Sandrine Oliver, because the only thing he'd ever be was bad. The world would have been a better place if he'd died instead of his mother. He didn't deserve the love of someone like Sandrine.

Dane couldn't control the actions of others, but he could control himself, and he'd decided that love wasn't worth the pain. He'd never lose his heart. Never marry. Never sire children. It was too great a risk to take.

"Your face has gone cloudy, Mr. Smith. What are you thinking about?"

"My family. Those that are left. My father died a year ago."

"I'm very sorry to hear it. Is that why you wear mourning garb?"

Mr. Smith stared broodingly at the garden wall. She'd noticed a darkness in him at times, an edge to his voice. He'd known suffering, she was sure of it. She laid a hand on his arm. "You don't have to tell me."

"It's not a secret. You already know that my mother died in childbirth." He spoke to the stone wall, not to her. She heard unshed tears in his voice, suppressed grief.

"My father and my much older brother never missed an opportunity to cast all the blame on me. They were angry with me for robbing the world of her smile, of her generous and kind heart."

Sandrine tilted her head, hoping he would meet her gaze. "You can't be blamed for that."

"Yet, it's true that my birth caused her death. They have the right to resent me. I wear these mourning colors to remind me of my dark origins. The light I stole from the world."

"Oh, Danny." She held his hand, threading her fingers through his. "You didn't do it on purpose."

"My brother has made it very clear that he will do everything in his power to sire sons so that there's no danger of a wastrel like me carrying on the family name. He has two girls already, but his wife is with child at the moment, and they're convinced that this one will be the male child he longs for. My brother's line will flourish, while I will never marry. I'm the blighted branch of our family tree. My line dies with me."

"Isn't that rather an extreme decision to make?"

"My brother's marriage was a society arrangement. I used to have foolish notions about falling in love, but I gave up all that nonsense long ago. Love means handing people the means to fatally wound you. I loved my older brother, and he used that devotion against me, time and time again. My friend, Deckard, left for war an engaged man, only to return and find that his fiancée had jilted him for his younger brother. He came home thinking that every scar, every sacrifice of war had been worth it to protect her. And then she married his brother and shattered his heart just as his body had been broken by combat."

"What a tragic tale." She was beginning to understand some of the desperation and pain she sensed under his teasing, confident exterior. This was the reason he raced curricles. He thought he didn't deserve to live. Maybe he even sought death.

She laid her head on his shoulder, wanting to be closer to him, to give him comfort.

It was very wrong to be here alone with him in the secret garden—her mother would be outraged if she knew—but Sandrine couldn't bring herself to feel guilty for following her heart and trusting this man. She'd only known him such a brief time, but she'd begun to believe that their chance encounter on the beach had been fated.

She'd been raised to be a good, obedient, faithful girl. And that meant marrying the pious Mr. Pilkington and living a safe, protected, ordinary existence.

Safe . . . and dull as mud.

Danny made life exciting and extraordinary. These sparks of attraction flaring along her skin where their hands met, the answering glow deep within her belly, the conflagration of joy in her heart: surely, he felt it too.

There was a connection between them, like the lavender that grew in both this garden and her own. Underground roots that touched, kissed, danced beneath the soil and sprang up in unexpected places, reaching for the sun.

She wanted to understand him more fully, to comfort him, and perhaps with time, make him see himself the way she saw him. It didn't matter what he'd done. He was here now.

He was *hers* now.

There were shadows in his eyes and on his soul, but if he allowed her to care for him, to love him, he would change, he would want to start a family with her, to grow ever closer through the years.

Perhaps . . . perhaps she wouldn't have to marry Mr. Pilkington after all.

Their hands entwined; their gazes locked. It was going to happen now. The moment she'd been longing for. He was going to kiss her.

She held her breath. Closed her eyes.

And nothing happened.

Disappointment tied a thick rope around her heart. She knew he wanted to kiss her. It was written plainly on his face, so why didn't he?

Perhaps he was promised to another. Perhaps he was already married. The devastating thought struck her heart like a stone sinking into the sea.

Silly, fanciful girl. Bring your head out of the clouds. What was she doing mooning about alone in a garden with a man she barely knew? She was only a small-village girl with big dreams. Maybe he saw her as something to pity. Like the manor house, lonely and unloved.

She pulled her hand away and rose, turning away from him. "I should finish gathering the herbs. My mother will be wondering where I am." She walked along the rows, blindly grabbing handfuls of lavender.

"Have I said or done something to offend you?" he asked, coming up behind her.

It's not what you did. It's what you haven't done.

"Ow!" She'd been walking so swiftly that she stumbled over a jagged rock and stubbed her toe. He steadied her with an arm around her waist.

"Did you twist your ankle?" He looked at her, brow furrowed, eyes clouded with concern.

She hadn't hurt herself, but the powerful grip

of his arm around her waist made her want to melt against him. She lifted her foot and leaned into him. "Not badly, but it does sting."

"Lean on me. We'll sit down for a moment."

His large, warm hand clasped hers, and his arm tightened around her waist as he helped her hobble to a stone bench. She sat down, and he knelt in front of her, lifting her foot and cradling it in his palms. He touched the top of her foot through the leather of her boots gently. "Does this hurt."

"Only a little."

He rotated her ankle. "How about this?"

"I think I'm all right." It wasn't pain making her breathing hitch and her heart pound. The intensity of his gaze, his palm sliding from her ankle to her calf. His fingers exploring beneath her gown. An insistent pulse beat in her neck, her wrists, her chest, and between her thighs.

She longed to be kissed, claimed, taken by him.

The sun was low in the sky, glowing with pink and persimmon. The lavender in the basket beside them scented the air.

The flutter of anticipation, the brightness of curiosity and attraction, flooded her mind. His hand glided higher, nearly to her thigh now.

Could this be the beginning of the most thrilling adventure of all?

They might kiss. Fall in love. Her life would never be ordinary again.

Chapter Five

What the devil was he doing?

Lips hovering close to hers. One hand up her skirts on her knee, the other resting on her trim ankle. Slide his hand up a few more inches and he'd be touching her garter. Her cheeks were rosy, and her full lips parted.

She was waiting for him to kiss her.

Dane wanted to devour her whole.

Scoop her up and lay her down on a bed of herbs. Cover her small body with his, wrap a hand around the back of her neck and feast upon her like a starving beast.

He couldn't kiss her. Wouldn't do it. But that didn't stop his imagination from running wild.

Slip his hand inside her bodice, cup her breast, and brush his thumb across her nipple until she moaned and arched her back.

Scents of lavender and rosemary in the air. His palms cradling that lushly rounded bum. Lifting her hips to meet him. Taking what she so freely offered.

Soft lips and sweet tongue tangling with his. Dip his head into the silk of her hair, kiss her neck, her shoulders. Tease her nipples with his tongue.

Make her come first with his tongue and then ride her to pleasure again. Lose himself in her.

Christ, you're a beast.

She's a good girl, innocent and trusting. If she wants you to kiss her, it's only because she thinks you're ordinary, honorable Mr. Smith.

He was a bad, dangerous rake. The kind of man that a girl like her should run from, should hide from.

She clasped her hands around his neck. "Kiss me, Danny," she whispered huskily.

Damn it all. Everything in him wanted to obey that command. Give her a first kiss and so much more.

The tip of her tongue darted out to moisten her lips. He couldn't help drifting nearer to those full, glistening lips. And she drifted closer at the same time.

Their lips touched, just a brush, the softest caress. He held still, steeling himself for what he must do. Pull away, leave her in the garden, leave Squalton.

And then she kissed him. He should have expected her to do something impulsive. After all, when he'd met her she'd been swimming in the sea all alone in nothing but her shift. Of course she dove into this kiss, wanting to rebel against her mother's control, wanting him to save her from that pious vicar.

She kissed him passionately, crushingly, and very, very inexpertly. He couldn't allow her to go away thinking that this was all there was to kissing, this mashing together of lips that she seemed so very intent upon.

He shifted his head back a little and wound his hand around her neck, taking control of the kiss. He was a bad, dangerous rake.

This was what he did best.

And this wasn't merely any embrace. He was kissing the luscious Miss Sandrine Oliver. He knew the shape of her breasts, the curves of her body. He'd been dreaming of her every night, fighting this longing. She tasted sweeter than sugar, and her skin smelled of lavender.

She melted against him and shifted her thighs, causing his hand to slide higher, dangerously close to where he was dying to explore. Careful, now. All he was doing was showing her a proper kiss. There would be no exploring beyond that.

As his lips teased hers, she crushed her soft breasts against his chest, and her thighs slipped open. Cock stiff and heart racing, he kept himself firmly under control, lifting his hand from her thigh and limiting their contact to lips only.

And tongue. Just the taste. Exploring the seam of her lips and slipping inside her mouth. She gasped, and her eyes flew open, but she didn't break the kiss. Oh no, not the newly brave Miss Oliver. She met his tongue with hers, and soon what had started as a soft, gentle kiss became deep and driving. Everything he gave, she demanded more. He could lose all his scruples in a kiss like this.

He could stay here and be Danny Smith forever.

Turn his back on the life he'd known. Give up the dissolute pleasures and replace them with worthier ones. Quit his friends, the Thunderbolt Club, the family that never made him feel welcome. Pretend to be someone else long enough that it became true.

Stay in Squalton and kiss Sandrine Oliver forever.

Impossible. He was here under false pretenses. She'd soon discover that he'd deceived her. He was going to sell her beloved manor house at the first decent offer, and she'd hate him for it.

All of this was wrong, so very wrong. He broke the kiss, gently removed her hands from his neck, and stumbled to his feet. "I must go, Miss Oliver. I shouldn't be here."

"What's the matter?"

Dane avoided the questions in her eyes, the confusion on her face. "I just remembered an appointment at the taproom."

"Then, I'll see you on Sunday?" An enticing smile. "You're meeting me at Mrs. McGovern's cottage, remember? We're going to have a promenade. And perhaps you'll even meet my mother."

He mumbled something about looking forward to it, handed her the basket of herbs he'd collected, and backed away. Even though he longed to stay and lay her down on the sun-warmed grass. Kiss her until she moaned his name.

His *real* name. He wanted her to say his name with gladness when he did something to make her smile. Breathe it huskily as he pleasured her.

But that was the heart of the problem.
She didn't even know his real name.

WHEN HE ARRIVED back at the Squalton Squire, he was greeted by his very large, very irate friend, Deckard, Duke of Warburton.

"There you are, you miscreant!" The deep scars webbing one side of his rugged face glowed purple in the afternoon sun. "You're damned difficult to find. First, I went to Brighton and they said you'd come here, but no one in this blasted village knows anything about a Lord Dane Walker. There's a Mr. Danny Smith rooming here, who sounds suspiciously like you. What the devil is going on here?"

"I'll explain, lower your voice, please."

"I'll bellow if I want to. I'm on an urgent mission to bring you back to London, and it's taking much longer than I anticipated."

"Come inside and have a pint with me. I'll explain everything."

"We don't have time for a pint." Warburton dragged him by the arm toward the stables. "Gladiator is saddled and ready to go."

"Why do we have to leave this minute?"

"Your brother has been gravely injured in a carriage accident. He's clinging to life. We may already be too late."

Spots danced before Dane's eyes. "That can't be true. Roman would never do something that stupid. I'm the one who'll die in a carriage accident, not him."

Warburton's steely gray gaze softened. "I'm sorry, Dane."

And that's when Dane knew it was true. There was nothing soft or emotional about Warburton. That pitying look in his eyes could only mean Roman really was at death's door. Warburton's iron grip on his arm was suddenly more of a support than an annoyance.

"Roman's really dying."

"He's been asking for you. Won't talk to anyone else. There's no time to waste. I already have your saddlebags packed."

"Can we make a stop on our way out of town? There's someone I must say goodbye to." He couldn't leave without making some explanation to Sandrine.

"Did you hear what I said? Your brother is asking for you, a dying man's last wish. We can't waste another second. Write her a letter, whoever she is," Warburton said impatiently, dragging Dane toward the stables. "We ride *now*."

Chapter Six

*A promise from a rake is as hollow and useless as
a well gone dry.*
> —Mrs. Oliver's Rules for Young Ladies

This thing—this misshapen, mute thing in the
bed—this wasn't his brother. His brother was
made of iron and barbed wire. His will was abso-
lute. His words cut to the quick. Dane had never
even considered the possibility of his brother being struck down at five and forty.

"Roman." He touched his brother's cold, limp
hand. "It's me. I heard you were asking for me."

His brother made no response beyond the rasp
of his shallow breathing.

There was no love lost between Dane and Roman. He was so much older and had always
treated Dane like a mistake, one that had cost
their mother her life. Roman had been convinced that this time his wife would produce
the heir that would secure his line.

"It won't be long now," said the family physi-
cian, a wizened man named Sneath. "He's lost
too much blood, and I fear he's bleeding inter-
nally as well." He cleared his throat. "The last
rites have already been given. I'll leave you alone
with him to say your goodbyes."

Dane didn't know what to say. Should he hold Roman's hand? His brother had always been cruel to him. He wouldn't want Dane's pity now. "Wake up, Roman," he said harshly.

Grief knifed Dane's heart, sudden and sharp. His brother was his adversary, but there'd been a time when Dane had worshipped him and would have done anything for his approval.

Now he'd do anything for another sneering lecture from his brother about Dane's exploits harming the family name and how he'd be cut off without a farthing if he didn't mend his wild ways.

"Wake up and curse me, you blighter!"

But Roman remained unconscious, wheezing, blood soaking the bandages wrapped around his torso.

Seeing him so helpless made Dane question everything. His brother was a bitter man, and his marriage was loveless, but at least he was doing something to better the world with his charitable concerns. Or was that Sandrine's voice in his head? Her soft voice had been with him the entire journey. That luscious kiss. What must she think of him for leaving so suddenly with no goodbye?

"Dane," Roman whispered, his eyelids fluttering.

Dane bent over. "Yes, yes, I'm here. What is it, Roman?"

"Dane . . . the charity ball . . . Piety . . ."

"Yes?"

His brother's eyes opened for one moment and then closed again, his head lolling to one side.

"You can't die, Roman." Dane gripped his brother's hand. "If you die and Piety has another girl, then I'll be the duke. You would never stand for that. Never. Doesn't that make you want to fight harder to live?"

"I'm having a boy." Piety entered the room, her hands wrapped over her large belly. She stopped beside the bed, and Dane rose.

"Piety." He inclined his head in greeting.

"You'll never be the duke." She was practically spitting, her hazel eyes lit by ire. "Roman hated you more than anything in this world."

He knew it was true, but to hear her say it still had the power to hurt him. "I don't wish him ill, Piety. I want him to live."

"You don't!" She pointed an accusing finger at him. "You want to be the duke so that you can squander the fortune on carriages and courtesans. You would cast me and my children out in the streets if you had your way."

"That's not true. How can you think that?" But he knew the answer already. Roman had poisoned her mind against Dane just as he'd influenced their father to hate him. "I swear to you, Piety, that you have nothing to fear from me."

"I don't want you here. He wouldn't want you here."

"He was asking for me. He said something about the charity ball, and he said your name."

"He spoke to you?" She flung herself down,

laying her head on his chest. "Roman, speak to me, not your brother." He made no response. "It wasn't like you to drive recklessly, Roman. Lord Dane is the reckless one."

She didn't have to say the words. They echoed throughout the room.

You should be the one to die in a carriage accident instead of Roman.

"You're a vulture, hovering over his bed wanting him to die."

"That's not true, Piety," Dane said forcefully. "I want Roman to live as much as you do. And I want your child to be male. Trust me, I don't want to be the damned duke."

Dr. Sneath reentered the room. "Your grace." He bowed to the duchess. "My lord. Let me examine him."

Dane attempted to help Piety rise, but she pushed his hand away.

The doctor bent over Roman, listening for his breathing, then felt his wrist for a pulse. "He's gone," he said solemnly, laying his hand over Roman's eyes.

"No," Piety wailed. "He can't die without telling me who's to blame and what to do."

"Who's to blame for what?" Dane asked.

"Nothing," she snapped. "Please leave me alone with him. Go to your club and drown yourself in brandy, for all I care."

"Good-bye, Roman," Dane whispered, a weight descending on his chest. Dane was now the heir presumptive. He was suddenly bone-weary from the journey and filled with grief. "I'll go to my apartments and have a rest. I'll be back in the morning, Piety."

"And I won't receive you," she said, head held high.

"SOMETHING'S DIFFERENT ABOUT you today, Sandrine," said Mrs. McGovern. "You have an air of satisfaction, like a cat who just caught a field mouse."

Sandrine smiled. It had been two days since Danny had kissed her, and her body and mind still hummed with the newness and thrill of those heated moments. Her head was firmly in the clouds, dreaming of all the extraordinary possibilities that kiss might open up.

"Has that dashing Mr. Smith finally spoken for you?" asked Miss Hodwell.

"Dodie," scolded Mrs. McGovern. "I told you that we don't trust Mr. Smith's intentions."

"Oh, I forgot," said Miss Hodwell with a crestfallen sigh. "But if it's not Mr. Smith making Miss Oliver smile so brightly, then what is it?"

"If you must know, it is Mr. Smith I'm smiling about."

"I thought so!" said Miss Hodwell.

"Has he spoken for you, then?" asked Mrs. McGovern.

"We've spoken of marriage and our families, and while he expressed a desire never to marry, I do believe that I can change his mind."

"Ah. And why do you believe that?" Mrs. McGovern asked with a frown.

"I know it deep in my heart." His kiss had been

a passionate promise as surely as any elegant proposal. She was sure of it.

"Have you been alone with him?"

"Perhaps."

"My dear, I must warn you about good-looking, well-spoken men who—"

"There's really no need, Mrs. McGovern. My mother has given me all the warnings I could require."

And Sandrine had thrown caution to the wind and ignored her mother's rules and warnings in the garden, but she didn't feel guilty about it because she knew that her mother would approve of Mr. Smith once he proved himself to be worthy.

"Then, where is Mr. Smith?" asked Mrs. McGovern. "He was supposed to be here a half hour ago."

"I'm sure he's been delayed at the inn. Perhaps his horse needed another shoe. I'll begin the reading, shall I?"

The two elderly ladies exchanged worried glances. Sandrine ignored them, blithely opening the history book she'd brought, and began to read.

Four long chapters later her voice and her spirits were beginning to flag. What could be keeping him from their appointment?

She closed the book. "I think I'll just run round to the Squire and ask after Mr. Smith."

"Yes, my dear," said Mrs. Hodwell with a gentle smile. "Perhaps that's for the best."

Sandrine kept her gait sedate, though she

longed to run the short distance to the inn. She stopped in at the stables to speak with Big Harold.

"Miss Oliver," said the gentle giant of a man, doffing his cap. "And how are you this fine afternoon?"

"I'm well, thank you. And how are your children?" He had six young children and another on the way.

"Lively as ever. They keep the missus busy, and that's no lie. How might I help you?"

"I don't see Gladiator in the stalls. Is Mr. Smith out riding?" She tried to keep her voice nonchalant, but Big Harold gave her a searching look.

"You don't know?" he asked.

"Know what?"

"Mr. Smith left two days ago. Rode off in great haste with a huge thundering beast of a man nearly as tall as I am." Big Harold shook his head. "Poor fellow had scars crisscrossing one side of his face. I heard the punters whispering that he was a duke and a war hero."

Danny had a friend who was a duke? Then Sandrine remembered the story he'd told her about his friend, who'd been both injured and jilted during the war. It could have been him. "Did they say where they were going?"

"I don't think so. The war hero had Mr. Smith's bags all packed and Gladiator ready to go. He wouldn't even allow Mr. Smith a moment to have a pint before he left."

"And you haven't seen them since?"

"He's gone, Miss Oliver. I'm sorry."

The pity in his dark eyes stopped her from saying anything else. She stiffened her spine. "Not
that it's any concern of mine. I only wondered because he had promised to escort Mrs. McGovern
and Miss Hodwell on a promenade today."

"Of course, miss. If I hear any news of him I'll
be certain to let Mrs. McGovern know."

"Thank you, Harold. Good day."

"Good day, Miss Oliver."

She walked back home, her mind churning.
Danny had been called away on urgent business,
but he would return as soon as possible. Or if
he couldn't return straightaway, he would at the
very least write her a letter explaining his hasty
departure. She would wait for the post every day
and intercept it before her mother saw what had
arrived.

Chapter Seven

Keep idle hands and fretful minds busy with useful work.
                    —Mrs. Oliver's Rules for Young Ladies

Several weeks later

I still can't believe that heartless Mr. Smith left without so much as a by-your-leave and then never even wrote you a letter to explain his departure," said Miss Hodwell.

"Don't worry about me." Sandrine attempted a carefree smile. "I've forgotten all about him. I have so much to occupy me now with plans for the benefit to raise funds for a new roof for the orphanage."

"Good for you, my dear," Mrs. McGovern said with a brisk nod. "You've a sensible head on your shoulders, unlike some I might mention. Do straighten your cap, Dodie. It's sitting sideways on your head."

Except that Sandrine hadn't forgotten Danny at all. She remembered every glance, every word, every touch. Some days she wished she'd never even met him so that she wouldn't feel so destroyed by his absence. She'd been happy in a subdued, restricted sort of way before she met him. She realized it now that her heart felt like it had shriveled to a dried husk rattling around in her chest.

Danny was gone forever. She'd dared to think he could be everything to her when she'd been nothing to him.

"Still, I'm very sorry, dear Miss Oliver," Miss Hodwell said. "I had hoped that he might prove to be a worthy suitor for you."

"I was nothing more to him than a passing fancy. I know next to nothing about Mr. Smith." The one that could leave so coldly and never look back. Never even write to her.

"Have a macaroon, my dear. I find they soothe all manner of ailments." Miss Hodwell thrust a biscuit at Sandrine.

"I wonder about Mr. Smith," said Mrs. Mc-Govern. "I can't help thinking that there's some mystery to him. That stallion of his was a fine specimen of horseflesh, the mount of a gentleman of social standing." She straightened the carnation pinned to her breast. "And now to find that he's only a common charlatan, a man that would dally with a young lady, give her expectations, and then depart so abruptly, so rudely. Well! We never should have allowed him inside our home."

"He never made any promises. He even told me that he didn't believe in love or marriage. I was the foolish one."

"If I ever see that Mr. Danny Smith I'll wring his neck with my bare hands," Miss Hodwell said fiercely. "I'll wrap him up"—she made twisting motions with her hands—"I'll squeeze him. I'll make him pay."

Sandrine giggled through the tears that were threatening to spill from her eyes, picturing the soft and petite Miss Hodwell strangling such a large beast as Mr. Smith.

"There, that's an improvement." Miss Hodwell handed her a rather sticky and dubious-looking handkerchief. "We've missed that bright smile of yours."

Sandrine wiped away a few tears. "I'm very afraid that Mr. Pilkington means to propose soon."

"Oh my. That is a calamitous thought, is it not, Dodie?"

"Calamitous indeed, Eve. I shudder to think of our sweet Sandrine having to share his abode. Much less his . . ." The two ladies exchanged glances.

"His what?" Sandrine prompted.

"His bed, dear."

"Dodie! We mustn't speak of such things," Mrs. McGovern scolded.

"Well, it's what we're both thinking, isn't it? He's bound to be as pitiless and dull as his sermons."

Sandrine had thought about having children with Mr. Pilkington, but she'd never been able to bring herself to imagine how that might be accomplished.

She shuddered. "I can't marry him."

"Oh!" Miss Hodwell pressed a hand to her hair, and then, realizing her fingers were covered with sugar, quickly lowered it.

"What is it, Dodie?" Mrs. McGovern asked.

"I've had the most wonderful idea. Why don't we take dear Miss Oliver with us to London when we go to visit your sister next week! Sandrine could petition the Duke of Rydell in person about the fate of Squalton Manor."

Sandrine sighed. "It's a lovely thought, but my mother would never allow me to go to London."

"Perhaps we can change her mind," Miss Hodwell said eagerly.

"You're very dear and kind to think of it, but I'm afraid it's not in the realm of possibilities, and I've determined that from this day forth I will keep my head out of the clouds, my hands busy with charity work, and my focus only on the task at hand."

DANE'S DAYS WERE spent at Rydell House with Cleveland, the estate's humorless steward, going over the record and account books and entertaining a seemingly endless parade of anxious uncles, solicitors, and business associates.

No one seemed to believe that he was capable of assuming the rigorous and taxing duties of being the duke. He was so occupied with those new duties that he hadn't had a chance to return to Squalton to explain everything to Sandrine, although he thought about her constantly.

His plans to find a buyer for the manor house had been placed on hold since he had much larger fires to douse now, with incomprehensible financial records and plans for the annual charity ball his brother always held this time of year. He also wanted to speak to Piety about her extravagant spending habits, but she was true to her word, refusing to see Dane and sequestering herself in her chambers, waiting for the babe to arrive.

Night was coming on as he finally finished for the day and set off on the short walk from Rydell House to his apartments. What was Sandrine doing at this moment? She was probably already tucked into bed with a sachet of dried lavender scenting her pillow. He was so wrapped up in thinking of her that he didn't even notice the shadowy figures lurking at the corner until they'd surrounded him.

He kicked and struggled, but there were three of them and they were bloody enormous. They held him flat against a wall, and one of them slid a flour sack over his head while another felt his coat pockets and stole his bag of coins.

They hadn't stabbed him yet, but Dane's entire body was tensed and ready for the thrust of a knife. He couldn't die like this. He hadn't even had a chance to apologize to Sandrine. He renewed his struggling and received another brutal punch to the ribs for his troubles.

"Take my . . . coin and be gone," he grunted.

"It's you we want." A knee to his kidneys. He doubled over in wheezing, twisting agony.

"Not . . . a fair fight. Take this hood off my head and give me a fighting chance."

"You think you can take all three of us?"

"Try me."

The accent and speech were rough. Only one of them was doing the talking, the other two were the enforcers.

"Stop struggling and listen to me. I've a message to deliver. It's about your brother."

That stopped him from twisting and attempting to break free. "What about my brother?"

"He owed our associate money."

"Lots of money," a new, deeper voice said.

"What was the debt for?" Dane asked, trying to keep his senses sharp, to differentiate between the voices, see if there were any telling lisps or patterns of speech that might give them away in future.

"You don't need to know that," replied the first man, the one who'd done most of the talking. "You don't need to know anything except that we have damning information about him. Information that, if published, would ruin you and your family name. So that's why you're going to pay his debt to us."

"What kind of information?" Dane groaned as another punch landed in his gut.

"I told you that you don't need to know everything."

"How do I know you're not lying?"

"Because your brother was in trouble," said the first man.

"Big trouble," the second man agreed.

"Will you stop repeating everything I say?" the first man said irritably. "Shut your mouth and use your fists. That's all you're good for."

"Pardon me for living," muttered the second man.

"I want proof," Dane said. "Hand over proof of this alleged information, and I'll think about giving you what you demand."

"You'll think about it, will you?" sneered the first voice. "Not good enough." A nasty, low laugh. "Your life is ours now. You'll do what we say when we say to do it."

Cold steel pressed against his throat.

Dane swallowed. "Tell me how much my brother owed, and I'll try to raise the full amount. Pay off his debt clean and simple. How does that sound, gents?"

"Too late for that, I'm afraid. Our associate will take your money, and you'll be called upon to do us small favors from time to time."

"What manner of favors?"

"It's easy enough. You and your reckless friends already spend your nights gambling and placing bets on sporting events. We'll tell you what to bet on. Then you'll tell your friends what to bet on. And when you win big, and they win big, you'll take a cut of their winnings, and we'll take it all."

"That seems risky to me, to my friends, and to you if the authorities—"

"One word to the authorities and—" The knife pressed to his flesh traced a rough line across his throat, hard enough to make him choke.

"Understood," Dane said shakily. The men holding his arms behind his back twisted harder, and he grunted in pain. "Easy, now. If you hurt me, I won't be able to do you any favors."

"You'll do the favors, all right," said the deeper voice, "or you'll have Mr. La—"

"Shut your mouth!" bellowed the first man. "You imbecile."

He'd been about to say a name that began with *L-A*, that much Dane knew.

"We'll be watching you," the man said. "You'll never know when and where we'll contact you, but be ready."

One more jab to his ribs, and then they were gone.

Dane ripped the sack off his head and ran back to the wider street. Passersby gave him curious glances as he stared wildly about, searching for a glimpse of his attackers, who'd managed to disappear into the night.

He leaned against a wall, quieting his breath. He'd never admit it in a million years, but he was scared. He didn't like being scared.

Whatever his brother had done for these men had been wrong. His upstanding, moralizing, holier-than-thou brother had been dealing in dirty money and nefarious deeds.

And now it was up to Dane to untangle the mess he'd made.

The ridiculous sun-drenched dreams he'd had at the coast were just that—dreams. Fantasies of a life he could never lead. Even more so now. Idyllic villages where everyone knew everyone, long walks on the sand with pretty, innocent Sandrine. It all seemed so distant now.

Danny Smith was gone forever. That stupid, silly fantasy he'd begun to have of abandoning his life in London and living a simpler, more meaningful life. Gone. All gone.

It might be his brother's sins he was paying for, but he'd sinned plenty in his life, and reparations were to be made.

Those foolish dreams he'd pieced together out of soft laughter, sweet looks, and blue skies had been brutally ripped apart.

THIS WAS THE beginning of the end for Sandrine. After the dessert course, Mr. Pilkington was going to propose.

She could barely choke down a few bites of custard. Her mind was in turmoil. She wanted to throw down her spoon, jump up from the table, run from the room, and keep running out of the house and away from her fate.

"Now, then," Mrs. Oliver said, catching Sandrine's eye. "I'll leave you two alone for a moment."

"Pray, don't leave, Mama."

"You may stay, Barbara," said Mr. Pilkington, wiping his lips with his serviette. "Since this is a mere formality. I flatter myself that everything is already settled."

"It is?" Sandrine asked, her heart sinking.

"It is. You know what I'm about to ask, Miss Oliver. Sandrine. May I call you Sandrine?" He didn't wait for a response. "My dear Sandrine, while it is true that you have no portion to speak of, and some gentlemen might consider that a deterrence, you are the most obedient, and most dutiful, and I daresay the prettiest young lady in Squalton-on-Sea. And I am the most eligible and sought-after of bachelors, and therefore our union is preordained." His voice took on the somber tones of the pulpit. "Preordained in the eyes of every villager, of your mother, and of the Almighty."

Sandrine opened her mouth to speak. There

hadn't been a question anywhere in that speech. Still, she was expected to be overjoyed that this man and her mother had come to an arrangement without her approval. She must fulfill her mother's every wish, do the right and obedient thing . . . but no sound emerged from her lips. She tried again, but still she had no command over her vocal cords. She simply couldn't force herself to respond.

A sudden, awful vision of her life swirled through her mind like a tidal wave, sweeping her into the dark oblivion of the briny depths of despair. She couldn't marry this man. She'd be expected to remain silent as he soliloquized, obedient to his demands, a meek wife and a selfless mother. He didn't truly see her. He only saw the version of her that her mother had painstakingly created and controlled.

"You're overwhelmed with gratitude, I understand. No need to speak, Sandrine. I comprehend from the zeal shining in your eyes that everything is to your satisfaction."

"Mr. Pilkington—" She'd finally found her voice, but he spoke over her.

"This winter, you and I will spend chaperoned time together. I will read to you from the scriptures while you embroider."

"Mr. Pilkington!"

"Yes, dear Sandrine?"

"I'm trying to say something."

"Sandrine," her mother said warningly, "this is not the time for flights of fancy. A simple *yes* will suffice."

Sandrine's mind scrambled about, desperately searching for a foothold on a ladder out of this nightmare. "Mr. Pilkington, I feel that I am not yet worthy of you."

"Nonsense, Sandrine." He smiled indulgently. "You are the most worthy young lady in all of Squalton."

"And yet I feel I must prove myself to you. There is one task I must complete. I've been invited to London by Mrs. McGovern and Miss Hodwell to accompany them to petition the Duke of Rydell on behalf of our historical society."

"You, go to London? I should think not!" exclaimed her mother, throwing down her serviette. "Have you gone mad?"

"Together, we three ladies will convince the duke to do the right, honorable, and charitable action and grant the manor house to the historical society."

Mr. Pilkington stroked his chin with his long fingers. "And you feel that this is almost a pilgrimage of sorts?"

"I do, I most heartily do. It's been my goal for so long, but our letters and petitions have been ignored. It's time to take action and meet the duke in person. I would travel with Mrs. McGovern and Miss Hodwell as their companion. Only for a fortnight."

"Out of the question," her mother said. "I refuse to allow you to visit that den of vice and sin. I would worry every minute you were gone. You don't know what it's like there. The dangers to young ladies that lurk around every corner. Tell her, Ernest, please tell my darling girl that she mustn't leave the safety of Squalton."

Mr. Pilkington steepled his fingers and regarded Sandrine thoughtfully. "Now, Barbara, while there are many evils in London, it's not the worst idea to present the petition in person. Pray think of the benefit to Squalton should your daughter succeed in her mission. The manor house could be restored, bringing visitors and new villagers to Squalton. It could also be used as assembly rooms for our Benevolent Society."

"But why must it be Sandrine?"

"Because it would be difficult for the duke, as hard-hearted and vindictive as he is, to say *no* to Sandrine, with all her many charms." He made an obsequious little bow.

Sandrine was thoroughly amazed. It seemed she had an unexpected ally. "Thank you, Mr. Pilkington. I will not fail your confidence in me."

"Go to London on your honorable pilgrimage with my blessing, dear lady. Fulfill your charitable mission, and then we may finalize our plans."

"Oh," her mother wailed. "I can't allow it. I simply cannot."

"It's only a fortnight, Barbara. She's going to do a charitable act. She will be prayerful in all that she does and will perform this act of service. Together, she and Mrs. McGovern and Miss Hodwell will melt the duke's heart and bring him into the light of loving kindness. The duke persecutes his brethren because he thinks that he is better than they due to his fortune and consequence. It will take a dutiful and blameless young lady like Sandrine to challenge the lion in his den and remind him that it is his good deeds, not his fine clothing, that will gain him access to the Pearly Gates."

"Perhaps you might write a short speech for me to deliver, Mr. Pilkington?" asked Sandrine. All she was doing was buying time, she knew that, but escaping from this room without saying *yes* to his proposal was her only goal at the moment. She would sort everything else out later. The rebellious spirt that had been awakened by her time with Danny wouldn't allow her to seal her fate this evening.

"I would be delighted, Sandrine. I shall begin work upon your speech immediately. I shall use the parable of the sheep and the goats. With my words and your soft looks and guileless smile, we are assured of success. I would accompany you myself, if not for my duties to the parishioners this summer."

Sandrine breathed a silent sigh of relief. That would have been a disaster. Her elderly friends would never have forgiven her if she'd arrived with Mr. Pilkington in tow.

"Are you quite certain that she should go, Ernest?" her mother asked tremulously. "I don't believe I can allow it. London is such a wicked, sinful place filled with dangers and temptations. I would never go there myself, and to think that I would allow my only child to—"

"I'm quite certain. Don't question me, Barbara,

and don't fret. You've done an admirable job raising your daughter, and she will be a credit to us, have no fear."

Mr. Pilkington thought to curry Sandrine's favor by taking her part, but she didn't care what his motivations were. The fact that he'd convinced her mother to consider allowing her to travel to London was nothing short of a miracle.

"Thank you, Mr. Pilkington," she said with real feeling.

"Please call me Ernest."

"Thank you so much, Ernest."

"As I said, Sandrine, I know we shall be of one mind on all subjects."

"Indeed, Ernest." She meekly bowed her head, but inside her heart was dancing to a new rapid beat. She was London-bound!

She wasn't going to waste this opportunity to achieve two of her longest and dearest dreams: visiting London, and convincing the Duke of Rydell to do the right thing.

She'd been meek and obliging her entire life. She'd been such a foolish innocent, thinking that she could change Danny's heart and somehow make him fall in love with her.

Her innocence had been bruised, but she wasn't beaten. She was determined to learn how to seize hold of life and truly live it, instead of allowing others to shape it for her.

And it all started with London.

Chapter Eight

London is a corrupt city filled with perils for young ladies, and must be avoided at all costs.
—Mrs. Oliver's Rules for Young Ladies

Ho there, it's our fearless leader!" Dane's friend Jeffrey Conway, Earl of Kenwick, shouted as Dane descended from his curricle and handed the reins to an attendant outside of the Crown Theatre in Covent Garden. "We know your brother died, Dane, and we're very sorry about that, but you've been back in London for ages and you haven't set foot in the club yet."

Kenwick punched his shoulder, which hurt like hell because his friend was built like a bareknuckle bruiser and towered a full head taller than Dane.

Dane returned the punch. "Sorry, friends. I've had the funeral, an army of solicitors, a sister-in-law who wishes I'd die too, and a monumental mountain of paperwork to contend with."

"Thought you'd forgotten about us," said Lord Barry Dudley, much shorter than Kenwick but just as barrel-chested, as he swaggered over to join them.

"You know I'd never forget my Thunderbolt comrades," Dane replied.

"Dudley's too ugly to forget, eh?" said Sir Michael Somersby with a grin, although he and Dudley were sometimes confused for brothers with their dark hair and square jaws.

"Too handsome, more like," Dudley retorted.

"Don't you just wish. The young ladies don't even look at anyone else when Lord Dane's in town."

"That's true," Dudley said. "Dane, why don't you go back to the seashore?"

Dane draped an arm over his friend's shoulders. "You're stuck with me, I'm afraid."

He'd missed his friends. Warburton, Kenwick, Dudley, and Somersby were founding members of the Thunderbolt Club, the best gentleman's club in all of London. Not some warren of dark, overheated rooms with ancient waiters pouring stiff tipple for pontificating lords, or one of the gambling clubs where ladies of the night joined young bucks for cards and bed sport. The Thunderbolt Club was all about racing. The faster the horse, the sleeker the carriage, the better. They lived to ride fast and ride hard.

"What have you miscreants been up to while I've been gone?"

"My new curricle arrived," said Kenwick.

"What did you name it?"

"*Lightning Streak.*"

"I love it." They all named their curricles. Dane's new one was *Firebrand*.

"Been waiting for you before racing *Lightning Streak* for the first time."

"You may want to schedule your first race without me. You have no idea the mess my life is right now. My uncles and their nervous solicitors are stuck with me as heir presumptive until Piety has her babe."

"Does that mean we have to start calling you Rydell?" Somersby asked.

"Good God, not yet! Hopefully never. I know you ruffians avoid churches, but can you all fall on your knees every Sunday and pray that the babe's a boy so I can return to my old life?"

Dudley's eyebrows shot up. "Now, there's a sobering thought. You, a duke. You'd become a boring stuffy old patrician like your brother with his parliamentary speeches and charity balls."

"Never! I'm still the wild and wicked rake you know and worship."

"Ha!" Dudley grinned. "That's a relief."

He'd always dabbled in dangerous pursuits, but now, with the threat from those cutpurses in the alley, he'd crossed a line. Knives pressed against his throat. Blackmail.

Any spare moment he had away from the ducal study was spent searching for the identity of his attackers, to no avail. He hated feeling out of control. Hated the feeling that they were watching him. Waiting to make their demands. What the hell had his brother become involved with?

"Actually," Dane said, lowering his voice, glancing around at the chattering throng of theatergoers eddying around them, "my brother had some mysterious and questionable dealings with some shady characters, and I've got that to sort out as well." He wouldn't tell them all the details yet, but he knew he could rely on his friends to back him up if it came down to that.

"Difficult to believe that Mr. High-and-Mighty would be involved with criminals," Kenwick scoffed.

"I know. He was always so morally superior, looking down his nose at us," Somersby said. "But we shouldn't speak ill of the dead."

"Sometimes I still can't believe he's gone," Dane said with a catch in his voice. "As you know, there was no love lost between us, but I never considered that he would up and die. Death could claim any of us, my friends. Any day. It's a sobering thought."

Kenwick nodded and punched him on the shoulder again, but this was a soft punch, his way of showing sympathy.

Kenwick cleared his throat. "Whenever I think about death, do you know what I do? I get riproaring drunk. And that's what we intend to do tonight. Are you with us?"

"I don't think so," Dane replied. He certainly couldn't stagger about drunk in public anymore: he must keep his wits about him and be ever vigilant for signs of the blackmailers. "I should probably have an early night. See the play and go home."

"Absolutely not," Dudley said. "We won't let you go soft on us. You need a reminder that you're the most swaggering cock of the walk in town. If you don't show yourself, all the lonely ladies in London will weep." Dudley wiped away imaginary tears.

"Probably left some saucy widow weeping at the seashore, am I correct?" asked Somersby. "Spill your guts. We want to know all about it."

"No saucy widows, I'm afraid." Only one very sweet and very wholesome young lady who haunted his thoughts and dreams like one of her manor apparitions. She must be so angry with him for leaving with no goodbye, no explanation. He hated himself for what he'd had to do. He couldn't reveal his identity now, since he was tangled up in the spider's web of his brother's dark financial dealings.

"Pity, that," Somersby replied.

"The properties I inherited are worthless. Squalton Manor is a crumbling money pit that's only fit to tear down. Though, it does command a sweeping view of the coastline."

"My uncle is looking for investment properties. Perhaps he'd be interested in viewing the land," Dudley said.

"I don't care about the properties," said Somersby, "I want to know about the village maidens!"

"Somersby, is that all you think about?" Dane asked.

Somersby thought about that for a moment. "Yes. Yes, it is."

"You're hopeless." Dane shook his head. "There was one young lady."

"I knew it!" Somersby crowded closer. "Tell us about her."

"The prettiest thing you ever saw, a heart-shaped face, a sweet smile, cornflower-blue eyes. I rescued her from drowning."

"She was probably pretending to have a cramp so you'd have to carry her to the shore," said Dudley.

"'Lawks! I'm drowning!'" Somersby pretended to swoon into Dane's arms. Dane pushed him away, but Somersby held on to his coat. "'Lord Dane, thank you for saving me. How can I ever repay you?'" He batted his eyelashes up at Dane.

Dane broke Somersby's grasp, none too gently. "Don't talk about her like that."

"What's wrong with you?" Somersby asked. "Didn't take you for an old maid."

"Gone prudish on us? Going to tell us to stop swearing and drinking?" Dudley asked.

Dane took a slug from his pocket flask. "'Course not." He wiped his mouth.

For some reason his friends' joking about Sandrine had put him on edge. The memory of their time together was something almost sacred. A treasured memento to marvel at when the noise of the sea lapping at the shore was long gone. A reminder of the man he'd dreamed of becoming to be worthy of her.

"It wasn't meant to be, that's all. She's an innocent young lady and I'm a bad, wicked rake. She's probably already engaged to the town vicar. He was about to propose to her when Warburton dragged me back to London."

Kenwick folded his arms. "Never thought you'd lose out to a curate."

"But it's not marriage our Dane wants," Somersby said. "You're always going on about never being caught in the marriage trap."

"Plenty of lovely ladies here in London who don't want marriage from a fellow," Dudley agreed.

"And they'll all be at Madam Avalon's Silver Palace tonight," Kenwick said with a wink. "We're going there after the play, and you're coming with us if we have to truss you up and carry you over our shoulders."

"I DON'T KNOW about this, Miss Hodwell." Sandrine clung to her elderly friend's arm as they were jostled by the crowd inside a Covent Garden theater. "My mother gave me a very extensive list of rules to follow while I'm in London."

"We won't allow you to come to any harm, dearie," Miss Hodwell said.

"I mustn't attend any balls for fear of being lured into the garden by handsome scoundrels who mean to harm me, or ride in open carriages with a gentleman, or ride in closed carriages with a gentleman, or drink any lemonade or punch for fear that it's been poisoned with spirits. And one of her rules is that I can't attend any events in Covent Garden."

"Then, how are you supposed to attend theatrical evenings?"

"I think that's the point."

"My dear Miss Oliver," said Mrs. McGovern, pursing her lips, "while your mother is a friend of ours, she has some very unreasonable ideas about London. With the proper chaperone, a young lady may enjoy the activities of town in a safe manner."

Miss Hodwell smiled kindly. "She'll never have to know if you break a few of her rules. We won't tell her if you don't. We think it's not healthy for you to be kept so rigidly confined."

"You need some diversion, and that is why I've asked my niece, Francesca, to meet us here." Mrs. McGovern lifted her hand. "Oh look, there she is now. Francesca darling, over here!"

A slender young lady with her hair piled into a tower of yellow curls approached them, with two other elegant ladies trailing her.

"Francesca, this is the young lady I wrote to you about, Miss Sandrine Oliver."

"Miss Oliver, how do you do?"

"Very well, thank you."

"She's nervous about attending the theater," Miss Hodwell said. "Her mother doesn't think it's proper for young ladies."

"But this is a morality play," said Francesca. "It teaches us morals."

"I suppose that might make a slight difference." But Sandrine was doubtful that anything would make her mother approve of any of this.

"And how are you finding London, Miss Oliver?" Francesca asked.

"It's very tumultuous." Nothing was ever predictable in London. People seemed to rush instead of walk, and there were so many new sights and sounds all in competition——the cries of costermongers hawking their wares, groups of ragged children playing in the reeking gutters, the hubbub of carriage wheels and crowds teeming about under the stony gaze of the imposing edifices she'd only read about in her history books.

"Miss Oliver," said Francesca, "these are my dear friends, Lady Roslyn Stockard and Miss Marta Maples."

"Charmed, I'm sure," said Lady Roslyn, a diminutive woman with daringly close-cropped dark curls framing her face, her gaze barely brushing Sandrine before returning to the crowd of fashionable ladies with feathers in their hair and men in stiff collars and tailcoats.

"Likewise," agreed Miss Maples. Statuesque and voluptuous, with russet-colored hair and gleaming red lips, Miss Maples was displaying more décolletage than Sandrine had ever glimpsed before. She tried not to stare, but it was difficult as her extraordinary bosom was directly at eye level.

"My aunt met Miss Oliver in Squalton-on-Sea and has brought her for her first visit to London," Francesca explained to them.

"Squalton-on-Sea? What an unfortunate name for a seaside resort," drawled Lady Roslyn.

Miss Hodwell's attention was caught by a waiter carrying trays of ices. "I think I'll go and see about some refreshments, dearies."

"Miss Oliver, you are quite charming. Isn't she, Marta? She has that fresh seaside air about her." Lady Roslyn looked Sandrine up and down. "Simple and unaffected."

Miss Maples tittered. "Simple indeed."

"Now, put away your claws, you two," Francesca admonished. "We must be lovely to Miss

Oliver because she hasn't had our advantages. This is probably her best gown."

Sandrine glanced ruefully at her simple white muslin gown. "I told Mrs. McGovern I didn't have anything fashionable to wear."

"You look quite lovely," said Mrs. McGovern.

"I adore your gowns, ladies," said Sandrine. "The vibrant shade of your matching pink sashes is so becoming."

"Our pink sashes are our signature adornment. We're the Pink Ladies," said Francesca. "No other young lady is allowed to wear this precise color of pink."

"I'm dying for the Season to begin," said Lady Roslyn. "We're going to rule the *ton* this year, ladies. You'll see."

Sandrine wasn't here to rule anything, except perhaps the Duke of Rydell when she had her audience with him.

"Will you be attending the Season, Miss Oliver?" asked Miss Maples.

"I'm going back to Squalton within a fortnight."

"Such a shame," Miss Maples said in false, treacly tones.

"I'm heartbroken," Lady Roslyn agreed with a blank expression. "How was your summer in Yorkshire, Francesca?"

"I had a flirtation with a baron, but nothing came of it."

"I collected three new beaux—all military gentlemen!" Miss Maples exclaimed, pulling a square silver case out of her reticule and opening it to reveal a folding book of miniature portraits. "Don't they look smart in their uniforms?"

"If you collect any more beaux you'll have to open a portrait gallery," said Lady Roslyn.

"And what about you, Sandrine?" Francesca said. "May I call you Sandrine? We don't stand on formalities. You may call all of us by our Christian names. Any eligible bachelors pining for you in Squalton-on-Sea?"

"I deflected a proposal of marriage from the vicar before I left."

"Is he handsome?"

"I suppose he's not bad-looking. Though, rather slender of limb."

"That's unfortunate. I do like a gentleman with substantial thighs," said Miss Maples.

"Miss Maples!" said Mrs. McGovern. "Moderate your topic of conversation, if you please. I have been charged with chaperoning Miss Oliver, and her mother is very strict and proper."

"What about this vicar's equipage? Does he own a curricle?" Francesca asked.

"A very prosaic coach and four."

"Still, that's something," said Francesca. "Why did you deflect his proposal?"

"He's always lecturing me about the narrow path of righteousness."

"Oh Lord. He sounds like a bore," said Marta with a frown.

"Then, you don't want to be seen with us, my dear Sandrine," Roslyn said with a cheeky grin. "Our path is crooked as they come."

"What do you mean?" Sandrine asked.

"Never mind Roslyn," said Francesca, linking her arm with Sandrine. "Perhaps your cap is set for another gentleman?"

"She did meet a gentleman this summer, a Mr. Danny Smith. Perhaps you know him, Francesca?" asked Mrs. McGovern. "He's very tall, almost excessively handsome, with dark hair and deep blue eyes."

"Sounds dreamy," Marta sighed. "Is he a military gentleman?"

"I don't think so, though he did have a friend who was a war hero and a duke. I don't know that much about Mr. Smith, to tell the truth. I'm trying to forget about him since he left Squalton suddenly and never contacted me again. The only thing I really know about him is that his mother died in childbirth, and he likes to race curricles."

"Race curricles, you say?" Roslyn raised her delicately arched brows. "That's very odd. We do know a tall, dark, and handsome gentleman who races curricles and has a war hero for a friend, but his name is Lord Dane Walker, and he's an infamous rake."

"That can't be him, then," Sandrine said. "Mr. Smith was a common man. Very charming, respectful, and honorable. At least I thought he was, until he left town suddenly without even saying goodbye."

"If he's in London, we'll find him and bring him to scratch!" said Marta. "I'm very good at finding handsome men."

"Speak of the devil and he appears," exclaimed Francesca. "Here's Lord Dane now, with his entourage of cocksure rakes and rascally rogues."

Sandrine followed her gaze, and her heart nearly jumped out of her chest. It was Danny! In crisp black evening attire, swaggering toward them at the center of a group of equally fashionably attired young rakes, who were joking loudly and jostling one another.

Mr. Danny Smith. Dripping with confidence and animal appeal, staring appreciatively at a woman wearing a scandalously low-cut red gown who was devouring him with her eyes. He was gorgeous, and he knew it.

He looked like a completely different person. His expensive clothing, his arrogant posture. Could it be the same man she'd met at the seashore? She must know.

Her feet set her running toward him before she could think about the propriety of a mad dash through a crowded theater.

She was breathless by the time she reached him. "Danny? It's me, Sandrine!"

Chapter Nine

*A lady must never display her temper in public,
no matter how severely provoked.*
        —Mrs. Oliver's Rules for Young Ladies

What in the name of creation? Sandrine wasn't supposed to appear at a theater in Covent Garden. Rushing at him with arms outstretched and eyes lit with pleasure, a vision of beauty in a simple white gown with pink cheeks and tousled sunshiny curls.

"What are you doing here, Sandrine?" he whispered, trying to draw her aside for a more private conversation. The Pink Ladies weren't far behind Sandrine, with knowing grins and gossip-hungry eyes.

"I'm here with Mrs. McGovern and Miss Hodwell for a fortnight. Why did you leave Squalton so suddenly?"

"I thought you said that your mother would never allow you to visit London."

"She changed her mind. You're not . . . happy to see me?"

For those first moments as she approached him he'd been utterly, deliriously happy to see her. It was as though the crowd had melted away around her, and she'd been the only woman in the room, her hair glowing in the gas lamps, her eyes the color of a calm sea at sunset.

In those first moments he'd wanted to run toward her, sweep her into his arms, and kiss her. Carry her to his curricle and take her home to his bed. Promise never to leave her again.

But then he'd remembered the fist to his gut, the rough voices, the cold edge of the knife pressed against his throat. *Your life is ours now. You'll do what we say when we say to do it.*

His life was in danger, and the lives of anyone associated with him might be in peril as well.

Sandrine must be sent back to safe, sleepy Squalton. She couldn't be associated with him. Not until he learned the truth of what his brother had done and why these ruffians were blackmailing him. He stepped back, closing ranks with his friends, who were giving him curious looks.

"Miss Oliver. Of course, I'm delighted to see you," he said stiffly. "And how is your good mother? Am I to give you congratulations on a proposal from Mr. Pilkington?"

The light left her eyes. Her hopeful smile faltered, wobbled, and fled. Her hand outstretched, as if to touch him, fell to her side.

"I don't understand. Why are you being like this?"

Lady Roslyn sauntered toward them. "It's very simple, sweet girl. This is no common Mr. Smith. This is Lord Dane Walker, heir presumptive to the dukedom of Rydell and a known rake. You've had the wool pulled over those big blue eyes," she drawled.

"Lord Dane Walker. Heir presumptive to the dukedom of Rydell. That can't be true!"

He'd wanted to hear her say his real name. Say it with gladness when he did something to make her smile. Breathe it huskily as he pleasured her.

This was all so dreadfully wrong.

His shoulders tensed, and his hands balled into fists. He hadn't wanted her to find out like this, in a room full of people. He should have told her. He never should have lied to her. "It's true, I'm afraid. I was called away suddenly from Squalton-on-Sea to attend my brother, who suffered a carriage accident and died."

"Then . . ." Her eyes narrowed. "Then, you lied to me?"

"Everyone in Squalton hates my family. I had to hide my identity."

"But the time we spent together. You could have told me then. But you were . . ." Understanding dawned in her eyes. "You were using me as your guide to Squalton and a way inside the manor without revealing your identity."

Hating himself more with every word he uttered, he pasted a mocking smile on his lips. "You do see the awkwardness there would have been if I'd used my real name. 'The bloody blasted Duke of Rydell, may 'e damn well rot in 'ell,' and all that."

Dudley laughed. "*Bloody blasted Duke of Rydell.* I like that."

With each word her face changed. A wrinkle appeared between her brows, her cheeks flushed, and tears misted her eyes. And then the hurt in her eyes hardened to fury.

"I see. I see exactly. You're nothing but a charlatan and a scoundrel!"

He wanted to beg her forgiveness. Fall at her feet. Instead he crossed his arms across his chest. "You're not the first lady to brand me so."

"And she won't be the last, eh?" Kenwick said with a mocking laugh.

Titters from the Pink Ladies. Shocked stares from the people around them.

"I wish I'd never met you at all!" She grabbed Lady Roslyn's glass of punch and threw it in his face before running through the crowd toward the exit.

Sticky pink liquid dripped down his face and stung his eyes as his friends erupted into howls of laughter.

"Temper, temper!" Dudley wagged his finger at her retreating back.

"She told you," Kenwick said with an amused chortle.

"Miss Oliver, wait!" Miss Francesca McGovern called. She glared at Dane. "Now see what you've done!" She ran after Sandrine.

"That was the famous young lady from the seashore?" Somersby chuckled. "Safe to say she won't be pining for you any longer."

Lady Roslyn smirked and clapped her hands together slowly. "Well done, my lord. Your reputation as a Rake of the First Order is intact."

I wish I'd never met you at all.

Dane wiped punch out of his eyes with a hand-kerchief. He'd made Sandrine angry, made her cry. Humiliated her publicly.

He'd done what he had to do.

Drive her away. Mock her. Make her hate him.

No woman would stay to endure more of that. She'd leave London immediately.

HER MOTHER HAD been right. She couldn't trust strange man, and certainly not a man like Lord Dane. He was exactly the man her mother had warned her about. A predatory London rake, roaming with his pack of howling wolves.

She'd been publicly humiliated by a man she'd thought was good. He was vile. He was horrid. He was a liar and a seducer, and she hated him. Loathed him with a passion so intense it was making her see red spots dance before her eyes.

Had she really been fantasizing about a life with him? This arrogant, mean-spirited noble-man, born to wealth and privilege. He'd laughed at her, made others laugh at her.

Why had she come to London? This had all been an enormous mistake.

"Sandrine!"

Francesca caught up with her outside the the-ater. "You can't go tearing off like that. We must wait for my aunt. It's not safe."

Sandrine looked around them. Francesca was right. Several men loitering about the entrance were eyeing them with interest.

"I'm sorry," Sandrine said and sniffed. "I wasn't thinking. I was so very angry and humiliated."

"Was he really the man you met in Squalton?"

"I thought he was an honorable man, bred in the country, and the entire time he was lying to me. He owns Squalton Manor, and that means that he holds the fate of the entire village in his hands. He must have been laughing at me the whole time. It was all a huge joke to him. Seduce a village maiden under an assumed name."

"Did he?" Francesca asked, her gaze intense. "Did he ruin you?"

"No, nothing like that. He seduced me with words and gentle glances, and with his gentlemanly behavior and the way he listened to me and made me feel so special."

"That doesn't sound like the Lord Dane I know."

"It was all lies. I never would have told him my innermost secrets and desires if I'd known he was a heartless nobleman and rake. How he must have laughed at my girlish fancies."

"Listen to me, Sandrine." Francesca gripped her wrists. "Men are beasts ruled by their basest instincts. Worse than beasts, really. They're fleas on beasts." She handed her a fresh handkerchief.

Sandrine wiped her eyes, smiling through her tears. "Thank you. My mother always told me the same thing, but I didn't believe her. Now I do."

Mrs. McGovern joined them outside. "What's all this commotion? Miss Oliver, are you weeping?"

"It's nothing, really. I . . . ."

Miss Hodwell came rushing out. "What's all this, then? Lady Roslyn told me there'd been a calamitous occurrence."

"The man Sandrine met at the beach, the one

you know as Mr. Danny Smith, is actually Lord Dane Walker," Francesca explained. "His brother Roman, Duke of Rydell, recently passed away, and now Lord Dane is heir presumptive."

Mrs. McGovern's face grew stern. "Why did he lie about his name?"

"He discovered how much the townsfolk of Squalton hate the dukes of Rydell and gave a false name," said Sandrine.

"The libertine!" Miss Hodwell jabbed her finger at the theater facade. "Courting you under false pretenses. I ought to go in there and teach him a lesson."

"Now, Dodie, we've caused quite enough of a public spectacle for the evening," said Mrs. McGovern.

"He's a notorious, unprincipled rake," Sandrine said. "And I'm the most foolish, gullible girl that was ever born."

"He's not worthy of you, my dear," Miss Hodwell said forcefully. "You're far too good and kind for the likes of him."

"I agree," said Mrs. McGovern. "You may have naively believed his lies, but that doesn't mean you're foolish. It only makes you innocent. And in my experience one's innocence is something to be cherished and not relinquished lightly. Now then, my girl, hold your head high, and we will view the play we came to see."

"I can't go back in there. I threw a cup of punch in his face. I made a terrible scene."

"You did? Good for you!" said Miss Hodwell.

"You should have seen him with punch dripping down his face," Francesca said gleefully. "I don't mind missing the play. Let's go home, and Sandrine and I will get to know each other better. Any lady who douses Lord Dane Walker with punch is sure to be a fast friend of mine."

Sandrine smiled. "That's very kind of you." As the hot flames of her anger and hurt burned down to smoldering embers, she realized something dreadful. "Oh no," she moaned.

"What's the matter?" asked Mrs. McGovern as they waited for her carriage.

"Don't you see why this is doubly horrible? I'm here in London to petition the Duke of Rydell on behalf of the Squalton Historical Society. Why didn't I think of that before I threw punch in his face?"

"Oh dear, I quite forgot. That does complicate matters," said Miss Hodwell.

"I can't face him. I must go back to Squalton." And she'd have to marry Mr. Pilkington and endure his endless sermons and his bony body pressed upon hers. Her thoughts spiraled deeper into the fathomless pit of a dreary, predictable future.

"Listen to me, Sandrine." Francesca held her shoulders. "You can't allow Lord Dane to drive you away. I know men like him, and they're always playing games. They only respect worthy opponents. If you want something from him, you'll have to play his game to get it."

"How can I be a worthy opponent to a ducal heir? I'm a girl who was raised in a tiny village. I know nothing of the games wicked rakes play."

"Perhaps not, but now you have friends who do. The Pink Ladies will help you seek revenge on Lord Dane and win him over to your property scheme in the process."

"I don't think your other friends much liked me."

"They can be a bit sharp, especially Roslyn, but she's quite soft inside, you'll see, and if I know her, she's already devising a plan to help you have your revenge upon Lord Dane. You need a night with the ladies. I'll invite them over tomorrow evening." She turned to Mrs. McGovern. "May she come stay the night at my house, Aunt Eve?"

"Certainly, dear, as long as your mother is there."

"We'll have ever so much fun, Sandrine. You can be an honorary Pink Lady until you leave London. We won't allow him to mock you again."

DANE WAS STILL stewing over the reprehensible way he'd treated Sandrine as he and the boys followed their familiar path to Madam Avalon's Silver Palace, a house in Covent Garden that hosted a nightly salon where artists, courtesans, and noblemen gathered for decadent pleasures.

He didn't feel like carousing tonight. He'd only agreed to accompany his friends because he wanted to speak with Madam Avalon. She was notorious for her role as queen of London's demimonde. He'd ask her to keep her eyes and ears open for any sign of a patron with animosity toward him or his family.

There was no way he could lose himself in empty pleasures this evening. He was still in mourning, and not just for his brother. For Danny Smith. For the dream of being good enough for Miss Sandrine Oliver. He could still taste the sticky sweet punch on his lips and hear her accusatory words ringing in his ears.

I wish I'd never met you.

Madam Avalon, a beautiful woman in her fifties, silver hair piled atop her head and ruby drops in her ears, proffered her cheek to be kissed upon arrival. Her blue eyes shining, she held him at arm's length.

"Lord Dane, it's been too long. But what's happened to you? Your hair is all sticky and you smell like a confectioner's shop."

"I angered the wrong young lady, and she splashed me with sugary fruit punch."

Madam Avalon laughed. "Always the rake." She accepted the elbow he offered. Her eyes were the same color as Sandrine's, a steadfast blue. "I was very sorry to hear of your brother's death. He was far too young."

"I still can't believe he's gone. And now I'm to be the family representative, God help us."

"Oh, you're not so bad as you pretend to be."

"I am though." What he'd done tonight was unforgivable. He'd never be anything but bad. He'd proven as much this evening.

You're nothing but a charlatan and a scoundrel! Sandrine's voice echoed through his mind and made his stomach heave.

"I suppose with all your new duties, I've lost you as an artist's model?" Madam Avalon asked.

"Would you take Kenwick in my place?" Dane thrust his friend forward.

Madam Avalon eyed the tall, solidly built earl, her gaze lingering on his groin. "Do you pad your trousers, Lord Kenwick?"

"What the devil kind of question is that? Of course I don't. This is all God-given."

"Turn around, Lord Kenwick."

He glowered at her but turned as ordered.

Madam Avalon examined his backside. "He'll do nicely, I believe. Be at my painting studio tomorrow after you've recovered from this evening's activities."

"What's in it for me?" Kenwick asked.

"Fame. Notoriety. Ladies clamoring to meet the artist's model."

His lips quirked to one side. "I suppose I can clear some time in my schedule." He drifted off toward a group of ladies who were admiring some portraits hung in the gallery, leaving Dane alone with Madam Avalon.

"May I have a moment of your time in private, madam?"

"Of course." She led him to a secluded bower.

"If I tell you something in confidence, can I be assured it will stay that way?"

She placed a hand on her heart. "I'm the very soul of discretion. Perhaps not when it comes to my bedroom exploits, but in other areas my lips are sealed."

"Something happened to me the other day. I was set upon by ruffians in a dark alley. They said my brother owed them a debt and that they had information that could be used to ruin my family. I don't think Roman ever visited you here, but through your contacts in the demimonde, have you ever heard any chitchat about my brother being involved with any nefarious characters, or getting himself into gambling trouble, or something of the sort?"

Her brow furrowed. "Your brother's reputation was spotless, as far as I know. But I'll keep my ears open now, and I'll let you know if I hear anything. Oh—wait, there is something. There was a gentleman who attended a salon last week, and he was asking questions about you. I quite forgot until just now."

"What did he look like?"

"Tallish, slender, thin mustache, and receding hairline. Annoying habit of sucking his teeth. Rather a loathsome fellow. I should have asked his name, but I was very occupied that evening."

"Not a regular patron."

"I'd never seen him before."

"Thank you. This helps immensely. At least now I have an avenue of inquiry to pursue."

"If I see him again I'll send word immediately."

"Thank you, madam. And now back to the ducal desk. No rest for the wicked, I'm afraid."

When they rejoined Dane's friends, Kenwick had already selected his companion for the evening, a curvaceous young lady who threw her head back and laughed heartily at every comment he made.

"I'll leave you to your evening, Kenwick," Dane said.

Dane made for the door but was stopped by Dudley, who staggered against him, already three sheets to the wind. "Leaving so soon?"

"My steward is attacking me tomorrow with an army of clerks bearing paperwork."

"That's not why you're leaving," Dudley slurred. "You're still thinking about that delectable Miss Oliver."

"I'm not." But of course, he was. He'd think about her until his dying day.

"You're smitten with her. What really happened at the seashore?"

History lectures. Herb gathering. The achingly beautiful dream of a simpler, better life with the most beautiful woman in the world by his side.

"What happened at the seashore was nothing but an impossible dream."

"You're halfway in love with her."

"It was a brief flirtation, nothing more."

Dudley jabbed at his chest with an unsteady finger. "I can tell when you're lying, you know."

"Maybe you're right, Dudley. Maybe I'm lying to myself. But it's all I know how to do."

He left then. Left the free-flowing wine, the lively conversation, the promise of secret, wicked pleasures. It all seemed empty and colorless tonight. He had perplexing financial records to sort through, blackmailers to expose and vanquish, and a host of other problems lying in wait.

He'd done what he had to do. He couldn't have innocent country ladies hanging about while he was embroiled in dangerous games with desperate criminals.

Chapter Ten

*Choose your friends wisely; a lady is judged by
the company she keeps.*
   —Mrs. Oliver's Rules for Young Ladies

She's too pristine to be pink," Sandrine overheard Lady Roslyn say in her sarcastic tones.
Sandrine had left Francesca's room to gulp fresh
night air on the balcony. Lady Roslyn had been
smoking a cheroot, and the smell had made her
feel sick to her stomach.

"Give her a chance," Francesca replied. "Aunt
Eve told me that her mother is terribly strict and
overprotective, and this is the very first time
Sandrine has been allowed to enter any kind of
society. I think she has pink potential. Did you
see the way she splashed Lord Dane with that
punch?"

"That was rather brazen of her," said Marta.
"Perhaps we could allow her to join the Pink Ladies while she's in London."

"One of our coveted sashes tied around that drab
old gown of hers?" Roslyn snorted. "I think not."

"And the way she wears her hair like an elderly
maiden aunt." Marta giggled. "All she needs is a
lace cap and a pair of spectacles."

"I'll help her dress her hair and lend her some of my old gowns," Francesca said.

"You'll never disguise her country accent and that wide-eyed innocence. 'Oh lawk, Lord Dane, keep those skintight trousers far away from me,'" Roslyn proclaimed in a soft, breathy voice.

Was that meant to be *her*? Sandrine pushed open the balcony door. "Are you poking fun at me, Lady Roslyn?"

Roslyn coughed. "Only a little."

"I don't have an accent, do I?"

"You do, rather," said Francesca.

Marta nodded. "You do."

"I suppose I'm only a gullible country girl who doesn't have a sophisticated bone in her body." Sandrine gathered up her reticule. "I should go back to your aunt's house, Francesca. I don't belong here."

Francesca sprang up from her chair. "Don't be put out. That's only Roslyn. She's like that with everyone. Come and sit with us." She pulled Sandrine over toward the fireplace.

"I meant that I don't belong in London. I should go back to Squalton-on-Sea."

"So that's it?" Roslyn asked. "You're going to admit defeat so easily and cry yourself back to Squalton? Your mother will be so proud."

"You can't leave and allow Lord Dane to win," said Francesca.

Marta leaped up from the bed she'd been lounging on fetchingly. "You must stand and fight!"

"I don't see as how I have a leg to stand upon.

I'm supposed to go to Rydell House tomorrow to present a petition to Lord Dane about the fate of Squalton Manor, but yesterday evening I lost my temper and made a public spectacle of myself."

"This is the perfect opportunity to make him pay for what he did to you!" Francesca crowed. "Your goal is to make him fall madly in love with you. Have him eating sugar from the palm of your hand like one of his stallions. And then he'll do anything you ask, including doing whatever you want with Squalton Manor. It's only afterward that you spurn him, as he did you."

"Spurn him?"

Roslyn nodded sharply. "Burn him to the ground."

"Trust us," Marta said. "We know men. They're very easy to manipulate. The problem is that he spends more time with his blasted Thunderbolt Club than at the social events of the season."

"And women aren't allowed in gentleman's clubs," Roslyn said. "Even if those women can ride circles around any man alive."

"You have the appointment at Rydell House tomorrow, that's good," Francesca said. "But we'll need to find other opportunities to throw you together."

"I don't know, Francesca. This plan seems to imply that I might drive a ducal heir mad with desire when obviously I'm only an unsophisticated country girl."

"Don't worry about that." Francesca tucked a

curl behind Sandrine's ear. "I'll give you a new image. What we need to worry about is ambushing Lord Dane at his places of leisure."

"What does a wicked rake do all day?" asked Sandrine.

Marta tipped an imaginary top hat, assuming a drawling low tone. "My dear Miss Oliver, what does a wicked rake do? Well, we don't rise until three of the afternoon, then we do manly things like compare the bloodlines of our stallions, order new boots, or buy new hunting dogs. Then we dine on beefsteak and brandy around eight, join a party at Madam Avalon's, or Vauxhall, spend far too much blunt at gambling or on champagne and courtesans, and then we don't go to bed until five of the morning. Then it's time to do it all over again."

"Or they're risking their necks racing their curricles with the Thunderbolt Club," said Francesca. "They have chariot races like the ancient Greeks. But the Grecian chariots were strong and sturdy, whereas these curricles are flimsy and easily overturned. I've seen too many of them flipped and smashed to pieces, the horses and the riders rolling in the dust."

"Is that what happened to Lord Dane's brother?" Sandrine asked.

"He wasn't a rakish sort. I'm not sure what caused the accident, but it certainly wasn't racing," Francesca replied.

"I witnessed an accident in Hyde Park just last week," Marta said. "The horse ran away, and one of the wheels of the curricle collided with the rising ground and the vehicle was upset, and Mr. Greville was pitched into the air, as if shot from a pistol, and thrown upon his head."

"Gracious! Did he survive?" asked Sandrine, her heart thumping.

"Yes. More often than not they pick themselves up with no broken bones and are back in their curricle the following day."

"I know dozens of ladies who are dying to ride in Lord Dane's curricle and have their necks put in peril," said Marta.

"When you go to have your interview with him, try to glean some details of his schedule so we'll know where and when you can surprise him," Francesca instructed.

"It all sounds rather complicated. I don't think Lord Dane will be in any danger of groveling at my feet."

"All you need is a little confidence and mystique," Francesca said. "Would you allow me to try something different with your hair?"

"How different?"

Francesca pulled the pins from Sandrine's coiffure and piled her hair on top of her head, pulling some tendrils about her face. "You should pin it up like this. And pinch your cheeks to give yourself a blush. And bite your lips to make them red."

"Goodness. It sounds painful."

"It's to achieve a certain effect," said Marta. "The slightly rumpled hair, pink cheeks, swollen lips, and a breathless little catch in your voice, as though you've just been thoroughly kissed."

She'd felt out of her element most of this evening with these gorgeous, sophisticated ladies, but she did know what Marta meant about the effects of thorough kissing. After that afternoon in the garden with Danny—Lord Dane—she'd been terrified that her mother would be able to somehow intuit that she'd been kissed, as though she'd been permanently altered by the experience.

"And you can wear some of my gowns," said Francesca.

"I couldn't do that. I might spill something on them."

"Poo! I don't care. I have dozens."

"But she needs something special. Something no one's ever seen before," Marta said.

"She needs a make-a-rake-grovel gown." Roslyn drew a curving silhouette in the air. "Something close-fitting in all the right places."

"I'll talk to my modiste. But in the meantime . . ." Francesca left the room and came back a few minutes later holding a cloud of pale yellow silk.

The ladies surrounded Sandrine, tugging off her gown and sliding thin yellow silk over her head. The gown slid down her with the softest caress against her skin, settling in elegant folds.

Francesca stood back and eyed Sandrine critically. "The bodice is too loose."

"Padding! I use it all the time." Marta pulled a wad of cotton from her bodice. "Here." She pushed her hand down Sandrine's bodice, lifted her breasts, and fit the padding underneath.

Sandrine glanced at herself in the glass. Her

bosom appeared far larger now, spilling over the bodice in an alarming manner. "I don't know. Isn't it rather . . . precarious?"

Marta adjusted the bodice of the dress even lower. "It's perfect. Trust me."

"We'll dampen your petticoats," Roslyn said. "You do have rather fine limbs, and you'll want to display them."

"My mother would never allow such a—"

"Your mother isn't here, is she?" Roslyn asked.

They didn't understand. Even if her mother wasn't here, her rules and fears constantly echoed in Sandrine's mind.

"A single pearl pendant around her throat to draw his gaze!" Francesca fastened a necklace around Sandrine's throat.

"French scent." Marta dabbed liquid from a cut-glass bottle behind Sandrine's ears until she coughed from the overpowering floral smell.

Francesca swept her hand toward the looking glass. "Well?"

The gown hugged her curves in an entirely indecent manner and her breasts were on display, but her hair did look nice piled up high like that. "I can hear my mother gasping in horror."

"You look a perfect dream. Won't Lord Dane be sorry!" Francesca crowed.

"Pretend I'm Lord Dane," said Marta. "And you're meeting with me to make your request." She widened her stance, crossed her arms over her chest, and dropped her voice to a low growl. "Good day, Miss Oliver."

"G-good day, Lord Dane. I hope you're having a pleasant morning?"

"No trembling, no stammering. Remember, you're an honorary Pink Lady. We don't allow any man to intimidate us," said Roslyn. "Try it again."

"Good day, Lord Dane," she said firmly, holding her head erect and meeting Marta's gaze.

"You're looking well, Miss Oliver, I must say. Is that a new style of gown you're wearing? There seems to be more of you on display than when last we met."

Sandrine giggled nervously. "He wouldn't say something like that, would he?"

"You'd be surprised," said Francesca. "I once had an inebriated earl compare my hair to a pineapple, my lips to cherries, and my bosom to ripe melons. Then he said he wanted to feast upon my fruit and lunged at me."

"What did you do?"

"Plucked a pin from my pineapple and poked him with it."

"Ahem, Miss Oliver," said Marta in her deep Lord Dane voice. "I'm a very busy man. What is it you want from me, Miss Oliver?"

Sandrine squared her shoulders, channeling the anger she still felt simmering inside her. "I want you to fall upon your knees and apologize for your abominable behavior, and then I want you to sign over the leasehold for Squalton Manor to my historical society."

"Too direct," Marta said, returning to her normal

voice. "Remember, you're meant to play his wicked game. First you disarm him with a little bit of this," she said and cocked her hip seductively, "and this." She wiggled her chest. "Then, you compliment his . . . desk."

"His desk? I'm not following."

"Every gentleman has a very large desk in their study where important financial matters are decided. And every gentleman is always fantasizing about draping young ladies over their desk and having their wicked way with them. You want his attraction to you to be tied up with his desk and therefore with helping your financial interests. Or you could literally allow him to tie you up on the desk?"

"Marta! She's an innocent." Roslyn rolled her eyes.

"I'm afraid I'm lost," Sandrine said.

"Never mind the tying-up. Keep it simple. Go to his desk, compliment it, make sure he's staring at your bosom or your lips, and then, when he's good and distracted, you slip your petition onto his desk. Then you sit next to it, and when he leans over to try to kiss you, you slide away swiftly, leaving him staring at the petition instead."

"All right. Desk. Bosom. Make him think I want him to kiss me, and then substitute the petition for the kiss."

"Very good, Sandrine. That's it exactly. You're a natural."

"I doubt that. You make it sound very simple. Honestly, I don't know why I must go through these maneuvers. He should want to help the people of Squalton from the goodness of his heart."

"A rake has no goodness in his heart," Roslyn said sternly. "You'll need to remember that at all times if this is to work. You must try to think like a rake."

"Lord Dane gazed longingly at you as you stormed out of the theater, Sandrine. You can do this. We believe in you," said Francesca.

Marta bounced on her heels. "Let's give her the initiation rites."

"The rites?" Sandrine asked.

"We have initiation rituals," Roslyn said. "If you want to become a Pink Lady, you have to drink from the sacred flask, smoke a cheroot, climb down a trellis or a drainpipe, and do something secret and scandalous."

"Sandrine," Francesca said softly, "you don't have to agree to any of this. You can go home to the seaside and live a safe, simple life. No harm in saying no. We won't think any the less of you."

This was another line drawn in the sand. She was here in London with these brave and brazen ladies. She could run home to her mother, or she could take a stand and fight for what she believed in. And if she became an honorary Pink Lady she'd have so many unpredictable and thrilling new things to add to her list.

Before her mother's voice could talk her out of it, Sandrine gathered her courage and stared into Francesca's eyes. "I want to pass your initiation tests. I want to become bold like you."

"I have a cheroot right here." Roslyn held out a slim cylinder. "If you're serious, that is?"

Sandrine took a deep breath. "I am."

"Then, we'll go to the balcony. Come along, ladies, live a little! Taste all that life has to offer," Roslyn said, opening the balcony doors.

It was a fine evening with a full moon overhead. Roslyn lit the cheroot and passed it to Sandrine. "Take a small puff at first and—"

Sandrine filled her lungs with smoke and began to cough and sputter. Francesca pounded her on the back while Marta giggled.

"I was going to say not to inhale, you silly thing."

"I did it!" Sandrine said, still coughing. "I smoked a cheroot. I don't much like it."

"It's an acquired taste. Take small puffs and blow smoke rings, like this." Roslyn demonstrated, looking very sophisticated.

"And now the ceremonial flask." Francesca produced a small silver flask. "Have you ever tasted brandy, Sandrine?"

"As a matter of fact, I have. I'm quite partial to it." She unscrewed the lid from the flask and took a sip. The taste reminded her of that morning on the beach with the man she'd known as Danny.

"Well, you're full of surprises. Pass it round." Marta held out her hand, and Sandrine handed her the flask. "I myself prefer bubbly to brandy—"

Marta was interrupted by a gruff, muffled

shouting from under their balcony. "Ho there, Pink Ladies!"

Francesca rushed to the balcony railing. "Be quiet, Kenwick! My parents will hear you."

"I want to talk to Roslyn. Send her down. No harm will come to her, I swear it on my mother's grave."

"Are you inebriated?"

"Usually."

Francesca glanced at Roslyn who gave a little shrug. "I'm going to live while I'm still young, ladies. Don't wait up for me." She climbed over the balcony railing and disappeared down a rose trellis.

Sandrine wanted to appear worldly, but she was shocked. "Won't this ruin her reputation?"

"Only if someone finds out," Francesca replied. "I know it's shocking and scandalous, but there's no stopping Roslyn. We love her, and we'll stand by her no matter what."

"I can't believe she climbed down that trellis!"

"We'll teach you how to climb down from this balcony another night," Francesca said.

Sandrine peered over the edge of the stone railing. "It's a long way down."

"It's quite safe."

"And what about the secret and scandalous thing?"

"It's going to be a surprise," said Marta. "But it will be something your mother wouldn't even think to put on her list of rules because she would never conceive that you might try such a thing."

A thrill rippled through Sandrine's body. "It will be at nighttime?"

"Yes, you can know that much."

"It won't be something dangerous to my reputation?"

"We'll make sure that you're not exposed," Francesca promised solemnly.

"Or dangerous to me?"

"There will be no actual danger involved. We always travel with stout, loyal, and impeccably discreet footmen. And all of us have undergone the initiation, and no harm came to us or our reputations."

Oh good Lord. What was she agreeing to? This was too much, too dangerous.

She'd never been allowed to have close women friends. Her mother always said that the wrong sort of friends might lead her to temptation and sin. But Sandrine was so tired of the fearful voice in her head proclaiming the rules of acceptable behavior.

Perhaps with a little help from her new friends, she could begin to find her own path in life.

"I want to do this. It's time for me to begin living my own life."

"Bravo, Sandrine!" cheered Marta. "What's your new goal?"

"To think like a rake," Sandrine replied.

"Yes," said Marta, "and?"

"To win the leasehold to Squalton Manor."

"And how will you do that?" asked Francesca.

"I'll beat him at his own game. I'll be disarming and flirtatious and make him fall madly in love with me, grant me the leasehold, and then I'll spurn him and leave him in the dust."

"Hear! Hear!" said Francesca.

Marta handed the brandy flask to Sandrine. It still tasted forbidden and sinful, but this time it also made her feel powerful. She raised the flask. "To making Lord Dane pay!"

Chapter Eleven

Flirtatious behavior such as fluttering one's eyelashes isn't proper for young ladies.
—Mrs. Oliver's Rules for Young Ladies

This is punishment for all my sins," Dane groaned, throwing down his pen. "I don't know how you stomach it, Warburton. Drowning in paperwork. Besieged by land agents. I'm not cut out to be the duke."

"It's not as bad as all that. You're new to it, that's all. My father died when I was twenty, and I quickly learned the tricks that make the job manageable."

"Do tell."

"It's simple enough. I engage a scrupulous and trustworthy steward, and I pay him an outrageous sum to keep such meticulous records that even a lout like me can follow the estate finances. I limit my appearances in Parliament because no one wants to see this scarred face give speeches. I spend most of the year at my ancestral pile in Surrey where life is uncomplicated by women or family, and I hunt and ride to my heart's content."

"You make it sound simple, but I don't have a scrupulous and trustworthy steward. I have Cleveland, a dour and pinch-faced fellow who apparently blames me for all the ills of the world, including my brother's death, my sister-in-law's ruinously expensive tastes, and the incomprehensible mess of these record books. For example," Dane said as he jabbed his finger at the book lying open on the desk, "why on earth do Piety's stockings cost three quid a pair? What are they spun from, silver thread and moonbeams?"

"That is exorbitant."

"And what, pray tell, is a master aesthetician? The fellow charges my sister-in-law truly shocking rates for weekly treatments involving tonics, stimulating massage, and plucking. Plucking of what, I wonder? What in the ruddy hell is going on around here?"

"Sounds like a load of bollocks."

"And then there are the record books about Roman's precious charities. The man was giving away our fortune at an alarming rate to at least thirty separate benevolent societies with names like"—he picked up the book and read from it—"The Society for the Charitable Relief of Poor, Misused, Infirm, Aged Widows and Single Women of Impeccable Character Who Have Fallen On Difficult Times in East Edston."

"That's a mouthful."

"And then there are ones like this: The Retired Hunting Hounds Welfare Society."

"That's ridiculous," scoffed Warburton.

"Do you really think my brother cared enough about hounds to donate two hundred pounds per annum? On the one hand, we have Roman throwing money at charities, and on the other hand we have a wife who thinks she's entitled to live like royalty. It doesn't add up, I tell you."

"It certainly doesn't. Call in this Cleveland fellow, and we'll have a go at him. I'll help you get to the bottom of this."

"Actually, I asked you here today to consult with you on another urgent matter." Dane closed the record book and left the desk. "Pour me some of that."

He'd asked the footmen to leave them alone because he was going to confide in Warburton about the blackmail attempt.

Warburton poured Dane some brandy. "Is it about that Miss Oliver from the seaside? Kenwick told me what happened at the theater. Wish I could have seen you dripping with punch. What did you do to make her so outraged?"

"She had no idea I was anyone other than simple Danny Smith. She's here to petition the Duke of Rydell to gift Squalton Manor to her precious historical society, but I've already found a buyer for the property. Dudley's uncle."

"Poor thing. First you deceive her with a false name, and then you sell the manor out from under her."

"She doesn't know about the manor yet. I'll go to Squalton soon and tell her in person, attempt to soften the blow and make my apologies."

"Has she left London, then?"

"I can't imagine she'd stay after I humiliated her in public."

"Sounds like she gave as good as she got."

"She'll be back in Squalton by now, safely sequestered with her anxious mother." And the thought nearly killed him. He wanted to chase after her, beg her forgiveness, and forget all about the bloody dukedom of Rydell, but his life was far too complicated and perilous for that.

"It's for the best," he said, still trying to convince himself of it. "She's not safe here in London."

"Not safe from you?"

"Not safe from the mess that it is my life. I asked you to meet me here because I must tell you something in confidence. Kenwick, Somersby, and Dudley are my good mates but they're too hotheaded. I wouldn't trust them to be discreet about this matter."

"Say no more. I'm your man," Warburton said gruffly. "Your secret's safe with me."

"The other evening I was accosted by a group of ruffians. They twisted my arms behind my back and beat me while I was incapacitated. One of them held a knife to my throat."

"What?" Warburton bellowed, slamming his glass down onto a table. "Why am I just hearing about this now? They can't get away with attacking you." He half rose from his chair, gray eyes stormy and hands curled into fists. "Who were they? They're going to be sorry they ever threatened a friend of mine."

Warburton was the man Dane wanted by his side in a fight. He was solid muscle and sinew from all the bare-knuckle boxing he practiced, with massive thighs from horse riding and shoulders that required an extra yard of fabric at the tailors.

"I don't know who they were. They threw a hood over my head. They said Roman owed them money and that they had information about him that, if made public, would ruin our family."

"They could be bluffing. Maybe they heard about your brother's death and decided you would be an easy mark?"

"Or it's completely possible, now that I've seen these tangled financial records, that Roman spread his money too thinly and had to borrow and then couldn't pay his debt."

"Or maybe he had a secret gambling habit. He won big, felt guilty about it, gave away money to charities, and then he lost big and the ruffians who threatened you were hired by the gaming hell."

"I have to find out who my would-be blackmailers are and if they have anything incriminating on Roman. They said that he'd been doing small jobs for them, and they expect me to do the same."

"Have you uncovered any clues to their identities in your brother's things?"

"Nothing here. While they were threatening me, one of them—not the brightest fellow—nearly said the name of his companion. It began with the letters *L-A*."

"Lang, Landon, Law . . . we can make a list."

"Madam Avalon told me that a first-time patron of hers, a tall, thin man with a receding hairline and a habit of sucking his teeth, was asking questions about me after Roman's death."

"Then, maybe he's your man."

A knock sounded on the door, and when Dane replied, his butler, Mosely, handed him a letter.

"My lord, this note was delivered by a young boy dressed in ragged clothing. The wily thing slipped through my fingers before I could detain him to ascertain the origins of the note."

"Thank you. You may leave us." Dane broke the seal. "It's from the blackmailers."

"Well?"

"They want me to attend a prizefight tomorrow. They'll slip me another note telling me who to have all my friends bet their money on."

"If they're fixing prizefights, then these are serious criminals."

"I know. I'll constantly be looking over my shoulder."

"We'll have to go on the offensive. You can't live your life looking over your shoulder. I know who can help us, my friend Osborne. He's helped me with certain tasks of a similar nature in the past. Go along with their demands for now, make them think you're compliant, but we'll be on the hunt for them, and we will bring them down."

"Thank you, Warburton." Dane clasped his friend's shoulder. "I knew I could count on you."

There was another knock at the door. "Yes?" Dane called.

"My lord, there's a representative of the Squalton Historical Preservation and Improvement Society to see you about a petition," Mosely said.

"A Mrs. McGovern? Tall, wears pearls and white carnations?"

"No, that wasn't her name."

"Then, a Miss Hodwell, a short elderly lady who probably offered you a macaroon from her reticule?"

The butler's eyebrows raised. "Er, no, my lord. It's a Miss Oliver, a very young lady."

"Safely back in Squalton, eh?" Warburton chuckled. "Seems she's braver than you give her credit for."

"I can't believe she'd visit me after the way I treated her."

"Apologies, my lord. Should I send her away?"

"Yes," Dane said at the same time as Warburton said, "No, no, show her in. I want to see who wins round two."

Mosely glanced at Dane questioningly.

"You just said that you owe her an apology and an explanation," said Warburton.

"Damn it," Dane grumbled. "Show her in, Mosely, but I'm not going to apologize. This time I'll send her packing in earnest. For her own safety."

"Of course you will," Warburton said with mock seriousness.

Miss Oliver entered the study, and Dane steeled himself for the inevitable swell of attraction.

It was as though the seashore had come to him here in this musty old study filled with dry books and ledgers. A breath of fresh sea air, sweeping through the study and rustling his papers. A wave sweeping through him.

Her beauty hit him anew each time he saw her, though she looked different today. She sashayed toward him, a vision in pale yellow silk, giving him a sidelong glance before turning the full force of that bright smile on Warburton. To her credit, she didn't flinch away from the sight of his scars.

"Miss Oliver, this is my friend Deckard Payne, Duke of Warburton."

"Very pleased to make your acquaintance, your grace. Lord Dane, you're looking well this morning."

Dane eyed her suspiciously. "Haven't brought any sticky beverages to douse me with, have you?"

"I brought no weapons."

Except herself. That warm smile, those heart-stopping curves. There seemed to be more of her bosom on display today, which made it difficult for Dane to form complete thoughts. And her hair was arranged in swirling curls on top of her head instead of in a simple knot at the nape of her neck.

"I assumed you'd left London, Miss Oliver," Dane said.

"You thought I'd be in a carriage on my way back to my mother, crying my eyes out, languishing limply and ruing my lot in life?"

Warburton grinned. "I told him you were braver than that."

"Oh indeed, your grace. Lord Dane is not the only one who becomes a completely different person at will. I'm a London lady now, both brave and bold."

London Sandrine smelled overpoweringly of a French rose garden and wore a gleaming pearl pendant nestled in her cleavage that made him want to go diving between her breasts with his tongue. And that's when he saw the pink sash tied around her waist.

"Aha! I knew it. Those Pink Ladies put you up to this. They did all of that"—he waved his hand at her hair and the mouthwatering display of her breasts—"and they've told you to use your feminine wiles to persuade me to grant you the manor house. But it won't work. I've already found a prospective buyer who'll want to demolish the manor and build something more modern."

Her smile faltered. "You can't demolish the manor. Where would Lucidora and Coraline live?"

It required a moment to remember that those were the names of the ill-fated spinsters whose ghosts she'd befriended. This woman had goodness baked into her soul like sugar into a macaroon. She even cared about the fate of ghosts.

"They'll have to find a new house to haunt. Squalton Manor is too far gone."

"This petition"—she pulled a scroll of paper from her reticule—"contains a detailed proposal for renovation work by a member of a guild who assures me that repair is possible."

"Put that petition back in your purse. I won't be perusing it today or any other day." He waited for Sandrine to give him a passionate lecture on historical preservation or lose her temper and throw brandy in his face, but she only regarded him with calm determination in her azure eyes.

"Is he always so disagreeable in London?" she asked Warburton with a silvery little laugh.

"Actually he's usually quite charming. I'm the grumpy, disagreeable one."

"Really? I find you charming, your grace."

"Why, thank you." Warburton preened, shooting an amused look at Dane.

"Perhaps it's just me who brings out this unflattering side of his personality? I wonder why," she mused, one finger lifted to her lips and head tilted fetchingly. "Could it be that I've gotten under his skin?"

Warburton chuckled. "One could draw that conclusion, dear lady."

"Enough," Dane said, heartily annoyed by their banter. He was supposed to be pushing Sandrine away so that she left London and stayed safely in Squalton.

"As much as I'd love to stay and continue our conversation, Miss Oliver, my friends are expecting me," said Warburton.

"Don't leave me," Dane whispered urgently.

"Round two for the dazzling Miss Oliver, I predict," Warburton said with another chuckle. *Turncoat.* Dane hadn't seen Warburton smile this much since . . . ever.

"I'll see you at the prizefight tomorrow, Dane. Good day, Miss Oliver."

"Good day, your grace. I do hope I'll see you again before I leave London."

Warburton bowed and left, leaving Dane alone with this new Sandrine who threw teasing glances and melted the cold, grumpy hearts of dukes.

"I'll call for a footman—"

"Afraid to be alone with me?" Sandrine asked, advancing toward him. Dane backed away until eventually his buttocks hit the edge of his desk. "Of course not." But he was afraid. Because all he longed to do was pull her into his arms and kiss her again, and that could never happen.

SANDRINE HAD THE advantage. He'd backed himself up against his desk and was staring at her lips.

If Marta knew her rakes, he was fantasizing about draping her over his desk.

She placed her palms on the smooth mahogany desk. Just as Marta promised, his gaze dropped to the ample amount of cleavage she was displaying. She wriggled her shoulders a little under the pretense of rearranging some papers.

His gaze heated, and his lips parted. Now Sandrine was the one picturing being laid across the desk and kissed by those firm, commanding lips.

"I—I like your desk," she said breathily.

He cocked his head. "I beg your pardon?"

"Your desk is so very large." She ran the tip of her finger over the edge of the desk, stopping inches from his thigh. She felt like she sounded ridiculous, but she'd come this far, so she followed Marta's instruction, hopping up onto the desk, which wasn't very comfortable. "So many weighty matters must be decided here. Upon this very large, very important desk."

His eyes had gone smoky and intense. He

turned to face her, placing his large hands on either side of her bottom. Marta hadn't said anything about being trapped by him against the desk. Now how was she supposed to wriggle away easily and leave him staring at the petition?

"My . . . desk likes you, Sandrine," he said huskily. His lips drew closer. The heat of his body surrounded her. Her thighs parted of their own accord, and he stepped forward, pressing her against the hard surface of the desk.

She couldn't remember her next maneuver. Couldn't think of anything except his long, lean body touching her, his strong arms bracketing her, his lips so close. She could lift her chin and kiss him. She longed to taste him, feel his tongue inside her mouth again. She could lie back, drape herself across the surface, and ask him to have his wicked way with her.

The petition. Squalton Manor. Think like a rake. Bring him to his knees.

His lips were nearly touching hers now. She waited one beat. Two. And then she made her move.

Placing her petition on the desk she jumped down and slipped under his arm, making her escape. He was left leaning over the desk, arms braced on either side of the petition. He turned his head.

"I do hope you'll consider our petition, your lordship," she blurted before making a run for the door. Once she was safely outside the room she leaned against the wall, catching her breath.

She heard a soft chuckle emerge from his study. Had she disarmed him?

He'd definitely disarmed her.

She'd been seconds away from losing sight of any goal other than being ravished by the handsome, infuriating Lord Dane Walker.

Francesca and Marta were waiting for her when she arrived back at Mrs. McGovern's rented town house.

"How did you fare?" Francesca asked.

"Did you disarm him?" Marta inquired.

"I'm not sure. I think it might have worked? Everything happened exactly as you said it would. He was staring at my lips, and when I wriggled my shoulders he stared at my bosom."

"Of course he did. He's a rake."

"And then when I complimented his desk and hopped up to sit upon it, his eyes went all smoky and he placed his hands on either side of me."

"Oh my," Francesca said. "And then what happened?"

"I almost forgot about the petition. He was so powerful standing over me, and honestly I was the one longing to drape myself across his desk."

"Oh, Sandrine, I do hope you didn't succumb to that temptation!" Marta said sternly. "You were there to control him, not the other way around."

"I remembered that just in time, and when he leaned forward to kiss me, I came to my senses, placed the petition on his desk, and ran away."

"Good girl." Marta nodded her head approvingly. "You'll be a Pink Lady in truth before long. Trust me, he'll read your petition. And he'll think about you the entire time."

"I hope it works. He said he already has an interested buyer for the property, and I nearly lost my temper but I kept myself calm."

"Don't lose heart. This is a long campaign. We'll have to throw you in his path again soon."

"Did you do any sleuthing about his schedule?" Francesca asked.

"His friend the Duke of Warburton was there, and before he left he mentioned seeing Lord Dane at a prizefight tomorrow."

"Excellent sleuthing. A public outing will be the perfect opportunity to needle Lord Dane."

"I've only read about prizefights. Do young ladies attend such bloodthirsty events?"

Marta winked at her. "Pink Ladies do."

Chapter Twelve

Gambling, prizefighting, horse racing, and other rough pursuits are unseemly for young ladies.
   —Mrs. Oliver's Rules for Young Ladies

I adore a good prizefight!" enthused Miss Hodwell. "The brutal pageantry of it. The pugilists circling like wild beasts. So invigorating for the blood. I have my money on young Dodgson—the odds are three to one in his favor."

"Dear Dodie, you mustn't excite yourself. You'll spoil your dinner."

"But Eve, don't you find it exciting?"

"I don't see the appeal. Two enormous brutes stripped to the waist and exhibiting themselves for thousands of spectators."

"Young Dodgson is no brute! He's highly educated, most eloquent, and skilled in the science of pugilism, and he's going to beat Tuckwell so completely that the match will be over in under thirty minutes, and he'll win the hundred guineas!"

"Is she always this bloodthirsty?" Sandrine asked Francesca in a whisper.

"Miss Hodwell has a voracious appetite for sport and other socially sanctioned acts of violence."

"It's an indecent spectacle," said Mrs. McGovern, sounding like Sandrine's mother.

"No more indecent than a ball. The boxers wear flannel trousers, while young ladies expose nearly as much in ballrooms and are grasped about the neck and waist by a succession of gentlemen."

"Dodie, don't be silly."

"It's true!"

The prizefight was held on Crowley Heath near Copthorne. It was a beautiful day, and thousands of spectators, mostly men, were gathered around a large square of ground with stakes at each corner and ropes between.

The Pink Ladies had dressed Sandrine's hair, chosen a rose-patterned gown for her to wear, and lent her a fetching straw bonnet trimmed with pink roses. Their efforts were not in vain. Gentlemen looked her up and down approvingly, and the few ladies present did the same.

"Everyone's staring at you, Sandrine," crowed Francesca. "They all want to know who our beautiful new friend is."

Sandrine didn't care about everyone. The only person she cared to make an impression upon was standing nearby, surrounded by his disreputable friends. His presence was a prickle along her spine, an awareness that permeated her entire body.

What would have happened yesterday on that desk if she hadn't slipped away from his embrace? He was studiously ignoring her, that much was evident. He hadn't even so much as glanced her way, and he stood with his back toward her, talking and laughing loudly with his friends.

But wasn't purposely ignoring someone much the same as staring at them?

"HAVE YOU ATTENDED a boxing match before, Miss Oliver?" asked Miss Hodwell.

"Never. My mother wouldn't allow such a thing."

"Do you see those men standing by Dodgson and Tuckwell?" Miss Hodwell said. "Those are the knee man and the bottle man. The one will kneel with one knee up for the boxer to sit on between rounds, while the other will keep him provided with water to drink and maybe even peel him an orange for a rush of energy. I should like best to be a bottle man. Then, I'd be right in the action. I'd taste the blood and feel the sweat upon me."

"Dodie," Mrs. McGovern remonstrated, "sometimes I do wonder about your sanity."

"If I were shaped less like a macaroon and more like an Amazon, I'd want to train in the pugilistic arts."

"Don't be ridiculous."

"You, Miss Maples, are very statuesque and pulchritudinous. Have you thought about pugilism?"

"Ah, no, Miss Hodwell. I would be afraid of bruising about my face. I do agree, though, a prizefight is most stimulating."

"The Thunderbolt Club is here in force," remarked Francesca. "And Lord Dane is ignoring you while the other fellows leer," she whispered in Sandrine's ear.

"I told you that our plan would work," Marta said. "You should ignore him as well. Don't look at him even once today. And if he approaches you, pretend not to see him and immediately start talking to someone else."

The rules for conquering rakes were more complicated than the boxing-match guidelines, it seemed.

"I see so many handsome gentlemen in their military uniforms," said Marta with a happy sigh.

"And they see you. Incoming, ladies," said Roslyn. "Sandrine, this is your chance to make Lord Dane jealous."

A tall, blond gentleman in a beaver hat and exquisite tailoring approached their group. "Dear Miss McGovern, won't you introduce me to this lovely creature?"

"I'd be most happy to, Baron Chisholme. This is my friend, Miss Sandrine Oliver."

He bowed. "Very pleased to meet you. Are you the young lady who doused Lord Dane Walker with punch? I've been longing to meet you. Everyone is talking about you and thanking you for putting him in his place. He had that coming to him for some time. I applaud you, Miss Oliver."

"Miss Oliver is a relation of the Earl of Amberly," said Francesca.

"You don't say. I went to school with Amberly. Why have I never made your acquaintance, Miss Oliver?"

"She's been staying in a seaside resort recovering from a touch of pneumonia," Roslyn said.

"You appear to have made a full recovery. You're as blooming as the roses on your bonnet, if you'll allow me to say so, Miss Oliver."

Francesca nudged Sandrine with her elbow.

"Oh, er . . . thank you very much, Baron Chisholme," she replied. "The sea air is quite beneficial. This is my very first visit to London."

"Well then, you must allow me to accompany you to see some of our more famous sites." He launched into a list of the destinations she must visit. He was taller than Lord Dane and very well-built, and she supposed he was handsome in a sleek, well-groomed way. Every gleaming yellow hair was perfectly in place, and his waistcoat was embroidered all over with golden pomegranates.

She hazarded a quick glance at Lord Dane. He was staring directly at her. *Glowering* would be a more accurate description. One point for the Pink Ladies.

She batted her eyelashes at Baron Chisholme and touched his arm, laughing delightedly even though he hadn't said anything remotely humorous.

LOOKS LIKE YOUR Miss Oliver has a suitor," Dudley said, elbowing Dane in the ribs.

"She's not mine," he replied through gritted teeth. Chisholme. The biggest, dullest lout in all of London. "And if she has a suitor, it means nothing to me."

"You don't care that Chisholme is standing so close and leering at her like he thinks he's won a prize purse?"

"Not even one tiny bit."

"So if I go over there and ask her to take a carriage ride with me in Hyde Park, you won't care?"

"Be my guest." Lies, lies, and more lies. All he wanted to do was gallop across the field and tackle Chisholme to the ground and box him about his ears until he cried uncle.

And the only thing he could do was stand here and pretend to watch the boxing-match preparations.

The second note the blackmailers had delivered had read: *Tomorrow. Crowley Heath. Tuckwell is your man. Bet large.*

Everyone knew that Tuckwell didn't stand a chance against Dodgson. The odds were three to one Dodgson. All he could surmise from the note was that they had fixed the match.

Sandrine must have noted Warburton saying that he'd see him at the prizefight. He couldn't think of any other reason why she and the Pink Ladies would be here today. They'd put her up to some sort of campaign to provoke him into granting that petition of hers.

And it was working.

Even though it would mean a loss of swift and sure income and be worse for Squalton in the long run, he almost wanted to sign the damned house over to Sandrine so she would leave London and he could be sure of her safety.

He mustn't be seen with her. He couldn't even

glance at her in public. The men who were attempting to blackmail and control him were here today. He wasn't worried about his friends from the Thunderbolt Club: they could take care of themselves. But he damned well wouldn't expose Sandrine to a threat he still didn't know enough about.

"MISS OLIVER, WOULD you care to take a brief promenade with me to the refreshment stands? We could fetch lemonades for your friends," Baron Chisholme said, offering her his arm.

Sandrine wanted to refuse because she was heartily sick of Baron Chisholme already, but Francesca gave her a stern look.

"I'd be delighted, Baron Chisholme." She took his arm, and they set off.

She risked another brief glance in Lord Dane's direction only to find that he wasn't there any longer. She searched the crowd and couldn't see him. Why was she strolling with Baron Chisholme, who was the dullest conversationalist she'd ever had the misfortune to be subjected to, if Lord Dane wasn't even observing her?

"Oh, I feel a little faint," she said.

"My dear Miss Oliver, you mustn't faint. Rest here, in the shade of this tree, while I fetch the lemonades. Don't move, for there are thieves and unsavory characters about."

"I won't move, I promise. I'll be right here in your view the entire time."

She rested her back against the large oak tree,

pleased that she'd successfully dodged a few minutes of Baron Chisholme's banalities.

And that's when it happened. A hand shot out, grabbed her arm, and yanked her behind the tree, while another hand closed over her mouth, preventing her from screaming.

Chapter Thirteen

Be wary of rakes who seek to lure you into se-
cluded trysts.
　　—Mrs. Oliver's Rules for Young Ladies

Sandrine bit down on her captor's hand and
stomped on his foot.

"Bollocks, that hurt!" The man released her
mouth, and she gathered air into her lungs to
scream.

"Don't scream! Sandrine, it's me." Large hands
spun her to face him.

"Lord Dane? You frightened me half to death."

"I'm sorry. I wanted to speak with you in private."

"You could have had a note delivered."

"Why are you here?" He was still holding her
tightly, pressed against his chest and the tree.
"Are you following me?"

"Good day to you too. And I don't believe I
have to consult you on every detail of my schedule. Miss Hodwell is a boxing enthusiast."

"Admit it. You overheard Warburton speak of the
match, and you decided to come and plague me."

"I'll admit no such thing."

"Your plan is working. I'm seriously provoked
by your presence."

"Excellent."

"But you don't have to play these games. You're the most enticing woman I've ever met, but that doesn't mean that I'll sign over the manor house to you. I must start making sound financial decisions since my brother has made a mess of the estate."

"You're the one playing games, pulling me behind trees and warning me to be a good, meek, silent young lady."

"That's not what I'm saying. It's not safe for you here," he whispered urgently. "These events are notorious gathering places for criminals."

"I'm perfectly safe with the baron and with my group."

"And you can't be seen speaking with me."

"Then, you should let me rejoin my friends."

"I'm serious, listen to me. No one here must suspect that we know one another."

"Because you're an unsavory character?"

"Because there are things that I can't tell you. Sandrine—" his grip tightened on her arms "—I know I've given you no reason to trust me, but I'm asking you, I'm begging you, to trust me on this."

"I absolutely will not." She thrust out her chin. "I'll never trust you ever again."

"It's for your safety. There are bad men here, men my brother owed a debt to, and they're blackmailing me. I don't know who they are or what they look like. I'm worried that any young lady I'm seen conversing with could become a target for them. I can't keep you safe if you persist in following me everywhere I go."

"Are you making this up?"

"I'm not, really. This is serious." His gaze was steady, his tone urgent, his grip punishing.

"Then, I will endeavor to help you."

He sighed and relaxed his hold on her arms. "Thank you. It will be best if you don't attend any of the same events that I—"

"I'll help you by keeping a watch on the crowd. If any man takes an inordinate amount of interest in you, I shall report back to you in a safe and distant manner."

"Good God, Sandrine, you're driving me insane. I forbid you from involving yourself in my investigation in any way, however safe or distant you think it might be!"

"Hush. Someone will hear you shouting at me."

"Promise me you won't do what you just said you'd do."

"I don't owe you any promises."

"And another thing. You can't entertain Baron Chisholme as a suitor."

"Suitor? I only met him today."

"And yet I'll wager he's already made plans to see you again, hasn't he?"

"He has been making a list of sites in London he'd like to show me, but I find him to be—"

"Forget about Chisholme."

"What right do you have to tell me who to step out with?"

"None whatsoever. Only think of your mother. Would she approve?"

"She certainly wouldn't approve of me held in

your arms, pressed up against a tree, where no one can see us."

She tried to laugh but the sound caught in her throat. He was so possessive of her. And she liked it. No, she didn't.

"What's wrong with Baron Chisholme?"

"He and I have a history, and he's only courting you to nettle me."

"Let me see if I comprehend correctly. What you're saying is that there's no way that the baron could be attentive to me simply because he finds me attractive? He's only speaking to me to infuriate you? Your arrogance knows no bounds."

"That's not what I meant. You're very attractive, and you know it. But this running about with the Pink Ladies and playing games with me, this isn't you."

"How do you know what's me? You don't know me at all."

"I met the real you at the seaside."

"You met a girl who was completely under her mother's thumb and had little idea of what freedom could be like."

"I want you to have your freedom. But I want you to be cautious, as well. And associating with me can only be bad for you, Sandrine."

"Anyone else I should add to my list of Forbidden Suitors?"

His expression darkened. "Go back to your friends. Don't leave their side. And ignore me."

"I can't ignore you when you're the reason I

came to London. Because you're the owner of Squalton Manor."

"I may have to hire someone to kidnap you, put you in a carriage, and take you back to Squalton."

"I'm sure my mother would thank you heartily."

HE COULD BE the one to kidnap her. He wanted to get her into a carriage. Alone.

The dangerous thought plundered his mind and made his blood pound like a pack of race-horses. Half of him wanted to whisk her away, to protect her, pack her into a carriage and take her back to the seashore and stay there with her forever. He'd become that man, the one he'd glimpsed in her eyes.

Someone who made her light up, made her laugh, a carefree man who frolicked in the surf, read out loud from history books, a simple, un-complicated man who wasn't running from extortionists and staring down the barrel of a dukedom.

The other half of him wanted to pack her into a carriage for a much less high-minded purpose. When he saw her, was near her, heard her voice. When his gaze filled with the decadent curves of her hips, her breasts and round shoulders, deli-cate fingers and ankles. When he was so close to the swoop of her lower lip, the pronounced dip in her upper lip that he wanted to kiss, to fit his thumb against. Every time he saw her he wanted to claim her.

He wanted to both protect her and claim her. Two things which couldn't coexist.

Protect her, keep her innocent, and claim her, do dirty forbidden things with her, tie her up with silk ribbons, watch as her lips opened around his cock, feel the heat of her mouth, her throat.

Christ! What the hell was wrong with him?

Standing here with her in his arms, her back up against a tree, sweating and wanting and warring with himself.

He was trying to keep this woman safe, and all he wanted to do was paw her behind a tree at a public event. It was all wrong. He was wrong for her.

He couldn't be anything to her.

"Sandrine. I care about you," he whispered. "I don't want you to get hurt."

"I'm London Sandrine now, remember? I have friends, and suitors, and I can take care of myself." She pulled away from him and left him standing there, still sweating, still burning with desire.

Chisholme returned, trailed by an attendant with a tray of lemonades.

Dane barely stopped himself from sticking out a foot to trip Chisholme and to wipe the pleased grin off his stupid face.

She's mine, Chisholme.

No, she wasn't. And she never could be.

When he rejoined his friends, the boxing match had gone seven rounds already. In the eighth, Tuckwell won, and Dane's heart sank. The men threatening him were powerful and not to be taken lightly.

The threat was real. The danger to him, and anyone close to him, was real.

Chapter Fourteen

*Set an example for others with the impeccable
morality of your words and deeds.*
— Mrs. Oliver's Rules for Young Ladies

I'm afraid that he won't see us," Sandrine said to
Miss Hodwell as they traveled by carriage to Rydell
House. Her friend had insisted on accompanying
her to see Lord Dane about the petition. Sandrine
also wanted to pass along the observations she'd
made at the prizefight yesterday.

"Nonsense, of course he'll see us. I have a plate
of my fanciest macaroons. Of course we have no
need of culinary bribes when you're in the room.
I do believe he appreciates you more than sweet
treats."

"He doesn't appreciate me. He wants me to
leave London, and he won't be pleased to see me
again."

"I won't allow him to dash your dreams simply
because he wants a quick profit."

"I'm willing to play any games necessary to
win the manor house."

"Is that what you're doing with that fetching
new hairstyle and those low-cut bodices? I think
it's a good plan to win his heart and bend him to
your will."

"You know about that?"

"I'm not blind, Sandrine. And I used to be a young lady myself."

"Why did you never marry?"

"Never wanted to. Eve and I have built a wonderful life together."

"You certainly have."

"I must caution you though. Protect your heart carefully, lest Lord Dane hurt you again."

"There's no possibility of that. Any feelings I entertained for him are but a distant and distasteful memory." She was no longer a foolish and sheltered girl. Now she wore a pink sash and played a rake's wicked games.

"That's the spirit. We'll vanquish him yet."

The same stern and dignified butler Sandrine had encountered before answered the door at Rydell House.

"Please tell Lord Dane that Miss Hodwell and Miss Oliver are here to see him," Miss Hodwell said. "And we've brought macaroons."

"Very good, ma'am. Please wait here."

He returned swiftly and escorted them into Lord Dane's study, where Dane was sequestered at his desk with a man who had a pockmarked face and wore spectacles and a drab gray suit.

"Miss Hodwell. Miss Oliver," Lord Dane said. "May I present the Rydell steward, Mr. Leo Cleveland?"

Mr. Cleveland bowed without smiling and turned back to Lord Dane. "We should finish discussing the charity ball, your lordship."

"Pleased to meet you, Mr. Cleveland," Miss Hodwell said cheerily. "We brought a peace offering for you, Lord Dane." She held out the silver plate piled high with macaroons. "Care to try one, Mr. Cleveland?"

"I don't eat sweets, madam," he said fussily, glancing at the plate with disdain.

"Lord Dane?"

He looked tired today but still breathtakingly handsome. It took a mighty effort not to stare at him. She'd so recently been pressed up against the rough bark of a tree by his formidable body. What she'd told Miss Hodwell had been a lie. She still had feelings for him, struggle as she might to banish them.

You have feelings for a man who doesn't even exist, she reminded herself.

"Thank you, but I'm afraid if I eat one of those I'll smudge the account books, and Cleveland will have none of that. These ladies are here about the fate of Squalton Manor, Cleveland. You recall their historical charity?"

"Oh yes, his grace sent a substantial donation to the Squalton Historical Society every year."

"He did?" Sandrine asked, puzzled.

"It's all recorded here." Mr. Cleveland found a book and opened it. "Three hundred pounds per annum for the upkeep of Squalton Manor to benefit the Squalton Historical Preservation and Improvement Society and the Squalton Benevolent Society."

"How very peculiar," Miss Hodwell said. "Miss

Oliver, did our society ever receive a princely sum such as that?"

"We never received even a farthing. I'm quite sure of it! There must be some mistake."

"No mistake, I assure you, Miss Oliver." Mr. Cleveland frowned at her. "The treasurer of your society would be the one to confirm the receipt."

"I'm the secretary of the society, and I record any charitable gifts."

"I see," he said, looking doubtful that any woman could serve in such a capacity. "The gentlemen of the society must know the whereabouts of the funds."

"Perhaps they were waylaid somehow?" Miss Hodwell asked. "Lost in transit. Highway robbery, perhaps?"

"Every year?" Sandrine asked.

"Please refrain from impugning the memory of the late Duke of Rydell," Mr. Cleveland said. "He lived for charitable concerns. His annual charity ball raises more money than any other event in London. Speaking of which, your lordship, I've been attempting to tell you that the ball is scheduled for next week, and there are urgent matters for you to attend to."

"No one will expect me to host a charity ball while I'm still in mourning."

"On the contrary, they will expect the ball to go on as planned as a memorial to your brother's life work."

"Out of the question."

"The tickets have all been sold, your lordship.

The soprano has been paid, and the orchestra contracted."

"Refund the tickets. Don't accept the donations."

"We can't give back all the money. I believe some of it has already been spent."

"What do you mean, spent? I thought all proceeds went to the various charitable beneficiaries?"

"Er, that is, I believe your brother used some of the funds for the administration of the event. It's all in this portfolio." He held out a thin leather folder. "And it was your brother's dying wish that you host the ball."

"He did say something about the charity ball . . . but I can't host an event such as that."

"Allow me to run through the portfolio with you. I want to show you the pamphlet that will be distributed at the event. I've notated several questions on some of the documents regarding your instructions for portions of the evening, specifically the auction."

"I can't host it, and that's an end to it. We'll postpone until next year."

"I have a wonderful idea, Lord Dane," Miss Hodwell broke in. "A perfect solution to everyone's problems. If the charity ball is to be held next week and it can't be canceled without causing an uproar, Miss Oliver and I will assist with the preparations. She knows more about charitable organizing than anyone else. In addition to her work with the historical and the benevolent societies, she also volunteers her time at the Squalton Orphan Asylum. Allow us to organize your ball, and you'll find it will be more successful than ever before. And then there is the fact that we could safely see the funds collected for the historical society back to Squalton."

"I was under the impression that Miss Oliver was leaving London expeditiously," Lord Dane said in a warning tone.

"I'm not leaving until the end of next week. I'd be more than happy to assist with the charity ball, your lordship."

"Then, it's all settled." Miss Hodwell sat back in her chair with a satisfied expression. "Hand over that portfolio, Mr. Cleveland, we'll have a look at your notes and ensure that all is prepared to your specifications."

Mr. Cleveland clutched the papers to his chest, glancing at her sticky fingers. "This is highly irregular."

"Oh very well." Lord Dane threw up his hands. "Give them what they want, Cleveland. I've learned the hard way that Miss Oliver is a very determined young lady when it comes to charities. You can help host the charity ball, but then you'll leave London directly, the very next day. Is that understood, Miss Oliver?"

"Yes, your lordship." She'd been planning to leave that day with her friends.

"Are you sure they're the most . . . suitable hosts, your lordship?" Cleveland asked.

"Give Miss Oliver the portfolio, Cleveland, and we'll talk more about this tomorrow."

"Very good." Mr. Cleveland didn't look pleased

about it, but he handed it over as instructed and left the study.

Did Lord Dane truly not want to host the event, or was he worried about the dangerous men who'd threatened him? He had a thunderous look on his face today. She had to tell him what she'd come to tell him.

"Why don't you want to host the charity ball, Lord Dane? It will be an excellent way to carry on your brother's legacy."

"I'd rather cancel the thing. I have enough to deal with."

"But you heard your steward. The tickets have been sold, the monies partially spent," Miss Hodwell reminded him.

"I know nothing of running charitable events. I always hated attending them as a boy. My father preening about, wanting everyone to pat him on the back for being such a virtuous man. All the other patrons only there to display their wealth and status."

"A very cynical view. I should think that some must have unselfish motives, and the charity ball gives them a chance to contribute in a meaningful way."

"Not many. They're hiding vanity and a passion for display under a veil of benevolence so that they can congratulate themselves on such meritorious duty. And now, if you'll excuse me, ladies, I have an appointment to keep with the Duke of Osborne."

"And we're on our way to an engagement with

Baron Chisholme," Sandrine said. "He's taking me to see the Tower of London."

"I told you not to associate with him," Lord Dane growled.

"And I told you that you have no authority over me."

Miss Hodwell eyed them with delight on her face. "I'll leave you this plate of macaroons for your dessert, Lord Dane."

He escorted them to the door, and Miss Hodwell was already in the hallway when Sandrine turned back to Lord Dane.

"I must tell you something," she whispered urgently. "I observed the crowd closely after our conversation at the prizefight, and there was a man who watched you intently the entire day. His gaze never strayed from you. He was tall, well-dressed, with a thin mustache and a nearly bald head. I orchestrated it so that I bumped into him accidentally and glanced more closely at his clothing, and I saw that he wore a curious stickpin in his cravat in the shape of a scorpion. I made a sketch of it." She handed the paper to him.

"You bumped into him on purpose?"

"He didn't know that."

"Sandrine. My God, you're not listening to me. You can't associate with these men, they're dangerous, do you hear me? Three of them threatened me with fists and knives."

"How about, 'Thank you, Miss Oliver, this is extremely useful information'?"

"It is useful information, but the risk of obtaining it was too great."

"You don't care if you live or die, racing your curricles, so it's up to others to take an interest in keeping you alive."

"Good day, Miss Oliver," Lord Dane said through gritted teeth, practically pushing her out the door.

DANE AND WARBURTON were shown into the town house of Dalton, Duke of Osborne, and ushered into a study to wait.

"That woman will be the death of me," Dane grumbled.

"If the extortionists don't knife you first."

"Believe me, they have nothing on Miss Sandrine Oliver when she wants to plague a man."

"She's only having revenge on the sorry way you treated her. What did she do now?" asked Warburton.

"Put herself in harm's way trying to help me. I'll tell you about it when Osborne arrives."

"She seems quite capable and intelligent. I think she can take care of herself."

"It's all a sham, this London sophistication, attack-the-lord-in-his-lair act. I know her, and she's the sweetest, most openhearted, innocent, and generous soul I've ever met."

"Has you hot under the cravat, it's plain to see."

Dane groaned. "That's the problem. I want her, Warburton." He gripped the arm of his chair. "I can't stop wanting her, and it's driving me to the edge of madness."

"Only natural. She's a pretty little thing."

"Who's a pretty little thing?" the imposing Dalton, Duke of Osborne, asked as he entered the study, followed by another man with the same sandy hair and height.

"Miss Sandrine Oliver, a young lady from Squalton-on-Sea," Warburton said. "She's here in London to convince Lord Dane to sign over a historical building to a charitable society, but she'll stop at nothing short of bringing him to his knees."

Osborne nodded sagely. "Never underestimate the power of a determined young lady to upend your life."

"That's certainly the truth," the other man said. "Case in point being how Thea tamed you, Dalton."

"Warburton, Lord Dane, this is my brother, Patrick. He's my legal counsel and assists me with all manner of investigations. I assume that's why you're here today, to continue the relationship your deceased brother established, Lord Dane?"

"What relationship are you referring to?"

"Your brother came to me a week before he died. He told me that he'd been the victim of extortion for years, and he was fed up. He wanted to extricate himself and hired me and Patrick to help uncover the identity of his blackmailers."

"And have you been successful?" Dane asked eagerly.

"Not yet. We were wrapping up another case first, and we didn't have a chance to begin your brother's request before he died."

"You're right that we're here about the same issue," Dane said. "I was set upon by three men in a dark alleyway. They placed a hood over my head so I couldn't see them. One of them, whose name I think begins with the letters *L-A*, told me that my brother owed them money and had also been performing illicit tasks at their insistence."

"Which corroborates what your brother told me."

"My brother and I were estranged. This is all a complete shock to me."

"Now that you're the heir presumptive, the blackmailers are trying to continue their lucrative scheme."

"They said they have incriminating information that could ruin my family. I want to know who they are and what, if anything, they have on my brother. I could not care less about my reputation, but I wouldn't want to see my sister-in-law and her children harmed. I'm fervently praying she gives birth to a boy soon."

"You don't want to be a duke?" Patrick asked. He had a peculiar accent. Dane remembered hearing something about Osborne's brother being stolen away when he was a boy and raised in America.

"Hell no!"

Osborne chuckled. "Typical spare. You haven't had to deal with any of the weighty responsibilities. You'd sooner shoot yourself in the foot than take a seat in Parliament. I know all about you and the Thunderbolt Club. Crazy lot of risk-taking scoundrels, eh, Warburton?"

"Excuse me," Warburton said. "You're one to talk when it's you who tracks down and prosecutes dangerous criminals."

"So that's why my brother came to you," Dane said.

"Let's just say that we help people out of complicated situations. Patrick takes care of the legal side of things, and I do the grunt work. Sometimes people come to us with matters that they can't bring to the authorities. We only take a case if it's worth risking our lives for. I wasn't certain that your brother was blameless in this matter. I've been investigating him as much as the blackmailers."

"And?"

"On the surface your brother appears to have been clean as whistle. But my instinct tells me he was hiding something, and when you discover the truth you'll know as much as the extortionists. What demands have they made so far?"

"I gave them two hundred pounds and bet on the man they told me to at a prizefight and handed over my winnings."

"That's good for now. Go along with their demands, within reason, of course. Make them think that you're an easy mark, that you'll do their bidding. Patrick and I will begin our investigation in earnest."

"We'll thwart them together," Warburton said. "We do have one interesting angle to pursue. There's been a man asking questions about Dane at Madam Avalon's Silver Palace and observing him in public. He's tall, slender, with wispy hair, a habit of sucking his teeth, and he wears a stickpin in the shape of a scorpion."

Patrick gasped. "A scorpion! Are you sure?"

"Here's a sketch Miss Oliver made."

Patrick and Osborne studied the sketch. "I know this insignia well," Patrick said. "Your man is a member of the Order of the Scorpion, or at least that's the public name, a shadow organization that some believe are the true rulers of this country. I hope it's not them behind your brother's troubles. These men are pitiless, obsessed with accumulating wealth and power."

"Our father was a member of the Order," Osborne said grimly. "You don't want to go up against them. They have their grimy hands in every facet of government, commerce, and law enforcement."

"I may not have a choice," Dane replied.

"Have a care," said Osborne. "I know from personal experience the dangers that you face. Pretend to be an easy mark, but don't be sucked into their crimes. If you pretend to be something long enough, the lines blur between pretense and truth. Don't swallow enough darkness that the light of honor is extinguished forever."

"I don't need your warnings. I've already sunk lower than you'll ever go."

"I doubt that," said Osborne quietly. The dangerous look on his handsome but battered face made Dane believe him.

"I'll do some discreet inquiring about a connection between your brother and the Order," Patrick said.

"And I'll speak to your brother's compatriots in Parliament. Don't quite know how it happened, but I'm known as a reformed scoundrel now. I walk in elevated circles."

"You know very well how it happened," his brother laughed. "You were reformed by Thea."

"Ah, she does allow me to continue my work, but she makes me promise to leave the fisticuffs to younger men. My shoulder's still creaky from too many fights."

"And my face has seen better days since the war," Warburton said. "What about you, Patrick? Do you have a wife?"

"Papa?" A young boy with mussed reddish-brown hair ran into the study.

"Van!" Patrick embraced him. "Did you escape your governess again?"

"I saw the curricle outside, and I want a closer look. It's such a beauty. Is it yours, sir?" he asked Warburton.

"It's mine," Dane said with a smile.

"Will you take me for a ride in your curricle? How fast does it go?"

"Lord Dane's too busy, I'm afraid," Patrick said.

"Some other time," Dane promised.

"When I grow up, I'm going to have the fastest curricle in London. Flor says she'll keep a fast carriage and ride astride, but I told her that's ridiculous. Ladies can't ride astride."

Patrick ruffled his son's hair. "Go back to your studies, Van. We'll go for a walk in the park later." The boy left, dragging his feet and casting glances back at the men.

"Bright child. His mother must be very proud."

"His mother passed away."

"I'm sorry."

"I keep trying to convince him to remarry, but he hasn't found any English roses to his satisfaction," said Osborne.

"Do you know where the Order of the Scorpion meets?" Dane asked. "Perhaps I can pretend to be interested in joining them?"

"I don't advise such a rash tactic," said Osborne. "They're far too secretive and powerful. Better for us to discover the identity of the man who was asking about you at Madam Avalon's salon. That's the first place I'd start. Go back there, ask the footmen, ask everyone if they know him or his name."

Dane nodded. "I'll go there right now. Though, I should change into evening wear first."

WITHIN AN HOUR he was freshly shaved, garbed, and ready to take matters into his own hands at the Silver Palace. This was much better. Instead of waiting for them to contact him, to manipulate him to their own ends, he was lying in wait for one of them.

"Do you have a guest list for tonight's ball?" he asked Madam Avalon.

"Of course. But sometimes I allow uninvited guests to attend. That's why I keep such a healthy contingent of strong footmen here. I don't want anything unwanted happening to any lady. I try to screen each guest personally, but sometimes the odd stranger does slip through. And then there are the young debutantes who do sometimes dare each other to sneak in during a masked ball for a little thrill. I keep a very special watch on those and make sure they go home early with their reputations unscathed."

Dane smiled at the notion. Never in a million years would he see Sandrine at a place like this. She was safe at home with Mrs. McGovern and Miss Hodwell. Probably wearing a high-necked virginal white nightgown.

She'd already knelt to say her prayers and she was tucked into her bed, dreaming about the innocent things that good girls dreamed of . . . rainbows and unicorns and valiant, honorable knights on chargers.

Chapter Fifteen

Never visit museums or portrait galleries. Viewing nude sculptures or paintings has a corrupting effect on young ladies.
    —Mrs. Oliver's Rules for Young Ladies

A re we really doing this?" Sandrine whispered.

"I've always wanted to attend one of these masked balls," Francesca said, her eyes sparkling with excitement behind her mask. "We'll observe for a little while and leave. We'll stay long enough for you to fulfill the secret and scandalous initiation rite."

Sandrine wasn't worried about her identity being revealed because the ladies had done a wonderful job with her costume. They were all wearing elaborate powdered wigs created by Francesca that hid their natural hair color. Francesca's wig was a pale pink color that truly was a sight to behold. They had beauty marks pasted next to their lips and powder on their faces. They wore molded satin demimasks with lace edges and feather adornments, and silk gowns with panniers embroidered in paste jewels, in the style of the court of Louis XIV.

Like the others, she was wearing a cloak, which she didn't have to take off if she didn't want to, and she had a fan to hide her face should that be necessary.

"All right. It's time to go in. We should speak as little as possible," instructed Francesca, "and if you see someone you recognize, act as though they are a stranger. And remember to use our code names."

Sandrine's code name for the evening was Lady Sapphire.

They entered through the marble-columned doorway into a long hall, their slippers making shushing noises on the thick carpet. Torch-lit portraits lined the hall. Sandrine expected to see stiff, unsmiling ancestors in velvet capes, and the paintings at the beginning were respectable enough, but as they progressed, more and more clothing disappeared. Women wore nothing more than necklaces. Men had white sheets wrapped around their loins and nothing else.

She stopped in front of one portrait. "He looks familiar." She stepped closer. "Is this . . . ?"

"Lord Dane Walker. In the flesh." Marta giggled. "He's handsomely endowed, is he not?"

"How can you tell with that fig leaf covering it?" asked Roslyn.

Francesca peered at the portrait. "It's a very large fig leaf. It must be symbolic."

Sandrine was too stunned to do anything but gawk at the painting. She'd pictured him without his clothing, but here he was. Nude. Reclining on a velvet couch with only a fig leaf covering his— what had Marta called it?—*endowment*.

That handsome, arrogant face with the deep

dimple in his chin. So much sleek, powerful muscle on display. The painting should be titled *How to Tempt a Good Girl to Go Bad*.

"Lady Sapphire's having a *very* good look." Marta poked her in the ribs. "Have you ever seen beneath a fig leaf?"

"I've seen village boys splashing about in the sea."

Her imagination ran rampant, delving under the fig leaf and painting his endowment in big, bold strokes. A shivery thrill of anticipation chased along her spine.

This. This was why she was here. To do something secret and scandalous.

Not *too* scandalous, her conscience warned her.

Tonight was another line drawn in the sand. On one side was her mother proclaiming that the world was a dangerous place and it was safer to stay indoors and only have a very small sphere of experiences and acquaintances. On the other side was something wholly unknown.

Who might she be without her mother's voice in her head? The constant inner monologue of rules and fears wasn't simply going to disappear. It would be with her every step of the way whispering, *This is wrong, scandalous, perilous. Bad things will happen. Don't do anything you'll regret. Nothing you'll have to hide.*

But there was a new voice now, and it didn't whisper: it rang out clear as a bell and told her that avoiding all regrets meant avoiding life itself.

She wanted to truly experience life for the first time on her own terms.

She was ready to cross this line.

"Shall we go in, ladies?" she asked.

"If Lord Dane's here in the flesh, which he's bound to be, you'll have another opportunity to make him fall madly in love with you and agree to give you the manor house," Marta said.

Sandrine agreed. If there was one place to find a wicked rake, it would be in this gardenia-scented demimonde filled with flickering candlelight and provocative portraits. "But I thought the point was to remain incognito?"

"Keep your identity secret until you see Lord Dane, and then whisper your name in his ear," Roslyn advised.

"Ladies of the court, welcome," spoke a musical voice behind them. "I'm Madam Avalon, your hostess. You are most welcome here this evening."

She was slim and small of stature, but something in her carriage gave her a commanding air of height and importance. She had high, sharp cheekbones, silver-streaked hair piled high on her head and accented by glittering diamonds, and eyes that were a clear, summery blue.

"I see you're admiring my portraiture."

"Did you paint these?" Sandrine asked. "They're very handsome."

Marta snorted. "She likes that one in particular."

"Ah, yes, one of my most popular portraits. I've painted several replicas on special order for ladies who wished to remain anonymous. I could make one for you, if you like."

Sandrine swallowed. Wouldn't her mother just

die if she arrived home with this nude portrait in tow?

"Have you ever painted the portrait of a military gentleman, Madam Avalon?" Marta asked.

"They tend to like to keep their uniforms and medals on at all times."

"Such a pity. Perhaps I can persuade one of my beaux to pose for you."

"In a sash covered in medals and nothing more," Roslyn suggested with a wink.

Madam Avalon gave a silvery laugh. "I have a new portrait that might interest you ladies. I'm still putting the finishing touches on, but it's nearly ready." She ushered them to the window where a canvas draped with linen sat on an easel. She pulled back the covering to reveal another tall, imposing man. This time there was no fig leaf.

Roslyn sucked in her breath. "Kenwick, as I live and breathe!"

"Do you know him?" Lady Avalon asked.

"Everyone knows the Earl of Kenwick," said Roslyn with a breezy laugh. She studied the portrait. "Have you flattered him, or is this to scale?"

"Very much to scale. He's been blessed, has the earl."

Roslyn devoured the portrait with her eyes. "This is highly enlightening."

"That's what this salon is all about, my dears. Enlightenment. I make my paintings for women to gaze upon. I upend the normal social standards of what is an acceptable subject for a painting. Or an acceptable subject for a woman to paint. And I'm condemned for it. But this salon is a safe place. I have a feeling that you are young ladies who would not like your identities revealed." She held up a hand. "You don't need to confirm or deny anything. Please know that the attendants I've hired this evening will pay special attention to your safety. You should leave before the stroke of midnight, for it is after that hour that the more . . . scandalous activities begin. Do I have your promise?"

The ladies nodded their agreement. They'd planned to leave early.

"Very good. Now, we should make haste because the evening's glittering spectacle is about to begin!"

They followed her down the hallway and through a set of doors into a spacious antechamber lit by crystal chandeliers and filled with the scent of the hothouse flowers garlanding the walls. "Enjoy yourselves this evening, ladies. I'll have my eye on you to see that you do."

"I've already enjoyed myself immensely," Sandrine said, thinking about the portrait of Dane.

"As have I," Roslyn agreed.

"She's very glamorous." Francesca watched Madam Avalon drift through the crowd, stopping to bestow a kiss or a whispered word among the guests.

"Are you ready, Lady Sapphire?" Francesca asked Sandrine.

"As ready as I'm likely to be, Lady Flame."

They wandered through a series of chaotic, gorgeous rooms filled with richly garbed revelers reclining on velvet cushions, drinking champagne, conversing, and laughing merrily. Sandrine kept close to Francesca, attempting to appear sophisticated and blasé about it all, though when she glimpsed what appeared to be two men and a woman all kissing one another, her heart began to gallop.

When they entered the ballroom, Sandrine saw Dane immediately. He'd made no attempt to conceal himself. He wore a simple black silk mask and his customary black attire. She met his gaze across the floor. There was no flare of recognition, only a flicker of interest as he studied her face and gown. His heated gaze was almost a physical weight on her body.

She shivered, imagining his hands, his tongue, following the same path down her body.

She'd come here to do something secret and scandalous.

She'd come here to bring Lord Dane Walker to his knees.

DANE RECOGNIZED HER immediately.

She might think she could fool him with that powdered wig, mask, and costume, but she was unmistakably Sandrine. The carmine stain applied to the lush contours of her lips made him long to kiss her, and her gown—sweet Lord! The bodice was a narrow strip of yellow silk that only covered the lower half of her breasts, barely skimming over her nipples.

She looked stunning, although no more stunning than she did in a simple white gown with a fresh-scrubbed face. She was spun from sunlight, blue skies, and proverbs. She didn't belong here. But maybe she did. Maybe she really was becoming someone new without her mother's overbearing, overprotective control. He wanted to know this new Sandrine who stared at him so boldly. He could dance one dance with her. That wouldn't be so terrible, would it? No one else knew who she was tonight.

Absolutely not, damn it. He wasn't here to dance, he was here to find the man with the scorpion stickpin, who could be a dangerous criminal mastermind that even the formidable Duke of Osborne feared.

All eyes went to Madam Avalon as she walked to the center of the ebony-inlaid dance floor. "Ladies and gentlemen, revelers of all stripes and predilections, you have entered my court. There is only room here for love, for exploration, for the worship of the beauty that lives within all of us. I have a little surprise for you this evening. Tonight we will not simply dance, we will perform for the honor of being crowned sovereigns of this ball."

Murmurs and exclamations of surprise rose around her. This must be something new.

"I will personally judge the dance competition. Couples on the floor will be evaluated on elegance, ingenuity, and sensuality. If you display none of these attributes, I will tap upon your shoulder, and you and your partner will have to leave the dance floor without a fuss and watch from the sidelines. The final couple left on the floor will be crowned the sovereigns of tonight's festivities and will preside over my court."

He watched Sandrine's bold expression become timid. She shrank back toward the wall, whispering to Miss Francesca McGovern and shaking her head. She must be refusing to enter the dance competition and determined to remain a wallflower. Elation flooded his mind, because if any other man had made a move toward her, Dane would have had to flatten him with a swift punch to the nose.

"I'll make the same speech I always make for the benefit of those who are new this evening," Madam Avalon said. "This salon is a safe space for all. Some are here to partake of the array of pleasures available, and some are here merely to observe. This must be respected by all my patrons. At the first hint of unwanted attentions forced on any guest, you will be forcefully ejected by my vigilant staff, all of whom were chosen for their discretion, loyalty, sizable fists, and even more sizable . . . limbs." Titters from the audience. "Now, with that, let the dance competition begin!"

With Sandrine safely hiding behind a potted plant, Dane searched the crowd for the man with the scorpion stickpin. He'd asked Madam Avalon and her staff to be on the lookout for him as well. If anyone saw him they were to give him a sign.

Several ladies were eyeing him hungrily. One never knew what might happen at Madam Avalon's—a lady was likely to be bold enough to ask him to dance. He drifted to the back of the room, moving closer to Sandrine's hiding place.

Only she wasn't hiding anymore. As the orchestra began playing, she moved closer to the dance floor, eyes shining and jeweled slippers tapping to the music. She wanted to dance. Damn it. Several gentlemen were eyeing her like ravenous beasts, and one had already started to head toward her.

Dane wasn't about to let anyone else claim her as a partner. If she wanted to dance, it would be with him. He strode ahead at a fast clip, cutting off the other man before he reached her.

He caught her hand and lifted it to his lips. "Madam, would you do me the honor?"

"I'd love to." She pitched her voice lower in a vain attempt to conceal her identity.

As the music swelled he brought her to the floor, clasped her by the waist and one of her dainty hands, and led her into the dance. It felt so perfect to hold her, to be close enough that one dip of his head would bring their lips in contact.

She was more enthusiastic than graceful, but she looked so delectable when she spun, her head thrown back, smile glowing brighter than the chandeliers.

He lost himself in the pleasure of touching her, of being the recipient of her smile. She gave herself to the dance, allowing him to lead and show her what to do. He guided her hips into a swaying rhythm, twirling her around to clasp her from behind, fitting her fine curves into his embrace.

Other couples were tapped on the shoulders and asked to leave, but they remained. He forgot all about the competition, forgot there were people watching them, and lost himself in her eyes.

THIS WASN'T ANY kind of dance they taught in finishing school. This was something that Dane was inventing as he went along, a sensual exploration of her body with his eyes, and then with his body, positioning her hips where he wanted them, swaying to the swooning violins.

He was a wonderful dancer. She wanted to stop and just watch him as he moved, sinuous and swaggering. Hip cocked, calling everyone's attention to his endowment sheathed in tight black trousers.

His fingers skimmed the side of her breasts. There were people watching them, watching him touch her. She should be ashamed of the hungry gazes, but she wasn't Sandrine Oliver, a country lady experiencing the London demimonde for the very first time. She was Lady Sapphire, a worldly courtesan. Finally she was acting out scenes from the history books she loved to devour instead of only reading about glamorous balls and lovestruck courtiers.

She leaned back and rested her head on his shoulder as his lips touched her neck. She was dimly aware that there were only three couples left on the dance floor. Roslyn was twirling in a sensual waltz with a gentleman whom Sandrine thought might be Dane's friend, the Earl of Kenwick.

Someone tapped on her shoulder.

She whirled around, but it wasn't Madam Avalon. Instead, a stunning woman with crimson lips, gleaming russet-colored hair, dark brown eyes, and voluptuous curves poured into a silk gown the color of rubies was cutting in to dance with Dane.

"Pardon me, miss," she said to Sandrine, "but this gentleman engaged me for a dance."

Sandrine saw the flash of recognition in Dane's eyes. Recognition and admiration. He dropped Sandrine's hand, gave her a brief bow, and danced away with the redhead, waltzing in lazy circles. They were perfectly matched in height and sensuality, their movements fluid as water.

The air left her lungs as if someone had kicked her in the stomach. Her first thought was to march up to the woman and demand her place back, but Madam Avalon had already tapped the final couple on the shoulder and was announcing that Dane and the mystery woman were to be crowned.

Sandrine didn't wait around to see more. Dane had abandoned her for a sophisticated paramour. He'd publicly humiliated her again. Had she really thought that she could win this game?

She ran out of the ballroom and toward the first door she saw. Maybe she'd only ever be a country lady, gauche and uncultured. Maybe that's how he saw her, even when she was dressed in decadent finery.

The door led to a balcony. She ran down the steps and toward the entrance to a manicured garden, following a path lit by lanterns.

"Wait!" a voice called. "Sandrine, wait a moment?"

But she only ran faster, thinking to lose him in the hedgerows, wanting only to be alone.

Chapter Sixteen

Be ever vigilant against forbidden carnal cravings.

　　　—Mrs. Oliver's Rules for Young Ladies

Dane ran after Sandrine, easily overtaking her. He caught hold of her hand. "Sandrine."

"Don't. Just leave me alone."

"That woman tapped you on the shoulder for a reason, Sandrine. She was acting on Madam Avalon's orders. She knew you were an innocent, and it was for your own protection. I never should have been dancing with you. I didn't know it, but the Sovereigns she crowned were expected to share a public kiss as part of their final dance. You could have been ruined in public. She never would have picked an innocent to be Queen."

She stopped attempting to run away and searched his face in the moonlight. "Does that woman have a name? You obviously knew her well."

"Her name is Carissa. And, yes, I do know her. She's a courtesan, and she and I had an arrangement many years past."

"I see."

"I don't want to hurt you, Sandrine. Intentionally. Unintentionally. It's the last thing I want."

"And yet you somehow manage to do it so well."

Dane sighed. "I know. Slap me, Sandrine. It might make you feel better."

"I don't want to slap you."

"Seriously, it will do you good. And don't hold back, really let me have it." He closed his eyes and offered his cheek.

"I don't want to slap you," she repeated. "Because I want to kiss you."

His eyes flew open. "Don't do that. No, we can't have any of that. I'm taking you back inside now." He clasped her arm.

"Not before you make it up to me."

She ripped off her mask and threw it to the ground. Then she started taking out hairpins from her wig, one by one, until she freed the hairpiece and set it on a marble bench.

"Sandrine, what are you doing?"

She fluffed her hair around her shoulders and it tumbled lower, covering her mounded breasts. All he could do was watch, entranced, not daring to breathe.

Her eyes glittered like gemstones in the moonlight. "I know you want to kiss me."

He cleared his throat, preparing to do the right thing and escort her back to her friends and see all four of those hoydens safely back to their carriage with strongly worded instructions to the footmen and outriders to deliver them home forthwith. And not to ever bring them out again.

"I can't kiss you."

"And why is that?"

"You know why. Because I'm a—"

"Bad, heartless rake, and I'm a sheltered, innocent young lady."

"Exactly."

"But I'm not Sandrine tonight. I'm Lady Sapphire, a worldly, experienced courtesan, and I've come here this evening expressly for the purpose of being kissed in the gardens by a notorious rake." She reached up and untied his mask, setting it aside. "From the look in your eyes you want to do more than kiss me. It looks to me like you have an entire list of depraved things you'd like to do to me."

"You may be right." Hell, she had *no* idea how long the list was.

"You wouldn't be doing things *to* me, you'd be doing them *with* me, at my specific request. And do you want to know why I chose you, Mystery Man whose name I don't even know?"

Don't ask her. Escort her back. End this now.

"Why did you choose me?"

"Because I saw a very nearly nude portrait of you in the entrance hall, and it gave me forbidden carnal cravings."

He tried not to smile and failed. "I'm heartily sorry for giving you carnal cravings. I'll have Madam Avalon take down my portrait."

"Too late. I've already seen it. There you stand, staring at the painter with challenging arrogance, confident in your attractions, your handsome face rendered perfectly, sensual lips and that dimple in your chin, and all with dark temptation in your eyes. One large hand holding a fig leaf over your . . . endowment. Leaving that alone to a lady's imagination. And I couldn't stop imagining what was under that fig leaf. I'm imagining it right now."

A choking noise emerged from his lips. She was imagining his cock right now with her innocent mind, trying to picture what it looked like. His cock responded by swelling against the placket of his breeches, informing him that certain parts of his body would be more than happy to satisfy her curiosity.

"Your body is so different from mine, Dane. You're sculpted from muscle that looks hard as marble."

"Especially when you're close by."

"What do you mean?"

"Merely a little joke."

"My mother was always warning me about carnal cravings, going on and on about how the serpent tempted Eve to sin, and now, for the very first time, I understand what she was on about. I'd never felt anything of the sort before I met you. It's a feeling like rushing water inside my body, a blissful glow in my heart, a quickened pulse, little thrills running up my spine. A longing to be kissed. I'm not leaving this garden until you've satisfied that craving."

"If I give you one kiss, you'll be satisfied?"

"Completely."

It was a very dangerous idea and twisted logic, at best, but his mind had ceased being logical, and desire had taken the driver's seat.

"One kiss, that's all you'll get, my worldly courtesan."

One soft brush of his lips against hers. Nothing more. Hands by his sides, not exploring her curves. Just a little taste inside her mouth. She opened for him with a sweet eagerness that shattered his resolutions. He caressed her hips and brought her closer, molding his body into hers. She shifted her hips, moving against his cock, her breasts crushed against his chest.

Too much.

He broke the kiss, but she pulled him back with her hands on his shoulders, pressing him closer until he was lost to everything but her. He deepened the kiss, skimming his hands down the sides of her breasts and lifting her bottom until he could fill his hands with her generous curves and settle her more tightly against him.

This was more than just a kiss. It was everything he'd been dreaming about since the moment he met her. This melding of bodies, hearts beating together, her soft encouraging moan urging him to lay her down in the grass.

He pulled back reluctantly. "There," he said, breathing heavily. "One kiss. That's all you get."

Her eyes were hazy blue in the moonlight, her lips swollen and red from his kisses. Her breasts rose and fell, nipples nearly visible below her low bodice. She made an erotic portrait. One he'd like to hang in his bedroom.

She held his gaze, and a smile teased her lips. "I want more."

"You can't have it." He wouldn't be the one to ruin her. She would regret it. And she would hate him. And he'd live with her hatred for the rest of his life. Like he'd lived with his brother's hatred.

"I'm here in your world, Dane. Show me, teach me, tell me what we would do together in this garden if I were a bold lady looking for pleasure and I picked you out of the crowd because I saw your portrait. What would you do to me? Tell me. Tell me *everything*."

"Everything."

"All of it."

He groaned.

She'd been molded by a restrictive mother trying to force her onto a narrow life path, but she wanted to stray. He read it in her eyes. Felt it when she brushed her fingers over his knuckles, her touch so tentative, more of a whisper than a touch.

She wanted him to corrupt her, teach her about life, awaken her passions, take control and give her the thrills she craved.

"You want me to tell you about it."

She nodded. "Only words."

He took a breath, struggling for control. He couldn't give her those thrills, but he could tell her about them. It didn't make sense, but he didn't care.

"I'd lay my coat down on the grass. Then, I'd ease you down onto it."

"That much we can do, no?"

Yes, they could do that much. And nothing more.

He laid his coat down and then eased her down onto it next to him and bent to whisper in her ear. "I'd take my cues from you. If you were eager, if you moaned my name softly and pulled me against you, we'd move swiftly. Or if you wanted me to take my time, to linger, I'd tease you first before I kissed you. Holding my lips over yours, not kissing you, not yet, learning the shape of you with my hands first, the silk of your skin. Touch before taste. I'd savor the lingering scent of the rose sachet you keep with your linens."

She shifted restlessly, laying her head on his shoulder.

"And finally I'd kiss you. Take your lips with mine, fill your mouth with my tongue, invade you, taste you. I'd wrap my hand around the back of your neck and tip you up for my invasion. I might use both hands, my thumbs tilting your chin up, so that you can feel how big my hands are, how small and delicate your neck is in my hands. I'd feel the pulse at the base of your neck with my thumb, press softly, show you that I'm in control. Listen for your response. And then, as our kiss deepened and you moved restlessly beneath me, I'd know that you wanted more. I'd whisper in your ear, 'I'm going to touch you now. Do you want me to touch you?'"

She made a little whimpering noise.

"You'd moan and command me to touch you. I'd slide my hands inside your bodice, fill my hands with your soft breasts, flick my thumbs across your nipples until they were hard and sensitive. I'd have to taste you there. I'd have to suck on your nipples, and while I sucked and licked and tasted my fill, you'd begin to squirm under me, your thighs would part, and you'd seek my arousal through your skirts, you'd grind up against me, and you'd feel me nudging between your thighs. I'd push your skirts up, spread your thighs with my palms, look at your body in the moonlight, spread you for my view."

She gasped. "You would look at me so openly?"

"I'd want to see your secrets before I tasted them."

"Tasted . . . ?"

"I'd give you pleasure with my fingers, inside you, moving over you. Then I'd move down your body, spread your thighs with my hands, hold them open while I slid my tongue over your secret places, dipping inside you, tasting your sweetness, bringing you to pleasure with my tongue. Only then, after I'd worked until you found your pleasure, then I'd think about my own. I'd ask if you wanted to touch me, discover what I'm famous for."

Sandrine snorted. "Famous, eh?"

"Deservedly so. And you'd say, 'Yes, yes!' and you'd wrap your small hand around my hard cock, and you'd thrill with the knowledge that you were in control, that you could give me pleasure or you could get up and leave me cold, sweating with need, praying for release. You'd look at me with a wicked glint in your eyes, and you'd ask if I wanted more and I'd choke out a *yes.* I'd tell you to use your mouth. I'd say, 'Take my cock in your hand and guide it between your lips. Swirl your tongue around the head.'"

He heard her sharp intake of breath and smiled against her hair. "Shall I continue my list of wicked things we'd do together, or have you had enough?"

"I—I would place my mouth on your . . ."

"Endowment. Or cock, as I like to call it. You'd suck me inside your mouth, and it would feel so heavenly I'd want to be inside you instead. I'd lift your head, and I'd tell you to lie back and spread your thighs. I'd wrap my cock with a protective sheath and then I'd position myself at your entrance, and I'd slowly enter you until I was deep inside you."

"Oh." She buried her head against his chest. "Go on . . ."

"You'd lock your legs around my hips and tell me to ride faster, harder."

Her breathing quickened, and her chest rose and fell rapidly.

"I'd rock into you," he whispered in her ear. "Then I'd lift you by your hips and place you on top of me in a seated position. Once you were on top you'd set the pace and how deeply I was allowed to reach. You'd drive me mad by lifting away, not allowing me to thrust deep enough. You'd enjoy teasing me, making me sweat and groan."

"I would be the one in control?"

"Completely. But then you'd relinquish that control to me. Your head would fall onto my shoulder, you'd moan and rock back and forth, your heels crossed behind my back. I'd hold your hips, and I wouldn't restrain myself any longer. I'm not good for much in this life but I'm good at this. I know how to give pleasure, and I know how to take it, master it, set you free by making you feel safe enough to relinquish control to me."

He stroked his finger down her cheek. The gentlest of touches. Only a fraction, the faintest hint, of how he wanted to touch her.

"I'd be so proud of the noises you'd make, the urgent plea in your voice. I'd bury my fingers in your hair and pull your head back. Bite your throat. Take control. You'd ask me to be a little bit rough with you. You'd want to be wicked. And I'm the devil who would get you there. I'd flip you over and ride you from behind. And the pleasure would grip us tightly, wring us out, so sweet and wild. And we'd ride the pleasure, the aftershocks, together, clasped in each other's arms."

Damn. Had he really said all of that? His cock was so hard it was about to break free from his trousers. And her hand was resting on his thigh.

"Dane?" she whispered. "I came here tonight to do scandalous things, not just to hear about them."

He set her at arm's length. "No. That was the deal. I tell you a list of wicked things I'd like to do to you, and then that's the end of it. You go home to your safe bed."

"What if I told you that I would go back into

that ballroom and find another handsome gentleman and take his hand and lead him into a
bower and kiss him?"

"I wouldn't believe you because while you want
a thrill, you also want safety, and that would be
one line too many to cross."

"You're right, I wouldn't do that. But I'd do this.
I'd ask for a little taste. One small wicked thing
from the long list you just gave me."

Dane knew that what she was asking wasn't
right. One little thing—did that somehow make
it better? Less depraved? It's only a safe, controlled debauchery with clearly delineated parameters. *I'm not going to ravage you, but you can
have one debauched item of your choice.*

"One wicked thing," he said.

"Only one, mind you."

She wanted to break free from her mother's
strict rules. He wouldn't take her virtue, but he
could do as she asked. Give her that small taste
of wickedness that she craved.

"If I agreed to your request, what would you
want?"

"To be touched."

Christ, that's all he wanted to do. Put his hands
all over every inch of her, glut himself on her soft
skin, her lavish curves. "Where would you want
me to touch you?"

"Here," she said and touched her breast, "and
here." She trailed a hand over her belly.

Watching her touch herself was his undoing.
He'd give her one thrill, and he'd take nothing

in return except the satisfaction of her sighs, her pleasure. He was selfish and good-for-nothing, but here in this garden he could unselfishly give her what he gave the best: pleasure.

"I won't do anything you don't explicitly ask me for, Sandrine. If you want to stop, simply say so. I'm not going to take anything from you. I'm going to give it to you, and your pleasure will be my only reward."

This was his reward. Pulling her backward into his embrace until she fit perfectly against his chest. Wrapping his arms around her.

He couldn't resist her whispered, dreamy-eyed request.

There were strict parameters. That made everything all right.

If he'd done his job right, she'd be primed and ready. He situated her back against his chest, his knees on either side of her. "Now, then," he murmured in her ear. "We'll start with this."

SANDRINE HEARD HER mother's voice in her mind: men are beasts, you can't trust them, they speak with the voice of the serpent, tempting you to sin, dooming the world to darkness.

She believed him though. He said he wasn't going to ravish her, and she believed that it was true. She was completely safe with him—if she wanted to be.

He would escort her back, and she could go home and think about this night and think about what a close call she'd had, how near she'd come to danger. How she'd held her hand out to the flame but hadn't been burned.

But she was already burning. His words had lit the fire of longing deep inside her.

She needed him to fan the flames higher.

She could flirt with disaster. With this man whom she trusted with her body in this moment. She could have a taste.

He slipped his hand under the edge of her bodice and cupped her breast lightly. She'd wanted him to touch her, to hold her. She was wrapped inside the circle of his arms, warm and protected.

When he shaped her nipple with his fingers, she had to bite down on her lip to keep from crying out with joy. She'd thought about him touching her as he talked, and the anticipation had built and built until she was stretched taut, quivering like an arrow pulled tight across a bow, ready to fly. He kept one hand in her bodice as his other hand drew soft little circles on her thigh, up her dress, over her garter.

"Spread your legs for me."

She didn't even think about disobeying. Her breath came in little gasps as he brushed his fingers over her inner thighs, coaxing them to fall wider. Her knees were supported by his, her back supported by his chest. She let her head fall back on his shoulder.

"Good girl. Relax. Close your eyes."

She turned her head and kissed his neck. He caught her lips with his and kissed her forcefully while one hand caressed both of her breasts and the other finally found the place that throbbed and ached for his touch.

His tongue thrust deeply into her mouth, and she opened her lips wider to take him, to match his movements. As his tongue told her to open for him, he spread her thighs wider, positioning her to his liking, and then he slid a finger inside her.

"Oh," she moaned, but the sound was muffled by his lips. He was inside her in two places at once, her mouth and between her thighs, one hand teasing her breasts all the while, lightly pinching her nipples until the need built inside her to a fever pitch.

"Sweet thing, moving your hips, you want more, don't you?"

"Mmm."

"What was that?"

"Yes. I want more."

Something wider, two fingers, or three, sliding into her body, then out again to touch her softly, learn her landscape, sketch her contours with a light touch, easily sliding inside again because she was melting for him.

"Now you're going to come for me, my good girl," he said in a deep, raspy voice.

Her body knew what he meant. She could feel it coming. There it was, starting now, as he stroked her. Her nipples, her secret places. Stroked and caressed her until she was shaking, clenching, with need.

"Now." A command. Spoken with authority by

this man who knew exactly what he was doing to her, knew how to make her body do unpredictable and thrilling things.

"I said now." And she obeyed. Arching her back, anchored by his hands, by his lips against her neck. His deep voice buzzing in her ear. She obeyed him, and she allowed pleasure to take her. Lilting bliss spiraling outward from her core to every part of her body. Such a beautiful surprise to fly apart and be reshaped by his arms.

"You're such a sweet, good girl," he murmured, stroking her hair.

"And you're good too. Stop pretending that you're not."

"I'm not, Sandrine. Did you hear what I told you? Did you feel what I just did to you? A good, honorable man wouldn't have said or done those things."

"You were granting a request. I don't think you were pretending to be someone you aren't in Squalton. I think you are that man, Mr. Smith, who holds balls of yarn for spinster knitters and picks herbs with young ladies and listens so intently to their ghost stories."

"And there it is." He pulled her skirts down and lifted her away from him. "There's the reason that this was a mistake."

"You're good, and gentle, and caring. You decide what you are. Not your father, or your brother, or society."

"Sandrine, listen to me, I'm not that man. I wish I could be, but I can't." He helped her stand up. "I'll only hurt you again."

Stung by his words, she gathered up her wig and mask, preparing to return to her friends. They were supposed to leave by midnight and she didn't even know what time it was.

"Lord Dane?" a voice called. "Are you here?"

"It's Madam Avalon," he said. "Here," he called.

She rounded the hedge and stared at them. "There you are, Lord Dane. And my charming guest. Your friends are looking for you. I'll take you to them."

"Do you have any news for me about the man with the stickpin?"

"He's here. My attendants are watching to make sure he doesn't leave the salon."

"Thank you. I'll go and talk to him."

"Is it the man I saw at the prizefight?" Sandrine asked.

"I think it could be him."

Sandrine handed him his coat. "Be careful."

He nodded and rushed away.

"Are you enjoying yourself, my dear?" Madam Avalon asked Sandrine.

"Very much so."

"And your little interlude in the gardens? I hope all was to your satisfaction?"

"He was a gentleman. He only did what I asked him to do."

"Of course. I never would have allowed you to go into the gardens with him otherwise. I saw you two dancing together. May I ask your real name, my dear? I promise to guard it closely. You remind me of someone I know."

"I thought the same about you. My name is Sandrine Oliver. I'm from—"

"Squalton-on-Sea."

"How could you know that?"

"I never thought this day would come."

"How do you know me?"

"Because, Sandrine, my dear girl. I'm your grandmother."

Chapter Seventeen

She had a grandmother? Sandrine's mind danced over the knowledge. She knew it to be true, deep in her bones. This woman looked familiar because it was like holding a mirror to what Sandrine might look like later in life. "I don't understand. My mother told me that you were dead."

A tear slipped down Madam Avalon's cheek, and she dashed it away with a gloved hand. "Is that what she told you? I wondered. For the past twenty years I've begged your mother to allow me to meet you. I've sent letters, gifts, offers of money to fund your schooling."

"I never received any of it. Whenever I asked about her parents, she always said that her father and mother perished in a fire. She refused to say anything else."

"I even visited Squalton once, but your mother slammed the door in my face. I stayed long enough to catch a glimpse of you, my darling granddaughter. It was a dagger to my heart not to speak to you. I had to be content with knowing that you were healthy, bright, and so very beautiful."

"I've longed to know my mother's side of the family. I've studied our ancestral tree, and your branch ended so abruptly. She said you didn't have any other children. That you were an only child yourself."

"I'm afraid that she lied. I have another daughter, your aunt, Dawn, and she has a daughter, your cousin, Sophia. They live abroad on a beautiful island in Greece. I'm going to visit them soon."

"This is overwhelming. I simply can't believe that my family tree has a whole branch I knew nothing about. Isn't your name Ruby?"

"That's right."

"I glimpsed your name once in a letter my mother was writing. I assumed she was writing to you beyond the grave, but she was contacting you in truth."

"Her letters were always very brief. She told me never to contact her or you. She wanted to pretend that I was dead."

"Why would my mother lie to me my entire life?"

"I am dead to her. She made that choice to bury me and be done with me. But how is it that you're here in London?" Her eyes filled with tears. "Is Barbara . . . is my daughter here as well?"

"She never leaves Squalton. She didn't want me to come to London. I'm here accompanying Mrs. McGovern and Miss Hodwell as their companion."

"Eve and Dodie? I know them well."

"You do?"

"They attend my salon on occasion."

"They do? I can't picture them here."

"As I said during my introduction this evening, I welcome revelers of all predilections. Those two ladies are life companions and enjoy the freedom the salon affords them."

Her grandmother was full of surprises. "I came to London to petition the Duke of Rydell regarding a property he owns in Squalton. When I arrived I found that Lord Dane owns the property."

"The infamous rake I caught you here with earlier. Is there something happening between you?"

"It's a long story."

"And you're short on time. It's about to chime midnight, and I'm sure your friends are worried about you. Shall we rejoin them?"

Her grandmother led her back toward the house. "We have much to talk about. Do you want to know me better? I wouldn't blame you if you prefer to follow your mother's wishes and pretend I don't exist."

Sandrine stopped walking and clasped her grandmother's hand. "How could I do that? I've only just found you. Of course I want to know you better."

"I'm so glad. Though, you should keep our family association a secret for now since it could prove disastrous for your reputation."

"Sandrine—I mean Lady Sapphire!" Francesca called eagerly, running to meet them. "We've been looking everywhere for you. We must hurry home now."

"I'll invent some excuse and come to see you tomorrow," Sandrine said.

Her grandmother clasped her hand and gave her a warm smile. "Shall I send an unmarked carriage for you at three?"

"That would be perfect. Send the carriage to Miss Francesca McGovern's house—only have the coachman wait a small distance away and I'll find him."

AFTER SEARCHING FOR nearly a half hour, Dane located the man with the scorpion stickpin drinking champagne and talking to an alluring woman with black hair and a silver-spangled gown.

"Excuse us for a moment," Dane said to the woman, taking the man's arm and bending it behind his back.

"Pardon me, I'm not going anywhere with you," said the thin gentleman with a supercilious sneer.

"You'll come with me or I'll punch you so hard your nose will be out of joint forever."

"No need to resort to such ruffianly tactics, Lord Dane. I'll spare you a few moments of my time. Wait for me here, my dear. I'll be back momentarily."

Dane guided him into an empty room and closed the door.

"Lord Dane, I was enjoying that conversation. You'd best have a good reason for cutting it short."

"You know my name but I don't know yours."

"Desmond Orleans."

"Why have you been asking so many questions about me, Mr. Orleans, and staring at me all through the prizefight?"

"I have a very good explanation, but I don't owe it to you."

"I know you're a member of the Order of the Scorpion."

"That is the name the public knows us by."

"Were you acting on their orders?"

"I was."

"Then is your Order behind this cowardly extortion attempt?"

"I know nothing of that."

"Let me speak more plainly. Did you hire those villains to threaten me, tip me off on the winner of the prizefight, and make me hand over my winnings?"

"Are you accusing me of fixing the outcome of a fight? This is outrageous!"

"Fixing prizefights would be nothing to a covert organization that some say acts as a shadow government."

"Believe me, we don't resort to petty threats. We have all the power and influence we require without it."

"Why were you blackmailing my brother?"

"Blackmailing him? Hardly. He'd been bribing us steadily for years to allow him to join our order. With little success, I might add."

"Then, why were you staring at me at the fight?"

"Again, I owe you no explanation, but I'd like to end this unfortunate conversation as swiftly as possible and return to my companion, and therefore I'll tell you what you want to know. I was scrutinizing you because your brother's application for membership in the Order is finally being judged. It's a membership for life and transferable to one's descendants. Rydell is an old and venerable dukedom. There are those in the Order who were seriously considering allowing him to join. However, when we heard of his death, the application was to be terminated. Still, one of my superiors asked me to study you to see if you might be a promising recruit if you become the duke."

"I've no desire to join your sinister order."

"Exactly the conclusion I drew from watching you at the match and on other occasions. We have no desire to grant you—a hotheaded, rash, indiscreet rake—membership in our exclusive group. Now, if you'll excuse me, I have a conversation to finish. And a very unfavorable report about you to write."

There was nothing about his demeanor or tone that led Dane to believe he was telling anything but the truth.

A curt nod of his head and the man was gone, leaving Dane not one step closer to knowing the identity of his attackers or the nature of his brother's misdeeds.

He rejoined Madam Avalon. "Did Miss Oliver make it back to her friends safely?"

"I delivered her into her carriage. She's safely home by now." She regarded him intently. "Tell me what happened in the gardens."

He'd proved that he was bad through and

through. He'd corrupted an innocent at a notorious pleasure ball. His warped mind had invented reasons why it was allowed.

"She asked me to kiss her. She wanted a safe little taste of wickedness."

"And you were happy to oblige."

"I kissed her only to satisfy her rampant curiosity. She said she'd developed carnal cravings after viewing my portrait."

"Ha! She's not alone. Ladies do like to stand in front of it for hours sometimes."

"Can you take it down, please?"

"It's my most popular portrait!"

"I never used to care who saw it, but after tonight I'm feeling some qualms of conscience."

"Things didn't progress too far, I presume?"

"They did not."

"Good, because I will have to murder you if you give her expectations and then let her down."

"Don't worry. I'll never be alone with Miss Sandrine Oliver ever again. She's helping me plan a charity ball, and I'll make sure she's chaperoned the entire time."

He'd already caused her enough suffering. He'd have to be honorable and chaste from now on. They should never be alone together again, but if they were, he'd be a perfect gentleman.

If her shift was soaked through, he wouldn't look. Not even one swift glance at a nipple. And if she experienced any more carnal cravings, he'd suggest that she try bonbons or brandy, and if that failed . . . he'd back away slowly and run like hell.

He'd be stronger and more resolute.

It wasn't only freedom she craved, it was affection and love. She was starved for it.

All he could give her was his body, and that would never be enough for a sweet, romantic lady like Sandrine.

Chapter Eighteen

Never keep secrets or tell falsehoods.
      —Mrs. Oliver's Rules for Young Ladies

Are you going to meet Lord Dane? Is that what this is about?" Francesca asked.

"It's nothing like that."

"Then, why can't you tell me why I need to cover for you today? Do you have an assignation with Baron Chisholme? I hope not, because he was only supposed to be the one to make Lord Dane jealous. He's not a worthy suitor."

"I'm not meeting a man. Trust me, Francesca, I want to tell you where I'm going but I can't, not yet. I'll be able to tell you soon."

"This is all very mysterious. Are you the same timid, naive young lady who arrived in London only a week ago? She would have trembled at the idea of lying to Mrs. McGovern and Miss Hodwell and haring off for a secret assignation."

"I'm not that girl anymore, Francesca. London has changed me."

"At least tell me what happened to you at Madam Avalon's last evening. You were gone for so long, and I was beginning to panic. Roslyn was off with Kenwick somewhere, and Marta was surrounded by a crowd of admirers. I was searching for you the whole evening."

"I'm sorry. I shouldn't have run off like that without telling you. But I was so angry when Lord Dane danced with that other woman. I ran off into the gardens, and then he followed me."

"Tell me all about it."

"I'll tell you soon. I'm off now. I'll be back later this evening. It might be quite late, but please don't worry about me. I'll be very safe. I told Mrs. McGovern I was spending the night at your house."

"Sandrine, I want you to make me a solemn promise that you won't do anything truly dangerous."

"I promise."

"We Pink Ladies are fearless and free, but we care for one another, and we'll do anything to protect each other."

Her grandmother's carriage was waiting for her on the next corner precisely as she'd said it would be. Sandrine was so excited to learn more about her grandmother, aunt, and cousin. Suddenly her world seemed so much more expansive and filled with possibilities.

The servants were still cleaning up after last night's festivities at the Silver Palace. Sandrine was ushered into the first conventional room she'd seen in the house, a small, comfortable sitting room with pale blue coverings on the furniture.

"I'm so very glad you came, my dear Sandrine."

"I'm glad to be here, Grandmother."

"Call me Ruby, won't you? How much time do we have together?"

"Mrs. McGovern believes that I'm with her niece, Francesca."

"And did you tell Francesca you were coming to me?"

"I kept it a secret as you asked me to, though I don't know why it must be a secret."

"Dear girl, I am quite notorious in this city, and I wouldn't want my reputation to taint yours."

"I don't care about such things."

"You say that now, but perhaps it will be best to keep our relation a secret. I want to give you the choice of if and when you will reveal it."

Ruby poured the tea. "You look so like your mother." Her hand trembled. "It was fate that brought us together, despite your mother's best efforts to keep us apart. I'm resolved to be truthful with you and allow you to decide for yourself whether you want me in your life. There are legitimate reasons why your mother doesn't want you to have contact with me."

"I suppose you might start there, then. Tell me what happened."

"Your mother was a good girl, studious and quiet. She always seemed to have the cares of the world upon her little shoulders. She never smiled or laughed or played like the other children. She was very grave. I felt that perhaps she was an old soul trapped in a young girl's body. I tried to give her every advantage, an education, and I fed her mind the books she craved. I kept her ignorant of the nature of my profession."

Had her grandmother been a courtesan?

"I can see that you're making assumptions. The same assumptions made by everyone, really. Perhaps I am what people call a *woman of easy virtue*, but not in the way that they judge me. I'm an artist, first and foremost. I was born with a paintbrush in my hand. I had this urge to capture what I saw on canvas, to render it through my eyes and present it to the world."

Sandrine helped herself to the plate of biscuits, excited to learn more about her grandmother.

"I tend to ramble on sometimes. You don't want to know all of this."

"On the contrary, I'm enthralled. I'm a historian by nature. I love to learn the history of people and houses. Tell me about your childhood. I want to know everything there is to know about you."

"I was always sketching as a girl, and when I discovered paints, my entire world lit from within and I knew that I was meant to paint. My parents recognized my talent and hired an art instructor. I spent many happy years learning the standard techniques. Painting still lifes, landscapes, all the acceptable subjects for a young girl of good breeding."

"Do I come from a family of consequence, then?"

"My father was a baronet. We weren't wealthy but we had enough, more than most. I was fortunate to be able to paint, but I chafed under the restrictions. When I visited museums and galleries I saw that male painters were allowed so much more freedom to paint what they wanted than I was. Scenes from antiquity that depicted strife, war, and other horrors. I didn't want to paint such gruesome subjects, but I also didn't want to only paint fruit arranged on a table or a park or an idyllic countryside. I wanted to paint real people. The girl who sold fruit from a cart and had such sad eyes. The man on the corner whose leg had been shot off by canon fire and who begged for alms and drank gin to ease his pain."

"Do you still have those paintings?"

She waved her hand through the air. "In a trunk somewhere. They weren't very good and they were the cause of much strife. My parents didn't understand why I couldn't paint acceptable subjects like other young ladies, so they sought to control me by handing me off very young in an arranged marriage to a much older gentleman who was anything but gentle. He beat me and forbade me to paint. I was miserable."

"Oh, Ruby, I'm very sorry."

"It's the fate of many young ladies in our society. I hope and pray it will never be yours. Does your mother have plans for you to marry?"

Sandrine nodded. "She wants me to wed the village vicar. I don't think he would beat me, but he would certainly lecture me for hours on end."

"You shouldn't be forced to marry someone not of your choosing. If there's one thing I'd like to instill in you, it's the truth of that. This is your life, Sandrine, not your mother's."

"I've begun to see that in my time in London. I don't think I'll ever be able to go back and live the life she's planned for me."

"I had your mother at twenty and I thought I

might die. I wanted to die. And then my husband died instead, and I inherited a small living and this property. I was so much luckier than most. My income wasn't sufficient for the life I wished to lead so I began painting again, accepting portraiture commissions. I discovered my taste for painting nudes—mostly male nudes."

"You're very talented. I loved your portraits." Especially the one of Dane. She'd committed every brushstroke to memory.

"Thank you, dear girl. I'm so glad you didn't inherit your mother's distaste for honest and sensual portrayals of the human body. It's a most shocking and scandalous profession for a widowed lady. If I were a man I'd be able to paint whatever I pleased with society's approval. A woman is only supposed to serve as the muse for the male artist. And do you know how many muses end up committed to asylums? It's shocking. They are the muses for the male artist, they give of their bodies and their beauty and are immortalized, but the moment they cause any trouble—poof!—they are made to disappear. And I am the one society vilifies. I who pay my male models good wages and never demand anything other than their consent to paint them. The Duchess of Osborne and I have a charitable foundation that offers scholarships to promising young women artists."

"A most worthy undertaking."

"And yet your mother wouldn't even approve of my charitable works. She's always attempted to adhere to the highest moral standards, and it nearly killed her when she discovered the means by which I had paid for her education. I wasn't a good mother in the beginning. I wanted my freedom and I did leave her alone too often. I led a very free existence. Well, you've seen how I live."

"It is difficult to imagine her at the Silver Palace."

"I didn't have the salon when your mother was a girl, but I did take lovers as I chose, and I'm afraid that I made mistakes. I'm not without blame in this situation, Sandrine. I was very young when I had your mother, and I sometimes drank too much and had despondent moods. I did love her and I wanted her to be safe, but I also wanted my own life and I was selfish. There were times when she felt neglected because of it. I've tried many, many times to make amends to her, but she persists in ignoring my pleas."

"Thank you for being honest with me."

"I'm telling you this because I want you to make your own decision about whether you want me in your life. Barbara grew to hate me, but her sister, Dawn, was more like me. A free spirit, a painter, and fiercely independent. I think what Barbara wanted was rules to follow, a conventional path prescribed for her, but I would never do that to a daughter of mine. I told her to live her life on her own terms."

"She does love her rules. She has so many of them."

"She hated having an unconventional and scandalous mother. She flew into a rage one day and said she never wanted to speak to me again.

She ran off with one of my models, a handsome viscount, and I never heard from her again. I know the viscount didn't marry her—I'm not sure exactly what passed between them. All I know is that she found and married your father and moved to Squalton and never contacted me again and ignored my letters and pleas for forgiveness."

"It seems a very harsh judgment."

"It's been the greatest sorrow of my life. I've kept informed of her life by hiring people to give me news. That's how I knew of your birth. You were my first grandchild and I've never even met you. And look at you! You're so beautiful, and goodness shines from your eyes. What manner of mother has she been to you? The reports I've received have alarmed me somewhat."

"She's been very strict and exacting. She's constantly worried about calamity befalling me and is always warning me about never talking to strange men."

"What would she say about Lord Dane?"

"She'd hate him. She says that all men are beasts."

"Perhaps. But they can be tamed if you find one worthy enough of the effort. Though, you must choose wisely."

"It's all such an interwoven chain, isn't it? You, her, me. No matter what happens, I'm glad I found you."

"And I'm so glad you're in my life. I leave you to be the judge of whether we should have further contact. I would love it so very dearly. I'll be journeying to Greece to visit my other daughter and granddaughter. Perhaps you might accompany me?"

The thought stunned Sandrine to silence. "On a ship? Across the ocean?"

"Yes. We'd have such an adventure."

"You can't know how much I long to go abroad. But my mother would never allow it."

"I understand. Your loyalty is to her, and rightly so. I'm not asking you to choose between us."

"I'd love to become better acquainted, but I'm meant to be going home in one week."

"Then, we must make the most of our time together, however short."

"I wish I could stay longer in London, but I leave immediately after the charity ball that I'm helping plan next week."

"Ah, yes. The annual Rydell Charity Ball. The scholarship program I administer with the Duchess of Osborne is one of the beneficiaries of that event from last year. But it was all very odd."

"How so?"

"A rather large sum was raised, but the duchess told me she's yet to receive more than a pittance."

"Really? That is odd. The exact same thing happened to me. The Rydell record books claim that my historical society was given funds from the charity ball, but we never received the monies."

"It could all be related to the threats made against Lord Dane by those nefarious criminals."

"You know about that?"

"He confided in me because he was searching for the man with the scorpion stickpin."

"What happened? Did he find him?"

"He did, but the man wasn't behind the blackmailers. He was evaluating Lord Dane for admittance into the secret society and concluded that he was unworthy."

Sandrine finished her tea. "I believe I'll pay the duchess a visit today. She helped her late husband raise the charity funds. Perhaps she'll know more about all of this."

"Are you sure you don't want to go to Rydell House for the express purpose of running into a handsome rake?" her grandmother asked with a wink.

Sandrine hoped her bright smile was convincing. "The thought never even crossed my mind. Lord Dane means nothing to me except as the future benefactor of the Squalton Manor museum and assembly rooms."

Ruby raised her eyebrows but didn't push the subject. "My coachman will take you to Rydell House and wherever else you wish to go. He'll be at your disposal. And I'll expect him to bring me back a report that you've arrived safely back at Miss McGovern's house. I've only just found you. I'm not taking any chances with you, dear girl."

BACK AT RYDELL House Sandrine informed the butler that she was here to speak with the duchess about the charity ball. She was shown into a suite of opulent rooms decorated with a lavish use of gold leaf and purple silk cushions.

"Miss Sandrine Oliver of the Squalton Historical Preservation and Improvement Society, your grace."

The duchess reclined on a pile of purple cushions, belly protruding and swollen feet propped up on a little stool. "I suppose you're here about the charity ball? Cleveland told me that two ladies, one young and one old, were going to help organize the event."

"We will do our best to make you proud, your grace."

"I'm simply heartbroken that I won't be able to attend this year because of my lying-in. I had the most exquisite gown embroidered with gold thread and a diamond tiara specially created for the occasion. Fetch my tiara, Prudence," she said to one of the maidservants in attendance.

"I'm certain you shall be resplendent at next year's event," Sandrine assured her. The duchess was a very attractive woman with abundant brown hair and high cheekbones, though there was no warmth in her cobalt blue eyes. "I'd also like to thank you for your family's generous donations to our historical society. Your and your late husband's philanthropy is legendary."

"Roman did love his charities. I'm not familiar with yours."

"I'm from a seaside village called Squalton-on-Sea. Our historical society raises funds for the renovation of the manor house to be used as a museum and assembly rooms for the benefit of the villagers, and the—"

"Yes, yes, I'm sure it's all very worthy and

benevolent and all of that, but let's go back to the ball. Are the decorations at the ready? The theme is to be fairyland. I did consider dressing the footmen as fawns, but they balked at the idea of wearing hooves."

"Ah . . . yes, that might have posed problems."

"I did have a dozen pair of gossamer wings sewn for the maidservants, however. They shall flit about hither and thither."

"I hear that you hired a famous soprano for the occasion?"

"That was Roman's idea. He did like his opera singers." The sour way she said it made Sandrine think she was referring to infidelity on the part of her late husband.

"And there is to be an auction of donated items. From the pamphlet that Cleveland gave me, there are some magnificent contributions."

"My charity ball is the place to see and be seen in London. No other event surpasses it for the opportunity to display one's wealth and consequence," the duchess said proudly.

"And of course it raises urgently needed funds for the worthy recipients."

The duchess gave a dismissive little shrug. "Of course, there is that."

The maid returned with a glittering tiara on a velvet cushion. "Oh, there you are, you gorgeous thing," cooed the duchess, caressing the tiara. "Put it on my head, Prudence." The woman arranged the tiara in her hair. "Ouch, have a care. You're so clumsy. Well? Isn't it the most stunning tiara you've ever beheld?"

Having never beheld a tiara before, Sandrine had to agree. "It's lovely." She couldn't help wondering how much a diamond tiara cost and whether it was the right choice to wear to a ball whose purpose was to raise funds for the poor and destitute.

"The ball is meant to be presided over by the Duke and Duchess of Rydell. Not my rakish brother-in-law who is merely heir presumptive and soon to be replaced by my darling boy." She patted her belly. "And some elderly ladies and a young lady from the seaside. No one knows you in London. I should have asked one of my titled friends to host in my stead, but it's all been such chaos with Roman getting himself killed and my lying-in being such a trial. This boy I carry is very active, and I can hardly leave my bed."

Sandrine decided to ignore the fact that she'd just been insulted. "Might I ask you some questions about the particulars of the ball?"

"Couldn't you speak with Cleveland?"

"You're the expert, your grace. Spare me a few moments of your time."

"Oh, very well. Ask me your questions."

"The donations are collected at the event?"

"Cleveland oversees all that."

"About the proceeds from the ball. You see, last year it was recorded that donations in the amount of three hundred pounds were given to our historical society, but we never saw the funds."

"Perhaps your treasurer absconded with them, for all I know."

"And the Duchess of Osborne's scholarship

fund for promising young women artists hasn't received their monies as of yet."

"That's no concern of mine. Talk to Cleveland."

"I was studying the pamphlet, and I wonder if you've personally visited the Society for the Charitable Relief of Poor, Misused, Infirm, Aged Widows and Single Women of Impeccable Character Who Have Fallen On Difficult Times in East Edston."

"I haven't personally visited them." She yawned. "I really don't care about them, do you? Roman loved to shower them with money. Simply piles of it. They're probably rolling around in it, those old crones. Are you finished? I'm rather tired. The charity ball is so dear to my heart, but I'm afraid this lying-in has been such a trial for me. I can't seem to muster the enthusiasm for all the charities like I usually do. It's more of a chance to see and be seen, do you understand? I hope you have an appropriate gown to wear? That one you're wearing is pretty, but certainly not grand enough for such an illustrious occasion."

"I'll be sure to make an effort with my appearance."

"See that you do. If you're representing me, you must be presentable. Now, I really must have my beauty rest. Go on about your business, Miss Oliver."

A maid showed her out. Sandrine stood for a moment outside the door, appalled at what she'd just heard.

Had the duchess really said she didn't care

about charity? There was something very wrong here. It was high time to do some investigating.

"STOP DREAMING ABOUT Miss Oliver and help me tighten this wheel." Kenwick shoved a wrench in Dane's face as they repaired his curricle in the yard of the Thunderbolt Club's rented premises near Hyde Park.

Fair caught. Dane bent to his task, but his mind stayed in the gardens with Sandrine. She'd been asking him to check off one more item from the list of wicked things he'd like to do to her.

Why couldn't he stop thinking about her? It was beginning to be a sort of madness. He'd never been obsessed by a woman like this before. Here he was thinking of Sandrine's shapely curves, when Kenwick's curricle itself was truly a gorgeous sight to behold.

Painted bright green, with black and gold details, the panels and footboard lined with green drab cloth. The body was ornamented with brass moldings. The springs, braces, and jacks were all top quality and built to withstand strain and speed.

"*Lightning Streak*'s a beauty," Dane said, slapping the wheel.

"I'm going to race it against Chisholme."

"You know he's not to be trusted. Remember how he attempted to sabotage me?"

"We'll triple-check everything this time. He's running around town making disparaging comments about Lady Roslyn. I don't like it."

"I thought you said you didn't care for her in that way."

"You know how it is with women. One day she's hot, the next she's cold."

"And every day you care about her."

"I try not to, but she gets under my skin, you know?"

"I do know. I know all too well."

"We danced at the ball last night, which led to a private chamber. Seems she was inspired by Madam Avalon's portrait of me."

"You're welcome. I've always thought you and Lady Roslyn would make a fine pair."

"We're always fighting. Except when we're passionately kissing."

"When will she make an honest man of you?"

"I don't think she wants to marry me. She only wants to take me for a ride. But what about you and that Miss Oliver, eh? You're bound to hurt that sweet little lady. She looks at you and wedding bells ring in her ears."

"I've been very clear that I'll never marry."

"That doesn't stop a girl like that from hoping that she can reform you. And damned if she doesn't have more of a shot than any other woman I've ever seen you interested in."

Kenwick held an iron rendering of the Thunderbolt Club insignia, a double-headed thunderbolt they'd found on an ancient Greek coin, against the door while Dane fastened it.

"There," Kenwick said. "I'm ready to race. Want to try my *Lightning Streak* against your *Firebrand*?"

Dane didn't much feel like risking his neck to day. His thoughts were in too much of a turmoil. Sandrine. Blackmailers. He wouldn't be able to maintain the focus required to expertly handle a horse and carriage at the speeds they ran.

"Ho, Dane!" called Dudley. "There's a lady here to see you. It's that Miss Oliver. Claims she has something urgent to say to you."

"What did I say? Ding-dong, ding-dong." Kenwick made bell-ringing motions. "First she ambushes you at your club. Next it's wedding bells."

"Leave off. She's helping me organize the charity ball."

"Is that what the young bucks are calling it these days?"

Dane rolled his eyes. Sandrine marched into the yard.

"So this is your infamous club." She glanced around the yard at the rows of curricles. "Do you allow ladies to join?"

"We would allow a woman to join if she had a high perch phaeton or a dashing curricle, a matched set of horses, and a sure hand with the reins," said Dane.

"We would?" Somersby asked.

"Why not? I thought women were all you ever thought about."

"True. And they'd be wearing form-fitting riding habits. I do like a tight riding habit molded over a round—"

"Somersby!" Dane said. "There's a lady present."

"And that's why I don't want ladies to join."

Sandrine laughed. "Sorry to spoil your fun. I must speak with you, Lord Dane. I was visiting with Madam Avalon today."

"You went back to the Silver Palace? Why?"

"It's a long story, I'll tell you all about it on the journey."

"What journey?"

"You're driving me to East Edston in your curricle. We leave immediately."

"No, we don't."

"Then, I'll ask another one of these handsome young gentlemen."

"I'll drive you to East Edston," Somersby said eagerly. He gestured toward his curricle. "Hop in, Miss Oliver."

"Oh no you won't," Dane growled.

Sandrine walked toward Somersby. "I require a ride."

"Can this wait? We're about to test Kenwick's new chariot."

"It can't. Help me up, Sir Somersby."

Dane muttered a curse under his breath. "You're not going anywhere with Somersby." The miscreant never thought about anything but getting underneath a lady's skirts. "You haven't told me what this is about."

"I spoke with your sister-in-law about the charity ball, and I've uncovered several discrepancies that might be pertinent to your quest for answers. You know, about your *brother*."

He escorted Sandrine a short distance from his

friends so that they could speak in private, since he hadn't yet told any other members of the club about being accosted.

"What manner of discrepancies?"

"Charities that never received the promised funds from last year's event. And charities that may well not even exist. That's where we're going today. To visit a charitable society in East Edston and ascertain its legitimacy."

"And where does Mrs. McGovern think you are?"

"With Francesca for the day and evening."

"And where does Francesca think you are?"

"I told her I'd return shortly. You're delaying, come along. I've been told the journey is less than one hour. We should be there and back expediently."

He'd sworn to never be alone with her again. Sworn to run like hell at the very idea. But she'd uncovered a new clue to his brother's potential wrongdoings. They had to follow up. He knew her well enough by now to know that she would find a way to accomplish her goals, with or without his consent.

"I don't like this."

"Are you afraid I'll take the occasion to ravish you?" she asked in a loud, challenging tone.

Somersby laughed heartily. "Do you need a chaperone, Dane?" he called.

"At least we'll put the cover up, so that no one sees us alone together," Dane grumbled. Although, come to think of it, it would provide excellent cover if she did decide to ravish him and he wasn't strong enough to resist.

No, no. They were only going on a short jaunt in the sunlight. Nothing more.

"Perfect. I've no wish to worry anyone."

Dane knew when he'd been outfoxed.

He had no choice but to hand Sandrine up into his curricle and take his seat next to his ravishing tormentor.

Chapter Nineteen

Riding in a gentleman's carriage is forbidden without a proper chaperone.
        —Mrs. Oliver's Rules for Young Ladies

It was a bright, sunny day, and Dane was acutely aware of the bright, sunny woman sitting so close by his side. She had a way of getting whatever she wanted from him.

"If my mother could see me now. I'm currently flouting at least three of her rules. I'm associating with a known rake, I'm alone with said rake, and I'm riding in his dashing curricle, brazen as you please. And I must say that it's quite exhilarating."

"You do know that your mother made those rules for a reason? I'm a rake, and you're not supposed to climb into my carriage and ask me to take you on a journey. I'm a bad man."

"Well, as it turns out, I'm scandalous as well. I'm going to confide something in you that I haven't told anyone else yet. Last night I discovered that Madam Avalon is my grandmother!"

Dane nearly lost control of the horses. "How is that possible?"

"You see the resemblance between us, don't you?"

Now that she said it, he did. "You told me that your grandparents were dead."

"That's what my mother always told me. It was a lie. She was raised in London and rebelled against her freethinking and free-spirited mother by disowning her, pretending she was dead, and settling in a small town with my very conventional father."

"It's astonishing. I've known Madam Avalon for many years. She's a very talented and generous woman."

"Isn't she?"

"Though, she is scandalous, of course."

"No more so than you are. Perhaps less."

"True." He couldn't argue with that. Society placed more blame on women who lived freely than men.

"I also learned that I have an aunt and a cousin living on an island in Greece, of all places. It's nearly overwhelming. I'm so overjoyed."

"I thought that you were exceptionally bubbly today."

"The branch of my family tree that I thought had withered and died is alive and well! I heard all about my grandmother's past today. And she told me her perspective about why my mother ran away. I don't know my mother's side of the story yet."

"She won't be happy that you discovered her secret."

"I'm not happy that she lied to me my entire life. Something bad must have happened to her in London. She taught me that men are beasts and not to be trusted, because they'll tell any lies necessary to steal your virtue and then toss you to the wolves. I never wondered why she thought this. Her marriage to my father seemed if not happy, at least congenial. My father bore my mother's flighty worries in stoic fashion. And after his death from a cancerous tumor, it was as though my mother blamed him for dying and leaving us alone in the world, as if the disease were somehow his fault. It was after his death that she began retreating from life, hardly ever leaving the house and not allowing me to leave, either."

"As for your mother's warnings . . . they're all true."

"They're not. You didn't take the opportunity last night to ruin me. And you could have. I was willing."

"I may be a rake, but I don't ruin innocents."

"Now I'm beginning to understand why my mother is so overprotective. She felt unsafe growing up and tried to give me safety."

"Or her mother hurt her, and so she hurt you, but in a different way. It's what families do. When people are bound together by blood, they know the very best ways to cause us pain."

"My grandmother creates scandalous portraiture. I don't think that's so terrible."

"In some circles she's one of the most respected portrait artists of our age. I've been to see exhibitions of her work at the Duchess of Osborne's gallery of women artists. They were very well-received."

"I'm proud of her, and I look forward to deepening our acquaintance."

They made excellent time from London to the outlying town of East Edston. Sandrine read aloud from the pamphlet. "It says here that the Society for the Charitable Relief of Poor, Misused, Infirm, Aged Widows and Single Women of Impeccable Character Who Have Fallen On Difficult Times cannot disclose its exact location for its applicants' safety but lies close to the town of East Edston. It provides sixty-five old objects and misused women a room, the use of a communal kitchen, a small garden, an allotment of coal in winter, and the sum of nine guineas a year. They call the women *old objects*? Not particularly flattering."

"If there are so many women housed there, it must be a structure of a substantial size."

"Perhaps a former hospital, or hotel? Or a cluster of cottages."

"Let's inquire at the village inn. They always know everything that's happening."

Sandrine followed Dane inside the inn. "Good day, sir. My . . . husband and I are subscribers to the Society for the Charitable Relief of Poor, Misused, Infirm, Aged Widows and Single Women of Impeccable Character Who Have Fallen On Difficult Times."

"Bully for you." The innkeeper barely glanced up before returning to read the paper he held.

"Husband?" Dane whispered.

"We're Mr. and Mrs. Smith today. Subscribers to the charity and concerned, respectable souls," she whispered to Dane.

"Do you know where the charity is located?" Dane asked.

"Can't say as I do."

"It's a large building, or a collection of cottages. There are sixty-five elderly women housed there. Surely you've heard of it?" Dane laid the pamphlet on the desk. The innkeeper glanced at it. "Never heard of it. Not around here. But if you're wanting to give money to a charity, you'll find lots of causes here. We haven't had any work since the mine closed."

"Are you quite certain? It says it's located near East Edston."

He scratched his chin. "I'd know if there were sixty-five ancient ladies living near me. There aren't. Perhaps it's a misprint? Could be West Edston. Bigger than we are."

"That must be it," Sandrine agreed.

"Thank you for your time."

Back on the street, Sandrine said, "That man was quite rude." She noticed men loitering about, hats pulled low and sneers on their faces.

"I don't like the way those men are looking at you. I was going to suggest luncheon here, but I think it's best to push on to West Edston. If it's a larger town and has all the custom this one used to, it will have a better-appointed inn, and we can dine there."

But the proprietor of the Hound and Hare in

West Edston proved equally uninformative, if more polite. "Can't say as I've heard of this society. Martha," he called, and a harried-looking woman bustled out from the backroom, "have you heard of this society for old objects?"

"The Society for the Charitable Relief of Poor, Misused, Infirm, Aged Widows and Single Women of Impeccable Character Who Have Fallen On Difficult Times," Sandrine clarified.

"Never heard of it. But I could use some charity, and I'm a woman of impeccable character whose husband misuses me most terribly. Works me night and day, and I never hear the end of his complaining."

"Oh, go on with you, you she-devil," said her husband affectionately. "I'm the one that will need an almshouse when you take up with a younger fellow behind my back."

"Are you quite certain that none of the elderly ladies are housed nearby?" Dane asked.

"There is an old sanatorium for consumptives and the like on the hill a short distance. Could be they've refurbished it without my knowing? Though, my Martha makes it her business to know everything wot goes on near here."

"There has been some activity there lately, comings and goings and the like," Martha said.

"That must be it, then," Sandrine said. "Thank you for your time. We'll take luncheon here."

"We've plenty of rooms at the inn, Mr. and Mrs. Smith, if you decide to pass the evening here."

After a quick bite, they said goodbye to the innkeeper.

"Don't tarry too long in the countryside. It's going to rain. I can feel it."

"What's he on about?" Sandrine asked. "The sky is brilliant blue with not a cloud."

The former sanatorium, while a cavernous building that could have housed a hundred elderly supplicants, was being transformed into a schoolhouse.

"I can't help thinking that this is all interrelated," Sandrine said. "The charity that can't be found. The threat made to you. Something very sinister is happening here. I don't like it."

"Nor do I. I'm beginning to think that my brother created a fictitious charity."

"And printed the name in his pamphlet? Wouldn't he have been worried about being exposed?"

"Either he did this knowingly, or someone was hoodwinking him."

"That seems more likely, don't you think? Perhaps he never checked on the charity personally but only relied on the word of others."

"I don't know what to think."

Dane pushed the door open for Sandrine, and they stepped out into a sky gone dark and tearful, rain pouring in sheets that soaked them to the bone in seconds.

"We'd better hurry home." He helped her into the curricle, gave a few encouraging words to the horses, who were eyeing the sky nervously, and they set off as fast as they could go over the rough lanes that led back to the main road.

The rain didn't let up, and soon the lane was muddy and the carriage lurched and heaved.

"We'll be stuck in the mud," Sandrine said.

"Don't worry, my horses are strong." And they were: they pulled them straight and true back to the crossroads. "We've reached the main road now. I'll have you back within the hour."

They hadn't gone more than ten minutes down the road when they encountered a long line of carts and carriages. Dane jumped down to make inquiries.

He was back in a matter of minutes, his face grim, rain streaming over the brim of his beaver hat and splashing his face. "Bad news, I'm afraid. There's a downed tree blocking the road. We can't pass through here until it's dislodged. I'd go and offer to help but I don't want to leave you alone."

"Go and help. I'll be all right if you secure the horses to a tree."

"I'll only be a few moments. They've made fair progress, and one more heave should do it."

Sandrine shivered. The covering of the curricle allowed a steady stream of rain to trickle down one edge and onto her back.

Dane was visible through the trees, as soaking wet as the first day she'd met him. His shirt had mud on it, and his hair was plastered to his head. He was nearly to the carriage when a loud crack of thunder sounded. One of the horses reared up, neighing loudly, and the carriage lurched dangerously to one side, throwing Sandrine against the door, her head hitting the hard edge of something.

"Whoa there," Dane shouted, grabbing the horse's bridle and righting the curricle.

He jumped into the curricle and gathered her into his arms. "Sandrine, are you hurt?"

"O-only shaken up. I hit my head on the door, but I'll be fine."

"I can't see anything in this light. You could be injured. We must make certain that you're all right. We're turning around and going back to the inn and fetching the doctor."

"I'm all right. I didn't hit my head very hard. Truly." She brought his hand to her head. "See? Only a trickle of blood. I don't feel woozy or faint. I was only frightened of what might have happened."

"My brother walked away from the carriage and was laughing and joking with people. He only had a cut on the back of his head. It wasn't until later that night that he collapsed with internal bleeding. I'm not taking any chances." His lips were bracketed by lines, and his jaw was rigid. "I'm taking you to see a doctor. Now."

Chapter Twenty

Never spend time alone with a known rake. He has only one thing on his mind: your seduction and ruin.

—Mrs. Oliver's Rules for Young Ladies

Mrs. Smith, you're perfectly well. No significant blood loss. Just a little knock on the head," the doctor pronounced after examining Sandrine in a chamber at the Hound and Hare.

Thank God. Dane's shoulders loosened.

He'd been so frightened when she hit her head. He was supposed to be keeping her safe, damn it, not exposing her to the elements, carriage accidents, and ruin.

He should have personally conveyed her back to Squalton when he'd had the chance. Instead, he'd involved her in his investigation, and look where it had led. Sandrine injured, her face wan, blood in her hair. This was a mistake of his making. He was so afraid that what happened to his brother would happen to Sandrine. He'd never forgive himself. Never.

"There's nothing to worry about." The doctor packed up his bag. "Everything is roses and sunshine. Well, perhaps not sunshine with all this unexpected rain."

"That's what I keep telling Mr. Smith," Sandrine said with a brave smile.

"Ah, but young husbands can be overly solicitous, in my experience. Any little scratch or mishap, and they come running to me, quaking in their boots, terrified for their dear, beloved wife."

"Thank you, Doctor." Dane walked him out and followed him into the hallway, closing the door behind them. "There's no chance that there could be internal bleeding? My brother had a carriage accident, worse than this, but he walked away, all smiles, then later that evening he collapsed and within two days' time he was dead."

The doctor shook his head. "In my opinion there's absolutely no danger to your wife. It's only a bruise. She'll have some swelling and discoloration but no chance of anything more serious."

"Are you sure?"

"One can never be absolutely sure. You saw the accident happen. Was the blow to her head forceful?"

"She slid slowly toward the door, and I don't think the impact was harsh."

"Precisely what I would have guessed. You really don't need to trouble yourself, Mr. Smith. Your wife only sustained a very minor injury. She'll have a small bruise, nothing more."

Dane clasped the doctor's hand. "I'm so relieved. Thank you so much, Doctor."

"Give her a small glass of hot wine and tuck her into bed. A little rest, and she'll be fully restored."

Dane paid his fee and returned to the room, nearly giddy with relief.

"Dane? I'm hungry."

Dane realized he was ravenous as well. "I'll go see about a meal."

The innkeeper was happy to provide a hot meal and mulled wine, but when Dane asked whether the roads were passable now, he shook his head. "This rain has settled in for the night. I just had two more customers who turned back from road. I think you and the missus are here for the night. I'll have the meal and more hot water and towels sent up."

Sandrine was dozing when he returned. She looked so vulnerable in the bed, so young and innocent. She was the one who'd told the innkeeper that they were married when they came to make inquiries. There'd been no time to explain that they wanted separate rooms. He'd carried her up the stairs, anguished and fearful for her safety.

"Sandrine."

Her eyes fluttered open.

"I have some very bad news."

"There's no food to be had?"

"It's not that. It's the roads. The innkeeper says he's already had several more guests who turned back because the road to London is still impassable. We're going to have to stay here tonight. Your reputation could be ruined."

"I'm not a London debutante jealously guarding her reputation."

"But if Mrs. McGovern learns you spent the night with me . . ."

"She won't. She thinks I'm with her niece. She and Miss Hodwell were going out to the theater. They always retire early. If we can make it back tomorrow morning, all will be well. You can take me to Francesca's house, and I'll sneak in before anyone is awake. At least we're not stuck in the curricle for the night. We have a nice comfortable bed, a fire in the grate, and a hot meal on the way."

"We do have a nice comfortable bed. But only one of them. You told the innkeeper that we were Mr. and Mrs. Smith. And now the other rooms are full so we can't request two rooms."

"Oh. There is that."

"I'll sleep in a chair." Easiest thing in the world. He'd done it many times when he came home too drunk and nodded off at a table instead of in bed. It did put a crick in one's neck to be sure, but the alternative was not to be entertained.

"Will you be comfortable?"

"It doesn't matter. It's only one night."

When the maid brought more hot water, he used a cloth and wiped the remainder of the blood from Sandrine's hair. "The doctor said that you'd only have a small bruise."

"On my temple, just here." She touched her face.

"It's already a fetching shade of mauve."

She smiled. "You were so worried when I really didn't hit my head hard at all."

"I was thinking about what happened to my brother. Sandrine," he said and dropped to his knees in front of the bed, "if anything had happened to you . . . I would never have forgiven myself."

She cupped his cheek. "But it didn't. Everything is rosy. Stop blaming yourself. I'm the one who forced you into giving me a ride in your curricle." She laughed softly. "Miss Maples told me that there are dozens of ladies in London vying for the chance to risk their necks for a ride in your dashing new curricle. And I beat them all to it."

She was the only young lady in London who made his heart thump so painfully. The only one he'd allow to touch his cheek, to give him that warm, caring look.

What was wrong with him?

He was so madly, deeply attracted to her. She smiled. She untied her bonnet strings. She quizzed innkeepers. And he wanted her. He wanted her all the time.

Everything about her. Not only the curves that had him perpetually aroused but her smile, her curiosity, the wide-eyed zest she had for new experiences.

He was tired of fighting this need. He was tired, full stop. And hungry. He'd been so desperately worried. He wasn't thinking clearly.

He rose and busied himself with wringing out the cloth and preparing the table for their meal. She watched him as he worked with a half smile playing on her lips, as though she were fully aware that she'd slipped beneath his defenses and was going to take full advantage of it later.

Sleep. That's all they would do tonight.

The food was simple fare that he ate quickly, avoiding her gaze. The mulled wine was on the sour side but did take the edge off the tension in his shoulders and neck.

Sandrine went behind the screen and emerged wearing only a thin white chemise, her hair tumbling in waves around her shoulders.

And there was the tension again, this time firmly centered in his groin.

She glanced at him before darting to the bed and snuggling under the covers. "Mmm," she said with a yawn, stretching her arms. "Surprisingly comfortable. Are you sure you don't want to join me?"

He'd never been less sure of anything in his life.

He wanted to peel those covers down her body and then lift that chemise over her head and then . . . No more mistakes. No more justifying bad choices with half-baked logic.

He dragged a chair to the fireplace with the back toward the bed and settled in without taking off any of his clothing or even his boots. He'd sit here all night in this hard chair, and he'd ignore the existence of the warm, snuggly, inviting woman in that bed.

His dream had come to pass. The wheel hadn't fallen off, the road was washed out, and the horse had bolted from thunder, but the outcome was the same: only one bed.

Ha!

"What was that?"

He must have spoken aloud. "Nothing. I was

only thinking about a dream I had when I first met you."

"About torrential rain and blocked roads?"

"About stopping at an inn with you and there was only one bed."

"And now it's coming true."

Not all of it. That dream could never come true. It had been a particularly dirty dream.

"What happened in the dream?" she asked.

"Nothing. It's an inappropriate topic. I shouldn't have brought it up."

"Are you telling me that you had a dream about us sharing the only bed and nothing happened? I don't believe it."

"Believe it. Go to sleep now. The doctor said you should have some rest. I asked the innkeeper to wake us at first light, and hopefully we can be on the road and have you home before anyone knows you're missing."

"If you won't tell me about your dream, I'll tell you about one that I had after the first day we met."

"Time for bed. Lamps out," he said desperately, turning down the wick. "Good night, Miss Oliver—"

"Don't you want to know what it was about?"

"I don't." He did. He desperately did. From the sultry tone of her voice, it had been naughty.

"I dreamed that when you rescued me out of the sea, it was a much chillier day, and you were very concerned that I would catch my death of cold. And you had to divest me of my wet garments. You grabbed hold of the bodice of my shift and you rent the fabric apart with brute strength and the garment split in two and fell off, and I was left entirely naked."

Good God. Despite his best intentions, his cock stiffened to granite. "One does what one has to."

"Do you want to know what happened next?"

He took another healthy swig of mulled wine. He'd certainly told her enough erotic things in the garden the other night. She should be allowed to tell him her fantasies. Words. Only words. There was a whole room between them. He was fully clothed. "Tell me."

"You stripped to your bare skin, and you whispered in my ear that you didn't want me to catch my death and that your body heat would keep me warm. 'Your lips are turning blue,' you said. 'I'll have to kiss you.' And then you kissed me so passionately that my whole body caught fire and my senses blazed to life."

"And then . . . ?"

"You transformed into the ravening beast my mother is always warning me about. You sprouted horns and cloven hooves and grasped me by the neck and held me down while you defiled me most vigorously."

Dane was barely breathing he was so aroused. His cock twitched and leaped, straining against his breeches' flap. The thought of holding her by the throat and thrusting inside her filled his mind. She had a filthy imagination. And he loved it.

"At the time, I didn't really know what defilement entailed. Beast-Dane was grunting loudly, and I was squirming about but I wasn't trying to stop you. I liked it. I wanted you to debauch me, to make me yours. I awoke with the most melting sensation, which I now understand was similar to how you made me feel in the garden the other night."

Dane choked on the wine and started coughing. She'd just described having an erotic dream resulting in orgasm. He hadn't even known women could have those.

"Is anything wrong?" she asked sweetly.

"I don't think we should tell each other about any more of our dreams."

"You didn't give me any details about yours."

"Go to sleep, Sandrine."

"Come to bed. You'll be more comfortable."

"I can't. You're testing your newfound freedom. You've recently discovered that you have a scandalous grandmother. We did one forbidden, wicked thing in a garden. But I'm not going to ruin you, Sandrine. It's not going to happen."

"I'm not suggesting bestial defilement. I was thinking more of gentle exploration with explicitly delineated parameters."

"No exploration, gentle or otherwise. Go to sleep."

She lay quietly for some time, and Dane's raging erection finally began to abate. He had almost drifted into a cramped approximation of sleep when her soft voice woke him.

"Dane, are you asleep?"

He pretended to snore.

"I know you're awake."

He lay still.

"You have no idea what it was like to be raised by my mother," she said softly. "To be so loved, so protected, that every scrap of clothing I wore, every word I spoke, every action was managed and chosen for me. Every friend I tried to make was driven away for fear they might corrupt me. Every innocent diversion was pronounced a gateway to immorality. I had no free will. I was made to believe that disaster would strike if I strayed outside of her strict rules of conduct."

She moved restlessly in the bed, and he wanted to hold her, stroke her hair and tell her everything was going to be all right. But he couldn't be the man who did that for her.

"And even as a grown woman," she continued, "she still chose my clothing and told me what I could and couldn't say, whom I could speak with, whom I should marry. I had no air to breathe. I was trapped in a net. And this week in London has given me a taste of what it would be like to be my own person. To discover who I am without my mother, without Mr. Pilkington, without the weight of having to be the perfect daughter and wife—biddable, chaste, maidenly, virtuous, selfless. You don't even value the freedom that society grants you because of your sex and your fortune. I want to be a little bit selfish. Is that so terrible?"

"Selfish doesn't make you happy. I can attest to that."

"Perhaps *selfish* isn't the word. I want to live on my own terms, in my own way. I've always wanted that. I used to write stories about little girls who ran away from home and had glorious adventures."

"Fairy tales."

"Perhaps. I stopped writing them when I was thirteen. The day I learned that there was no escape from my life. I woke in the morning with a dreadful cramping in my belly and blood on my sheets, and I knew that it was because I'd written another one of the bad stories about a girl who ran away from her mother. I'd hidden the story under my bed, and this was my punishment. I was dying. I knew it. I ran sobbing to my mother and confessed everything. I asked her to call for the vicar to give me my last rites."

"Oh, Sandrine." His heart was breaking for her. He pushed the chair around to face her. Dragged it closer to the bed. "Your monthly courses had begun."

"I didn't know that at the time. I thought it was a punishment, and my mother confirmed it. This was the curse given to all women because we are the original sinners. Bad and unclean. Every month I would receive this reminder of the sin inside me that must be wrestled with and overcome. She made me watch her burn the story I'd written, then she made me scrub my own sheets, and I wept and begged her forgiveness. I promised to be good and obey her and never think about being disobedient again."

Dane couldn't stand it any longer. He had to give her some comfort, and all he had to offer was himself. She was sitting up in bed. He sat next to her, on top of the covers, and held her hand.

"Sandrine. That was very wrong of her to instill shame in you for something so natural, something which should have been viewed as normal."

"I realize that now, but at thirteen all I saw was my wickedness. My body was shameful. Something to be hidden away and denied."

"Your body is beautiful, Sandrine. Something to be proud of, to be celebrated."

"Seeing the nude portrait of you made me start thinking about nakedness in a new way. You're obviously proud of your body. You display it for anyone to see. I only want you to know what I battle. A legacy of shame and restriction. And I want to leave it behind like a snake leaves its dry old skin. I want to be something new. I want to inhabit my body in an unfettered way. It's not my adversary, something to be ashamed of, but a gift, a precious gift, and these carnal cravings aren't something to be denied and suppressed."

He stroked her hand softly. "Your body is a temple, and I long to worship it, I want you so badly. But I can't offer you the connection, the commitment, or the love that you deserve."

"I'm not asking for commitment, Dane. I'm asking you to be my partner as I seek freedom, as I break free from the shackles of shame. Shouldn't a notorious rake be able to help me with those goals?"

"Believe me, I want you to reach those goals so badly it hurts. But you deserve, you want, more than I can give."

"Not even one more item from the list of wicked things you whispered to me in the garden?"

"Not even one." It cost him everything to say those words. "Sandrine, I told you from the start that I was bad, that I'd misspent my life, and I couldn't be the man you want me to be."

"What if we really were Mr. and Mrs. Danny Smith? What if you were the man you pretended to be at the seashore? Maybe things wouldn't be so complicated between us."

Her words were a spell woven of beach grass, sunshine, and longing. He wanted to be that man so badly. And he wanted things to be uncomplicated. Because in that moment it didn't seem too complex. He wanted her. She wanted him.

There was only one bed.

"I watched you calm your horse. You spoke gently, and your touch made him feel safe. I want you to do the same with me. I want to feel safe and gentled by your touch."

She wanted to feel *loved*. And he couldn't give her that. And if he couldn't give her that, then he couldn't give her any of the other things she asked for.

But damn it! She just kept talking in that soft, honeyed way about unbearably sensual things, and he was at his breaking point.

"One more forbidden, wicked thing. Not *the* thing. Only the next thing on the list," she said, glancing at him from under her lashes.

"I can't remember the list," he lied. He remembered every second of their encounter in the garden. All he wanted to do was write the whole damned list on her body with his tongue.

Wrap those shapely legs around his neck, lift her, open her thighs, and taste her. Tease her until she moaned his name.

His real name.

"You have a look of fierce concentration on your face, Dane. What are you imagining?"

"The next item on the list."

"So you do recall the wicked list."

"I do." Voice hoarse, mouth dry, palms sweating. *Retreat! Get out of this bed. Go sleep in the stables.*

"I've been thinking about the next item ever since you whispered those naughty, unexpected words in my ear. You said . . ." She faced him, looking into his eyes, fearless and beautiful with her hair unbound, the curve of her breasts visible beneath the thin muslin of her shift. "You said you wanted to spread my thighs and hold them open while you slid your tongue into my secret places."

Jesus God. Had he actually said that to an innocent young lady in the gardens of a notorious pleasure salon?

"I shouldn't have said that."

"Oh, but you did. And ever since you said those words, I've been wondering exactly what you meant."

"I think you know what I meant."

"Maybe I do, maybe I don't. There's only one way to be sure."

The look in her eyes was pure temptation. Sh

wanted him as badly as he wanted her. And if they didn't go too far, he could be the one to pleasure her, to satisfy her fantasies and wonderings.

"Show me, Dane," she whispered.

And he stopped fighting himself. He could deny her nothing.

She wanted gentle explorations. He would worship her body with a light, reverential touch. It was all about her. Coupling was usually a wild tangled chaotic experience. This would be different. Tonight he was painting a portrait of a young lady on the verge of a sensual awakening. A woman who wanted to fully own her body and the pleasure it could give her.

She lay back, trusting, smiling, anticipating.

He lifted her arms and tugged her chemise over her head. She shifted her hair to hide her breasts and covered the joining of her thighs with her hand, squirming uncomfortably.

He gently moved her hair away from her breasts and her hand away from her sex. He moved to stand beside the bed. "Let me look at you."

He drank in the sight of her, the generous breasts, small waist, curve of her belly, rounded, dimpled thighs, the curls between her legs, the trim ankles. He traced a meandering line from her shoulder between her breasts over her navel and down one of her thighs. "You're beautiful. So damned lovely it's physically painful to look at you. I'll make it so good for you, Sandrine. Let me do all the work. Lie back and relax."

He skimmed his hands over her throat, her breasts, the lyrical line of her belly. He was still fully clothed and standing by the bed. It felt safer that way, somehow. To keep a cloth barrier between them. Like the blockade he'd built around his heart. Give her pleasure, nothing more.

Her fingers brushed his cock through his breeches. Pure, teasing agony.

"Show me," she said again.

He moved her on the bed, sliding her forward until her thighs hung off the edge.

He laid her back gently, positioning the pillow under her head. "If you begin to feel light-headed, if you have any pain in your temple at all, tell me to stop, or tap me on the shoulder."

She nodded, her eyes flashing wickedly. "And if you begin to feel light-headed, my lord, and faint from desire, let me know."

Minx.

Her legs were clamped together. He coaxed them apart with gentle kisses on her thighs and soothing touches on her belly. Her thighs parted one inch, then another.

"That's right," he said. "Open for me."

When her thighs were spread wide, he placed his palms on her thighs, holding her open. He gazed at the beautiful, mouthwatering delicacy of her sex, and then dipped his head to taste her.

"Oh," she said huskily. "I thought that was what you meant."

"Mmm. And this." He pushed his tongue inside her. The honeyed flavor saturated his mind with desire. More, more. He craved more.

He kept his touch gentle and light, his movements soft as he stroked her with his tongue.

holding her thighs apart. Varying the location and tempo until he found a pace and a pressure that made her thighs clench and unclench and her breathing hitch. When she started making soft little moans he knew he was on the right track. Maybe a little faster now? A little harder?

He hadn't spoken out loud—his lips and tongue were far too occupied for that—but she answered his question.

"Yes," she moaned. "Yes. Dane."

His heart overflowed with pride. He'd win this race. The finish line was in sight.

It wasn't quick and it wasn't without effort, but he'd be happy to stay here and lick her all night until she reached her climax.

There was a moment when he thought she was about to, when her thighs began to quake and one of her hands wound into his hair to press his head closer, but it didn't happen.

"That's all right," he whispered. "Don't try too hard. It will come, sweetheart, it will come."

"Dane?"

He lifted his head.

"This is rather embarrassing. I have to . . . I have to use the chamber pot," she whispered.

"Of course." He jumped up. "You won't be able to reach your release until you tend to that. Nothing to be embarrassed about." He held out his hand and helped her out of the bed, giving her privacy as she went behind the screen.

She was a little shy when she came back, covering herself with a towel.

Lying back down, she spread her legs of her

own accord this time, and he smiled, a swell of fierce pride in his chest. "Now, where were we?"

It was quick now. She'd been holding back because of the call of nature. Only a few flicks of his tongue and a gentle sucking pressure and she came, pulsing under his tongue, moaning softly and clutching the back of his head with her hands.

His cock strained against his breeches, harder than he'd ever been.

When he'd teased the last ripple of pleasure from her and she lay back limply, spent, he moved her back lengthwise on the bed, pulling the covers up over her and kneeling by the bed.

She hid her face in the pillow.

He caught her chin and turned her to face him. "You did very well. I'm proud of you."

"You're very good at that."

"I've made it something of an art form." He knew that not every man was as focused on bringing his partner to pleasure. It was something he loved and something he was proud to excel at.

"I feel so languid now."

"A climax will do that."

"I'd like to give you . . . I want to do one wicked thing to you."

"I'm all right. I'm off to my chair now."

"No, Dane." She caught his hand. "I want to at least see you. In the flesh, instead of oil on canvas. At least remove your boots."

He removed his boots. "There."

"Now your coat. You won't want it to be wrinkled tomorrow."

The coat went over a chair back.

"Now your cravat and shirt," she whispered, a naughty gleam in her eyes.

He shouldn't do it, but he did. She'd already seen it all, anyway. He undid his cravat and tugged his shirt over his head.

"Unfasten your breeches," she said. He could hear a transformation in her voice from shy and hesitant to brave and bold. He could reward that boldness. And he did, stripping to his bare skin.

He adopted the pose he'd used for his portrait, only standing instead of reclining. Shoulders proud, stomach muscles tensed, both hands covering his privates, gazing out into the distance or, in this case, the rough plank walls of the inn.

"I like that pose. But it's not quite right. I believe your hands were at your sides."

"I don't have a fig leaf."

"I know."

He dropped his hands by his sides, and his cock sprang forward, pointing directly at her.

"Oh. My." Her eyes grew huge in the flickering firelight. "You're even bigger than Kenwick."

"Pardon?" he choked out.

She giggled. "I saw his unfinished portrait. There wasn't any fig leaf."

"I don't suppose he was in a state of arousal."

"No, he wasn't. I suppose I can't compare you until you're not aroused."

"Not likely to happen with you in that bed."

"May I . . . explore you?" She licked her lips, staring at his cock.

Hellfire and damnation. He was being tested.

And he was going to fail. Miserably. There wa
no way he could refuse a request like that.

He lay down beside her on the bed.

"I want to touch your—" she glanced dowr
and he held his breath "—chest."

That hadn't been what he was hoping for, bu
he'd take it. He'd take anything she chose to giv(
A warm soft hand over his heart. The brush c
her lips against his.

He willed himself to remain still and allow he
to explore.

"I might even wish to explore a little lower.
He tensed the muscles of his abdomen as sh
used both hands now to touch him, caressing hi
stomach, his hip bones.

"Do with me what you will," he said, flingin
his arm dramatically over his eyes.

She laughed. "Your virtue is my prize."

"Afraid to say that my virtue has long fled. Bu
yes, I'm your prize. Have your wicked way."

He fervently hoped that her prize was his coc!

"This . . . this is what I seek," she growle(
And thank the Lord! She circled his cock wit
her fingers. He nearly came right then and ther
Something about a good, innocent girl daring t
explore him so freely, pretending she was a m.
rauding pirate.

He would do anything, endure anything, f(
this woman. She really could have him ar
which way she wanted. Have his body. Pulsir
and eager for her touch.

Have his heart. Damaged and rusty with di
use but ready to beat again.

Damn. He was in the grip of lust. And the grip wasn't quite tight or rough enough.

"Don't spare me," he said, sliding his hand over hers, wrapping her fingers tighter and showing her how to move her fist up and down.

He collapsed on the bed, closing his eyes, imagining that he was inside her, where he really wanted to be. Inside her welcoming heat, skin to skin, sweaty and hot and riding for the sunset.

"Faster," he grunted, unable to play any more games, needing release now.

She watched his face intently as she pumped her fist, wanting to be good at it, wanting to please him.

She fantasized about being a worldly siren, and he felt the opposite, almost like this was his first experience with a lover. Her hand the first to touch him, besides his own. That gasping, brand-new, starry devotion to her touch.

Her lips parted. Her breasts bounced, the ends of her long hair brushed his chest.

He touched her lips, bringing his thumb to her mouth, pretending he was inside her mouth. She sucked instinctively on his thumb.

Then she pulled away. "Oh yes, I remember now. That was what you said, about guiding it between my lips and swirling my tongue around the head."

She followed words with deeds. He groaned and flopped back on the pillow, all thought of stopping this gone. Miss Sandrine Oliver's lips were stretched around his cock.

And it was the most exciting thing that had ever

happened to him. He'd thoroughly corrupted her, but what could you expect of a wicked rake like him? He was only living up to expectations. Making sure he wasn't any of the things she'd pronounced him to be last night. Good. Gentle. Caring.

"Suck harder," he growled, longing to fist his hands in her hair and guide her. Instead, he clutched the bedsheets until his knuckles were white. Her movements were inexpert and tentative, but damned if it didn't feel like heaven.

"No teeth," he moaned.

She mumbled something unintelligible.

"What was that?"

She lifted her head, and his cock popped free of her mouth. "Show me what to do. I don't know what you like."

She resumed her position, staring up at him. He should stop this, but he didn't want to. He wanted to bury his cock in her hot, wet mouth for eternity.

He wrapped her long hair around his fists, guiding her with his hands, sinking deeper into her mouth, applying a light pressure to her hair that allowed her to move freely but gave him some control.

She gripped him with her lips, sliding up and down in the tempo he set with his hands. He wove his fingers more tightly into her hair, lost in the silken feel of it and the erotic sight of her swallowing his cock.

He lifted her head.

"Was that right?"

"More than right." Voice raspy, breathing ragged. "Then . . . more?"

"No, no more." He clasped her shoulders and slid her on top of him until her breasts rested against his erection. He placed her hands on either side of her breasts, showing her how to cradle him. Then he began to move in the soft valley between her breasts.

He covered her hands with his, gripping tightly, pressing her breasts around his cock and stroking her nipples with his thumbs. It didn't take long. A few long, hard thrusts and he reached a long, shuddering climax.

"Sandrine." He thumped back against the bed, breathing heavily. "Damn."

She plucked a towel from the chair beside the bed and wiped his chest, and hers, and then snuggled against him. "I don't believe that last item was on your wicked list."

"That list was by no means exhaustive. There are so many ways to find pleasure together." Realization of what had happened began to sift through the fog in his mind. "And you won't be learning any more of them from me. This must stop, Sandrine." His tone grew serious.

"I know," she said. "It must stop. We can't do anything else on the wicked list. I know. Let's get under the covers."

When they were warm under the covers and she was nestled against him with her arm over his chest and her head tucked into his neck, she kissed his ear. "I trust you, Dane. I think you have more to give than you think you do.

You think you're untrustworthy because you blame yourself for something that wasn't your fault."

"The world would be a better place if I'd died instead of my mother. It's a fact."

"It's a lie. The truth is that we can't go back in time and change anything. So we have to live with what we've been given, this one life. You think that you don't deserve to be happy, but you do."

He wanted to believe her, but he'd been believing the opposite for so long. "I'm the stunted limb on my family tree, Sandrine. I loved my brother, and that made me weak and vulnerable. He took advantage of my vulnerability and taught me a harsh lesson about love. When you love people, when you let them close, they stab you in the back."

"What did he do to you?"

"He blamed me for my mother's death in childbirth. He was ten years old at the time. Life was perfect before I came along, according to him. A loving mother, a doting father, and then I ruined everything. The loving mother went cold and silent and was buried in the ground. The doting father became bitter and angry and difficult to please without the tempering sweetness of his wife."

"But they must have known that it wasn't your fault. How could it have been? You didn't ask to be born."

"I caused my mother's death. Roman never forgave me. I used to trail after him, five years old to his fifteen, wanting to be him, worshipping him, and he would do deliberately cruel things. Lock me in dark cupboards. Pour water on me and tell my nurse I'd wet myself. And when I went off to school, he spread false rumors about me, that I cheated on exams and stole valuables from the headmaster. He set me up. Created these elaborate schemes to make me the scapegoat of the school. Anything he could think of to make my life hellish. Then he'd report my fabricated crimes to my father to gain favor, to turn him against me. It worked."

"That's awful."

"You know, the pitiful thing is that even after he did all of that, I still wanted his approval, I still worshipped him. But eventually his campaign to break me, to make me pay, worked. I believed that I was the bad seed. That I'd never be anything but bad. That my birth was a tragic mistake. And that I can only make mistakes. And yes, I'm not thickheaded, I know that my mother's death wasn't my fault. And my father drinking and becoming bitter wasn't my fault. But I still feel that guilt and remorse. I can't shake it. It's always been there. The weight of it piled over my head, word by word. Falsehood by falsehood."

She rested her hand over his heart. "You know they were falsehoods. Now you must believe it with your heart."

"And now my brother, my tormentor, is dead, leaving me feeling even guiltier for resenting him. Blood isn't thicker than water. Blood is cold water closing over your head. Drowning your goodness. Loved ones know the best ways to hurt you."

"And so you became a reckless, immoral rake to escape those thoughts, if only briefly, with your drink, your pleasures."

"I'm stunted, I'm hollow. I can't love. You were safe and content in your little village, and then I came along and ruined everything. It's all my fault."

"I might have been safe, but I wasn't all that happy in Squalton."

"When I met you, I remember thinking that you always had a sunshiny smile on your lips and blue skies in your eyes."

"Because I was making the best of it. Because I knew no other way to live. I had to settle for what I'd been given."

"All my life I've been told that my brother was the good, upstanding, dutiful one. And if he wasn't good, if he was mixed up in something dangerous, or keeping funds meant for charities, then that would mean that he was bad and cruel to others, not only to me. And if he was bad, what does that make me?"

"You're a good man, Dane. You just haven't realized it yet. Stop blaming yourself for everything. All the ills of the world are not on your shoulders. Inside . . . in here," she said and laid a hand over his heart, "this is what truly matters. You're good. I know you are, even if you don't know it. All you need to do is forgive Roman." Her voice drifted into a whisper. "And forgive yourself . . ."

She fell asleep with her hand still covering his heart.

Her words echoed through his mind as he lay in the dark, listening to her soft, rhythmic breathing, and holding her close. Wanting, more than anything, for her to be right.

But knowing that it was too late for him to change.

Chapter Twenty-One

Mother knows best when it comes to choosing a spouse.
　　　—Mrs. Oliver's Rules for Young Ladies

Sandrine arrived back at Francesca's house in the early hours of the morning before the household was stirring. She climbed up the trellis, as the Pink Ladies had taught her to do, and onto the balcony. She tapped on the glass doors in the prearranged signal, and a sleepy Francesca let her in.

"Sandrine? Gracious. What time is it? You said you might be late, but it's practically morning. I was worried about you! Mercy me, you look a fright. Your hair is all mussed—and is that a spot of blood on your pelisse?"

"Nothing to worry over."

"Here, let me help you." She unbuttoned Sandrine's pelisse and removed her bonnet and gown. "Now crawl into bed."

Sandrine sank under the covers gratefully and Francesca joined her, rolling onto her side and facing Sandrine. "If you weren't here in the morning I was going to have to raise the alarm. But I didn't even know where to start looking."

"I'm very sorry for worrying you. First I went

back to Madam Avalon's, then I spoke with the
Duchess of Rydell, and then Lord Dane and I
went for a carriage ride."

"You promised you weren't meeting him."

"My plans changed."

"I do believe *you're* what's changed. And were
you with Lord Dane all night?"

"We were only going to be gone a few hours.
There are some troubling discrepancies in the
Rydell accounting books regarding charitable donations, and I wanted to go and investigate one of
the charities. We drove to East Edston but they'd
never heard of the charity we were trying to find.
So we drove to West Edston only to encounter the
same befuddlement. But by that time the weather
became inclement and the road was muddy and
a tree came down . . . To make a long story a little
shorter we had to go back and spend the night at
an inn until the rain stopped and the roads were
passable."

"Did you stay in separate rooms?"

"We couldn't. I had told the innkeeper earlier in
the day that we were a married couple. I thought
it would explain why I was traveling alone with
Dane. I didn't think we'd have to go back and
stay the night there."

"So you stayed all night in a room with the
most notorious rake in all of London? Sandrine
Oliver! You are utterly, completely ruined."

"I know."

"Except no one knows but me. So you'll be all
right. Unless—" she clasped Sandrine's hands
"—unless you could be with child?"

"No chance of that."

"What happened? Tell me everything."

"He was a perfect gentleman. I was the one who . . ."

Francesca's eyes grew huge. "You . . . ?"

"I suggested some exploration. He refused. I'm afraid I convinced him. Don't worry, we didn't go too far." More than far enough. Even the hint of being out with him after dark and she'd be shunned by society. Her mother would be destroyed.

"You're getting to be more brazen even than Roslyn."

"I know."

"You might want to leave London before something irreversible happens."

"Too late."

"But I thought you said that you stopped before things progressed too far?"

"What's irreversible is how hopelessly devoted I feel to him."

"Oh no," moaned Francesca. "You silly thing. You can't fall in love with Lord Dane. You simply can't. Use him for pleasurable explorations if you must, but don't make the foolish mistake of falling for a rake."

"I can't help myself. Even though he says he's bad through and through and he'll hurt me and he can't give me commitment or love."

"Listen to the man." Francesca shook her by the shoulders. "Listen to him, Sandrine! He's telling you the truth. I've known him much longer than you have, and I've seen young ladies make fool of themselves over him, pining and threatening to throw themselves in the Thames. Nothing ever pierces through that swaggering, arrogant exterior of his. Don't let him make a fool of you twice. He'll never marry. Although, if he becomes the duke he may be forced to. Becoming a duke would do wonders to rehabilitate his reputation. He'd become the biggest prize of the Season."

"I'll challenge any young lady to a duel if she so much as looks at him," Sandrine said, only half-joking.

Francesca giggled. "I'm going to miss you, Sandrine."

"Come visit me in Squalton."

"I'd like that." Francesca yawned. "Now go to sleep. We still have a few hours before my maid comes to wake me. And then we'll have hot chocolate, and you can tell me more about those explorations."

SANDRINE'S PLAN HAD worked. She arrived back to Mrs. McGovern's house in Francesca's carriage with no one the wiser. "Mrs. McGovern, Miss Hodwell, I'm back," she called.

"Oh, Miss Oliver! Such a to-do." Miss Hodwell hurried into the entrance hall. "Your mother is here. And so is Mr. Pilkington."

Her heart plummeted like a pigeon shot by a hunter. She wasn't ready to face her mother. And Mr. Pilkington was here?

"They're very angry with you. I'm afraid we haven't been very good chaperones. Oh dear, oh dear. And they won't take any refreshment. All they do is sit there in the parlor, stiff as boards. Eve is off visiting with a friend for the day, and I haven't known what to do, what to say."

"It's all right, Miss Hodwell." Sandrine smiled cheerfully, though inside her emotions were churning between abject terror and a strong urge to turn around and run anywhere but here. "I'll go in and speak to them. Why don't you go and have a lie-down? Perhaps with a plate of biscuits and a good novel?"

"That does sound just the thing." She brightened, straightening her lace cap, which had gone askew. "Are you sure you don't want me to be there?"

"Quite sure. This isn't your battle. You've been nothing but kind and good to me."

Sandrine led Miss Hodwell to the stairs and then prepared to face her mother.

At least Francesca had lent her another gown and insisted on dressing her hair properly before she returned. She was presentable.

She took three deep breaths, rubbed her temples for a few moments, and pushed her shoulders back. Right. She could do this. She wasn't the same person who had left Squalton.

She was London Sandrine. Someone her mother had never met before.

"Sandrine! There you are. We've been worried sick about you, haven't we, Mr. Pilkington?"

"Indeed, we have."

"Mother." She kissed her cheek. "Mr. Pilkington."

"I'm sure you're wondering why we've come," said her mother.

"I do wonder because I am scheduled to return to Squalton soon."

"We couldn't wait any longer. We had to come and rescue you from making a terrible mistake."

She couldn't know about Dane, could she? Sandrine's heart flip-flopped in her chest. She knew from experience that she didn't need to ask her mother any questions. The accusatory words would tumble out with no prompting.

"We've heard the most alarming report, Miss Oliver," said Mr. Pilkington.

Sandrine swallowed. They had only arrived this morning. They couldn't have heard reports about inns with only one bed. But perhaps something had reached their ears about the masked ball?

"A most alarming report," her mother echoed, "about you from Mrs. Philpot, who was visiting her daughter in London last week. She said that you've befriended Lady Roslyn Stockard, a young lady whose reputation has recently been sullied."

"Lady Roslyn is my friend. You don't know her at all."

"London has corrupted you, exactly as I said it would. I can see it in your eyes," her mother said. "You must come home with us at once. Before anything truly bad happens."

"I'd like to stay the full fortnight, thank you very much." She'd never contradicted her mother before. It made her heart race and gave her a sick feeling in her stomach. But she mustn't roll over and play dead as she had so many times before.

"I don't think you understand the gravity of the situation, Miss Oliver. An innocent girl like you must never hear the things that Lady Roslyn has been accused of. It beggars disbelief," said Mr. Pilkington with a curt nod of his sharp chin.

"She's a brazen girl who has been defiled and deserves scorn!" her mother exclaimed.

"She's my friend. Don't speak of her that way."

"You're shocking me, Miss Oliver." Mr. Pilkington stared down his long nose at her. "This isn't the conduct of the young lady I know and revere."

"I don't think you really know me at all, Mr. Pilkington. I didn't even know myself. I'm only now beginning to see that."

"Don't hold it against her, Mr. Pilkington. It's because she's been poisoned by this Lady Roslyn creature. This hussy who defies society's dictates and must pay the price."

Sandrine's shoulders shook. Whatever Roslyn had been accused of, Sandrine had most likely done nearly the same. She was tainted in their eyes, deserving of scorn. A fallen woman. A hussy.

"Like your own mother pays the price of society's scorn?" Sandrine asked.

Her mother's face blanched. "Pardon me, young lady?"

"I know all about my grandmother. She's alive and well and living in London. I've met her, Mama, conversed with her, and I—"

"You have a grandmother in London?" Mr.

Pilkington cocked his head. "Barbara, I thought you told me that your parents were deceased?"

"Ernest, would you allow me a moment alone with my daughter?"

"I believe it my right to be here."

Her mother fell upon a sofa, threw her head against her arms, and started wailing.

"Now, Barbara," the vicar said, rushing to her side, "do stop crying. I don't understand what this is all about. Who is this grandmother, Miss Oliver?"

"Her name is Ruby Avalon."

"Oh," her mother wailed, crying and hiccuping. "You can't tell him that."

"But it's the truth, and I'm not ashamed to say it. Why didn't you tell me I had a grandmother and an aunt and a cousin? All this time I thought that I had no living relatives in London, and I found out, quite by chance. You know I've always longed to have a large family."

"I forbade you to visit Covent Garden. You disobeyed me, you wicked girl."

"You lied to me my entire life."

"Ruby Avalon?" Mr. Pilkington's brow furrowed. "Surely not the notorious Madam Avalon who runs a scandalous salon called the Silver Palace, which encourages all manner of iniquity and subversive activities?"

Sandrine drew herself up. "Don't talk about her that way."

"And don't take that tone with me, Miss Oliver."

"I never should have allowed you to come to London," her mother said, her breath hitching.

"How can you say that? We have family here, Mama. How could you turn your back on your own mother and hide her very existence from me?"

"She was trying to protect you from sin, Miss Oliver. Well. This changes everything." He began pacing up and down the room. "Everything." He stopped in front of Sandrine.

Her mother raised tearstained cheeks. "If only you had accepted Mr. Pilkington and stayed in Squalton, none of this would have happened."

"Pardon me, madam, but there were no proposals definitely given or accepted."

"You were going to propose, though, weren't you?"

"I may have entertained the notion, even though she would be a portionless bride, but now, given her kinship with that woman, I couldn't possibly lower myself to marry her." He glared at Sandrine. "I have had a narrow escape. I was nearly hoodwinked into marrying the granddaughter of a notorious bawd. Thank heavens this came to light when it did!"

"She's not a bawd. She's a wonderful woman, a brilliant artist, and a benefactress to other women artists," Sandrine said vehemently. "She helps young ladies not harms them. Which is more than can be said for you, Mr. Pilkington. Why must your sermons dwell upon wrath and punishment, instilling fear and shame? Why can you not preach love, forgiveness, and hope?"

"I won't stand here and be insulted a moment longer. Barbara, I'm leaving."

"Ernest, pray reconsider! No one in Squalton

knows about my mother. We can all go back and pretend none of this ever happened."

"That's not possible, Mama. I can't go back and pretend to be that naive girl who follows all your dictates and allows fear to rule her heart."

"I will pray for you, Miss Oliver. You've obviously been corrupted and turned from the path of righteousness. Barbara, I can't marry your daughter, and there's an end to it."

"You can't marry her, you pontificating toad of a man, because she's already engaged to me!"

The thunderous voice sounded from the doorway. Dane stood there at his full height, face glowering, arms crossed, looking so deliciously handsome she wanted to wrap her arms around his neck and never let go.

"Engaged to you?" Mr. Pilkington stuttered. "Mr. Smith, isn't it?"

"Not Mr. Smith. Lord Dane Walker, heir presumptive to the dukedom of Rydell. Now, Mr. Pilkington, you will apologize to my fiancée. And make it eloquent, or I'll rearrange your face."

Chapter Twenty-Two

Honor thy mother and obey her in all things.
    —Mrs. Oliver's Rules for Young Ladies

Will you excuse us for a moment, Mother, Mr. Pilkington?" Sandrine grabbed Dane's hand and marched him out of the parlor, down the hall and into a sitting room.

She didn't look happy. Why didn't she look happy?

"Dane, what on earth was that?"

He tugged against her hand, still seeing red. "Let me go back, Sandrine. I'm going to rearrange that vicar's face with my fists."

"Dane. Why did you say that?"

"He was insulting you. He was saying he couldn't lower himself to marry you. No one speaks to you like that!"

"And so you dove in and rescued me. Even though I had the situation under control."

"I couldn't stand by and listen to that loathsome excuse for a man insult you!"

"Did you stop to think before you decided my fate?"

"I wasn't thinking at all. I was reacting. And I'd do it again. Just to see his mouth flop open."

"Did you ever think that I might not want this?"

"Wait." He laid his hands lightly on her shoulders. "Are you saying that you don't wish to marry me?"

She sniffed. "I'm saying that I don't wish to learn of my engagement before there's even been a proposal."

"Point taken." He gathered her small hands into his. "Miss Sandrine Oliver, would you do me—"

"And I don't want a proposal given not from love but from a desire to protect me from scorn."

She was being stubborn. They had no other choice. Now that the deed was done, all Dane could think about was their wedding night. He'd obtain a special license. He could have her in his bed within a week. "Well, too bad. We're already engaged."

"Go in there and tell them that you were mistaken."

"I won't."

"Why not? Dane, you've told me that you'll never marry. I'm not going to be the woman who you'll resent the rest of your life for forcing you into a union you never desired."

"I won't go back in there and tell them it was a mistake because it wasn't. It might be the first time I've done something right in my entire blighted life."

"Dane, you're not thinking clearly. We had a long night."

"We certainly did. And by any polite standards, the night we shared would be reason enough alone for me to announce our engagement."

"Without consulting me first."

"That's the thanks I get for making an honest woman of you?"

"Now you want me to thank you for deciding my fate without consulting me?"

"Sandrine, you're being stubborn. You know this is our only option. I would have proposed anyway."

"And yet, you didn't. And anyway, I wasn't angling for a proposal. I won't marry a man who doesn't love me. And I told you before that I don't need rescuing. I'm finally beginning to live my life on my own terms, and I don't need you to swoop in and try to rearrange everything to soothe your pride."

"I thought at least you'd want to marry me so that you could continue your campaign to save Squalton Manor."

"You announced our engagement because you care about me and my reputation. I thank you for it. But I release you from any obligation."

"I don't want to be released."

SHE LONGED TO capitulate, to throw herself into his arms and say, "Yes, I'll marry you," but she couldn't, and he was being obtuse about it. "You never would have proposed if you hadn't witnessed Mr. Pilkington being horrid to me. I'd wonder our whole lives whether you regretted those hasty words, spoken without thinking, spoken in anger."

Though, it had been stirring, she must admit. It had given her carnal cravings to see him stare down the vicar and offer to defend her honor with his fists.

"Sandrine, it doesn't matter why the proposal was given. You're marrying me. After last night, it's the only option."

"You're not listening to me." She balled her hands. "You can't ruin someone if what they're asking for isn't ruination but salvation. Calling it *ruin* is a way for society to shame women, make them feel like victims. I'm not a victim. I don't feel as though I've fallen into a dark, redemptionless pit. I feel, for the very first time in my life, as though I'm standing on my own two feet and I can bravely face what the future brings."

"You're mine now, Sandrine." He glowered at her and gripped her shoulders with his strong hands. He was going to rescue her whether she wanted it or not. And suddenly she was drowning, her head underwater, and only his arms surrounding her would allow her to breathe again.

"I can't seem to push you away, Sandrine. Those blackmailers are still out there. The threat isn't gone. And now we're bound to each other. I will protect you." His grip tightened until it was almost painful. "Do you hear me? You're mine. I won't let anyone hurt you."

He claimed her lips fiercely. The danger, the pleasure of coming together, lips exploring hungrily, hands tangling in hair, his fist in her hair, pulling her head back. His lips on her throat. She ached for him. Yearned for him.

His palm closed around her breast, a possessive claiming that thrilled her. She wanted him so badly. Last night hadn't been nearly enough.

She wanted him to take her here in this prim and proper parlor with pink roses papering the walls and dainty furnishings.

"I can't get enough of you. Sandrine—" her name on a deep, low moan "—I can't keep my hands off you."

"Then, don't."

He gripped her hips with both hands and pulled her against him, showing her how stiff he was, how much he wanted her. She was lost to anything but the desire flowing through her veins. She wanted to open for him. Take him inside her.

He pushed her bodice down roughly and dipped his head to suckle her nipple.

"Dane," she moaned, her head falling back. He captured the back of her head with his palm, and his hand moved lower, circling the back of her neck, holding her motionless for the sensual exploration of his lips on her breasts and throat.

"Sandrine Oliver!" They both turned their heads to see her mother standing there, jaw slack, eyes bulging. "You . . . you wicked beast! Mauling my daughter in broad daylight. Get away from her!"

Dane set her down. They were both breathing heavily. Sandrine adjusted the bodice of her gown and attempted to smooth her hair back into place.

"I can kiss my fiancée, Mrs. Oliver," Dane said coldly. He took her hand, and they stood shoulder to shoulder, facing her mother.

The horrified expression on her mother's face triggered a rising tide of guilt and shame that threatened to engulf Sandrine's mind and send her begging for forgiveness. But she fought it. She wasn't the same timid girl who'd left Squalton.

She willed her voice to be steady and calm. "You may as well know, Mama, that this isn't the first time Lord Dane and I have kissed."

"My God, do you hear yourself? Is this my devout and obedient daughter?" her mother sputtered. "You've been led astray by this devil. He'll never marry you, Sandrine. He's lying. That's what rakes do. They lie and then they leave you. They leave you alone and heartbroken."

"I absolutely will marry her," Dane said.

"Dane," she whispered. "I think I need to speak with my mother alone." It was time for an honest conversation. Time to stop hiding who she really was and claim her own space.

He searched her face, his eyes clouded with concern. "Are you sure?"

"I must do this. It's the only way for me to make my own way in the world."

He closed his eyes briefly. "I meant what I said about protecting you. I'm sending a carriage for you in one hour. Pack your things. You're moving into Rydell House."

"Don't bother with your corrupt commands, Lord Dane," her mother said with an icy glare.

"Sandrine will be going home with me to Squalton this very afternoon."

"Mother." Sandrine clenched her jaw. "We need to talk."

Dane gave her hand a squeeze. "I understand that you need time alone with your mother. I'll be waiting for you at Rydell House. Mrs. Oliver." He nodded at her mother on his way out.

Her mother watched him leave, then turned to Sandrine with loathing in her eyes. "And so that man pretended to be a commoner to win your heart and now he's ruined you. Is that why you begged to come to London? You were already under his spell. My poor, deluded girl." She rushed over to Sandrine. "Tell me that you haven't been compromised in truth. Tell me there's no possibility of a babe out of wedlock."

Sandrine stood stiffly in her mother's embrace. "There's no possibility of that."

"Oh thank the dear Lord! I couldn't have borne it."

"Mother," Sandrine said evenly, "did something hurtful happen to you when you were a girl in London? Is that what this is all about?"

Her mother dropped her arms and stood rigid and shaking with fury. "This isn't about me."

"But it is, isn't it? It's all about you. I want to know what made you so fearful of living your life and so restrictive of me living mine."

"You want to know what happened to me in my childhood? I'll tell you. I don't even know who my father is. My mother doesn't know. It wasn't the elderly man she was married to, that much she told me. And if that wasn't enough, she raised me with no moral compass, no rules. I was allowed to do as I pleased. I was lost at sea, tossed and turned about with no one to guide me."

"I know. She told me as much when I went to see her yesterday. She admitted that she'd made mistakes as a young mother."

"She raised me and my sister in a scandalous manner. It wasn't a proper environment for children. The men that came to our house, her artist's models, were sometimes inappropriately attentive. One of them seduced me, promised that he would marry me. I was so desperate to leave that house that I believed his lies. I was such an ignorant fool. I hadn't been taught right from wrong. I'd never been taught to be cautious and measured in my actions. And so I succumbed to the first wicked rake who made me pretty promises. And he took my virtue and abandoned me, left me in the gutter."

"I'm so sorry that happened to you."

"I was only sixteen, Sandrine. And my mother didn't protect me. I didn't love your father, but I married him because he was an honorable gentleman, one who was willing to marry a ruined woman who'd been used and discarded like a soiled handkerchief. I married him on the condition that he take me far away from London. I vowed never to return. From that day forward I determined that my mother was dead."

"She's so very sorry, and she's changed. She wants to apologize to you, to try to make amends."

"She was never there for me when I needed her. She was there for her midnight friends, her parties and her entertainments, but not for me. And she won't be there for you, either."

"She's changed. She's a loving mother to Dawn and to her granddaughter Sophia. She's going to visit them abroad. We have a family, Mama. Don't you want to meet your niece? Don't you miss your sister?"

"My sister is dead to me as well. Selfish people like them never change. They only chase passing thrills. And don't think that Ruby can replace me. She'll never be a good mother to you."

"I don't need a mother, I have you. And you've kept me safe, and you've given me confidence and allowed me to be secretary of the historical society, and I thank you for that quiet, useful existence. But it's time for me to leave the nest. It's time for you to allow me to spread my wings."

"It's not spreading your wings, it's clipping them. You'll be dragged down into the mud by this rake and by your new friends. I can't bear to think of you being exposed to the depravity my mother encourages around her. She's turned you against me. Even after everything I taught you, all the warnings. You're making the same mistakes that I made. That handsome rake won't marry you, he's only using you. You have your head so far in the clouds, my girl, that you can't see the muck your feet are mired in. And if he becomes a duke? Do you think he could marry a girl who is the granddaughter of the notorious Madam Avalon? This is what I was trying to protect you from. The knowledge of our sordid connections and the hot coals of shame that society will heap upon your head once they know."

"I'm sorry, Mama. But I must live my own life." It cost her everything to say those words. "And my goal isn't marriage. My goal is freedom."

The familiar guilt sat atop her chest like a boulder. The desire to please her mother, to be what she so desperately needed her to be, was still strong. She understood her so much better now. Understood why she'd been so harsh and restrictive.

"I've done everything for you, lived my life for you. How can you do this to me?" Her mother staggered to a chair and sat down heavily. "You are mimicking my mother's words. She always said that freedom was her ideal, but it's a deadly trap. Can't you see that? You're angry with me, you're trying to hurt me, when everything I've done has been to protect you and keep you from harm. What have I always told you about London? It's true, all of it. Look at how it's infected you, twisted your mind to sin. Come home with me now, and we'll rebuild the life we had. We don't need Mr. Pilkington. Let it be you and me, together, as we always were."

"I love you, Mother." Sandrine knelt beside her. "I'm not making this choice lightly or to hurt you. I'm making it because you've made all my choices up until this point. You've been the one to decide every aspect of my life, and I don't know who I am. I don't know what I want. It's for me to discover. And I might make mistakes. I'll be less than perfect. But I won't stop loving you. And I hope you can find it in your heart to forgive me and love me too."

"I won't forgive you, Sandrine. Not if you continue associating with that woman. That would be unforgivable. I'm begging you to come home with me." Her mother clutched her hands. "Forget about my scandalous mother. Forget about that arrogant rake who will never, ever love you the way you love him. Come home, and we'll start all over again."

"I wish I could do as you ask because I don't want to hurt you or disobey you. But it's too late. I can't forget everything I've learned. I have much to do here in London. I am helping Lord Dane host a charity ball, a worthy endeavor. I want to become better acquainted with my grandmother. I think society is wrong to shun her. I honestly believe she's changed, and I want you to come with me to talk to her."

Her mother's gaze hardened and she sat stiffly on the edge of her chair. "If you choose to stay here, Sandrine, then I wash my hands of you."

"Mama, you can't mean that!"

"I'll pray for you."

Sandrine bowed her head, grief gnawing at her heart. "Don't do this."

"When you are disgraced and your rake leaves you, and all the hollow pleasures of London turn to ashes in your mouth, when you are brought low and humble, then I may accept you back out of charity." She rose and straightened her skirts.

"When you are properly remorseful, you may appeal to me." She turned and walked away.

"Mama!"

The door closed. Sandrine fell against the arm of the sofa, hot tears soaking the cloth. It hurt too much. But she couldn't run after her mother and beg forgiveness. She couldn't go back to her old life.

She heard Mr. Pilkington's voice outside, and her mother's, and then the sound of a carriage leaving.

"My dear, what has happened?" Miss Hodwell asked, rushing into the parlor. "Is your mother leaving already?"

"She's gone."

"Are you crying? Oh my dear." She sat next to Sandrine and offered her a handkerchief. "Tell me all about it."

Where to start? "My life has become very complicated."

"Has it, dearie? I'm afraid I haven't been paying close-enough attention, then. Is it Lord Dane? I thought I heard his voice."

"Mr. Pilkington became very angry when he learned that Madam Avalon is my grandmother."

"Pardon me? Madam Avalon, the hostess of the Silver Palace salons?"

"The very same. I understand you are acquainted with her. I visited her and discovered our connection. She's the reason my mother never wanted me to come to London. My mother is ashamed of her and decided to pretend she was dead. I have a grandmother, and an aunt and a cousin. I can't simply undo that knowledge. They are my blood, and I've always, always longed for a large family."

"How astonishing! Eve and I know Ruby well. You should have told me that you were visiting her. But it was very wrong of Mr. Pilkington to cast aspersions upon you simply because you're related to Ruby. She may be considered scandalous, but she's one of the most vibrant and generous women I know."

"He said he could never stoop to marry someone like me. Lord Dane overheard him and informed Mr. Pilkington that he could never wed me because I was already engaged to Lord Dane."

"Heavens! What an exciting moment that must have been with Lord Dane putting that smug vicar in his place. I'm sorry that I missed it."

"It was the most unpredictable and thrilling moment of my life, though it was also confusing because I felt that he wasn't proposing out of love. He only sought to save my honor."

Miss Hodwell's response was lost in a flurry of activity and voices in the entrance hall. A maidservant knocked on the parlor door.

"Yes?" Miss Hodwell called.

"Lady Roslyn, Miss McGovern, and Miss Maples are here to see you."

"Send them in! And bring some tea and macaroons."

The ladies entered the room all pink sashes and pink cheeks.

"Kenwick is preparing to race Baron Chisholme

because Chisholme insulted Roslyn," cried Francesca.

"And the ruddy fool's had too much whiskey to calm his nerves, and now he's not fit to ride," Roslyn said angrily. "He'll break his neck!"

"Come, Miss Hodwell and Sandrine," Marta urged. "We have to stop him!"

Chapter Twenty-Three

*Contrary to what you read in novels, a rake can
never be reformed.*
    —Mrs. Oliver's Rules for Young Ladies

Kenwick and Chisholme were assembled on the
track, the two curricles lined up side by side with
their matched sets of horses.

Dane clapped his hand onto Kenwick's sub
stantial shoulder. "Kenwick, you've had too
much tipple. You're in no shape to drive."

"I'm all right."

"Walk a straight line for me."

Kenwick attempted to walk in a line, then wob
bled and had to throw a hand against the car
riage door to steady himself.

"That settles it. You're not racing."

"Have to race, Dane, old friend." Kenwick
threw an arm around his shoulders. "Chisholme
called Lady Roslyn a strumpet, so I challenged
him to a race. First I'll conquer him with my cur
ricle, and then I'm going to beat him with my
fists."

"You're not beating anyone with anything.
You're going home to sleep this off."

Baron Chisholme swaggered over. "Trouble in
paradise, lovers?"

Kenwick lunged for him but tripped and fell, hitting his head on the carriage wheel.

"Uh-oh." Chisholme laughed nastily. "I win by default."

"I'll race in his place," Dane said grimly, motioning for Dudley to help Kenwick off the racing green.

"Look lively, then. I haven't got all day." Chisholme retreated to his curricle and swung into the seat. His friends surrounded him, laughing and jostling one another.

"Dane, the Pink Ladies are here!" Dudley shouted, gesturing toward the far end of the field where Dane could see a line of grim-faced ladies in matching pink sashes marching toward him. When he saw Sandrine in their midst, his heart soared. She hadn't left London with her mother!

He should have wanted her to leave, to be safely back in Squalton, but he couldn't bring himself to want that anymore. She was meant to be here with him. He would keep her safe.

She approached him with concern written across her face. "Are you going to race?" she asked.

"Kenwick's too inebriated. I can't allow him to race. It's for Lady Roslyn's honor. I overheard you defending her today. I'm doing the same, in my own way."

"But what if . . . what if the traces break? What if you're thrown from the curricle like a shot from a pistol?"

"Don't worry. I've raced this course hundreds of times. It's dangerous, but I'm the best there is. Tell her, Dudley."

"He's the best. He's the king. No one mightier."

"You're waiting to find out if you'll become duke. You have responsibilities now."

"Sandrine." He skimmed her cheek with the back of his hand. "This is who I am. I'm a wild risk-taking rake. But I promise you that I'll win this race, and then we'll celebrate my victory." He bent closer to her, inhaling the delicate scent of lavender and rose that clung to her skin. "We'll celebrate with another item on the wicked list," he whispered.

Her cheeks flushed. "Dane, we have to talk."

"First I race."

Dudley took Sandrine by the arm and ushered her to the sidelines where she joined Lady Roslyn, Miss Maple, Miss McGovern, and Miss Hodwell. Lady Roslyn blew him a kiss.

His matched set of grays pawed the ground, ready to fly.

His focus sharpened as he swung into the curricle seat, gathering up the reins. The horses eyed each other nervously, the whites of their eyes showing.

Dudley and Somersby inspected the fastenings and the wheels one last time. Somersby patted the side of the carriage. "All good. Give him hell!"

"For the Thunderbolts!" Dudley roared.

Dane could already feel the wheels flying over the turf, his body jostling, teeth knocking together, the thrill of victory in sight.

"On your marks, gentlemen," one of the baron's friends shouted. "And . . . go!"

The curricles set off in a cloud of dust. Sandrine's heart thudded in time with the horses' hooves as she watched.

"I fear Lord Dane's not accustomed to Kenwick's curricle," Francesca exclaimed.

"It's a new chariot, Francesca," Dudley said. "Nobody's accustomed to driving it."

"'The smoking chariots, rapid as they bound, now seem to touch the sky, and now the ground,'" quoted Somersby. "That's from Homer. I always liked that description. Touching the sky."

"Faster, Dane!" Dudley shouted. "Ride fast, ride hard, ride far!"

"Your motto?" Sandrine asked.

Dudley nodded, keeping his gaze fixed on the sleek curricles streaking across the field.

Kenwick raised his head from his slumped position against the wall of the clubhouse. "Go, *Lightning Streak*!"

They rounded the bend, and Dane's green curricle swayed dangerously.

His death flashed before her eyes. He lay on the grass, unmoving, his spine broken, his eyes sightless.

He couldn't die today. She loved him. She knew it with blinding clarity in that moment. She'd fallen in love with humble and honorable Danny Smith. And she'd hated wealthy and mocking Lord Dane. But the man she loved was a complicated mixture of both: attentive and arrogant. Large-hearted yet scared to love. If only she could make him see that love gave you power, instead of stealing it away.

"Go faster, Lord Dane!" Miss Hodwell shouted. "Crush him, mangle him, make him eat your dust!"

They were on the final stretch now, racing neck and neck. Dane rose in his seat, urging his horses to go faster.

"He'll topple from the carriage!" She squeezed her eyes shut. She couldn't look. "Tell me when it's over."

"It's all right. Look, he's righted himself," said Somersby.

She opened her eyes. Chisholme's chariot veered sharply to the right, heading directly for Dane's. Sandrine held her breath. They were going to collide.

"I told you Chisholme's a dirty one," Dudley said. "He'll get them both killed."

Dane had to maneuver out of the way, but he kept his curricle upright.

They thundered toward the finish line. At the last possible moment, Dane's horses surged and left Chisholme in their dust. He crossed the finish line and eased the curricle to a halt. He threw the reins to Dudley and jumped down. His hair was wild, his cravat had come undone, and he looked just like the disreputable scoundrel she knew him to be.

He rubbed his hand down each horse's flank, whispering in their ears. The horses whinnied and nuzzled him.

The baron's friends helped him down, and he staggered away, swearing and glowering.

Dane swaggered over and the group sur-

ounded him, clapping him on the back, laugh-
ng and cheering. He laughed and responded to
heir jubilation, but his eyes sought Sandrine's
nd held her gaze. A wave of intense desire
urged inside her.

"You could have been killed!" she chided.

"But I wasn't. And now we have something to
celebrate." His eyes sparked with teasing sensuality in the noonday sun.

*I can't get enough of you. I can't keep my hands
off you.*

"Let's celebrate with some champagne!" Dudley
said, bringing over a bottle.

"Kenwick's had enough, and I'd rather celebrate
with my fiancée," Dane said.

"Your *what*?" Dudley asked, his jaw dropping.

"What's this, Sandrine?" Roslyn asked. "Are
you making an honest rake of our Lord Dane?"

"You heard me," Dane said.

"Ding-dong, ding-dong," muttered Kenwick,
propped up against the wall. "Whadiditellya?"

"Dane, can I talk to you?" Sandrine pulled him
around the side of the clubhouse.

"Alone at last." He leaned in to kiss her, but she
ducked away.

"Dane. Behave. You can't just announce to everyone that we're engaged. You're doing it again.
Planning my life without consulting me."

"I'm riding high, and to the victor go the spoils."
His face grew serious. "How did it go with your
mother? I'm very sorry if I was the cause of strife
between you."

"It's not your fault that we argued. It was mostly about my grandmother. My mother gave me an ultimatum. She said she'd wash her hands of me if I continued my relationship with Ruby. She shouldn't ask me to make that choice. I'm not giving up hope on her. There may be a way to reunite her with her mother."

"Always the optimist. The way you look at the world is so rosy and hopeful, even when things are falling to rubble around your ears. It's like you thinking that a few ghosts and some new paint will make Squalton Manor a sought-after attraction for travelers."

"It will! Or how I believe that you could be good under that cynical, teasing exterior?"

"Yes, most of all that."

"You think your birth was a mistake," she said softly. "Whereas I think the world is a better place with you in it. I won't stop trying to convince you of that."

"And I won't stop announcing our engagement because it's a fait accompli. I'm afraid you're stuck with cynical me."

"The engagement hasn't been settled yet. Besides the fact that you acted hastily and without consulting me, my mother said something after you left that I hadn't even considered. You can't marry me for the same reasons that Mr. Pilkington can't marry me. As much as you don't want to, you might become a duke, Dane. And then I would be the duchess with a scandalous grandmother, no fortune, no training in the art of duchessing, and a mother who will carry on about the iniquity of the sinful city of London at every social gathering."

"You'd win everyone over. Don't you know the effect you have on people?"

"Dane, there you are." The Duke of Warburton rounded the corner of the clubhouse. "Miss Oliver." He bowed to Sandrine. "Osborne's found something," he said in his usual gruff, direct way. "Or rather, someone. Your Mr. *L-A*, whose full name is Larken. He has him at Osborne Court for questioning."

"How did he find him?"

"Followed the money trail from the prizefight. We're to go and help question him."

"Go," Sandrine said, reading the question in his eyes. "Go and uncover the plot against your brother so that we can all sleep easier at night."

"I'm still sending my carriage for you."

"We'll see about that," she said.

"Fait accompli, my dear Miss Oliver," he replied with a devastating smile and a wave as he walked away with Warburton.

Sandrine's heart galloped. This was another line drawn in the sand. If she gave herself to him, there would be no going back. He desired her, that much was clear. But he'd never said that he loved her or even cared for her.

Would she be strong enough to resist him the next time he whispered wicked things to her? She must find the fortitude to fight this attraction.

She had to know that it was love, and not merely
lust, motivating him to claim her.

She must win the race for his heart as the Pink
Ladies had instructed her to do. Make him fall to
his knees. Make him grovel.

Chapter Twenty-Four

Indelicate topics must never be discussed by young ladies.
—Mrs. Oliver's Rules for Young Ladies

Osborne had Larken trussed to a chair in his cellar with a handkerchief stuffed inside his mouth.

"Does your wife know about this?" Warburton asked him.

"She's at her art gallery. I don't interfere with her work, and she doesn't interfere with mine." He raised his huge fists. "Shall I get to work, then, now that you're here to help?"

"This is where I leave you, gentlemen," Patrick said. "As your lawyer, I don't want to know what goes on in this cellar."

Larken whimpered, eyeing them warily.

Dane had no intention of hurting the man, but with three large men surrounding him with their fists raised, he hoped to frighten him into talking.

He approached the chair, and Larken flinched. "I don't like hitting a fellow who's tied up. But when you accosted me in that alleyway, I asked you for a fair fight and you kept me blindfolded and restrained. Turn and turn about."

"I'll ask you one more time," Osborne said. "A[r]e you ready to start talking? Nod your head *yes*."

Larken's gaze darted from Warburton to O[s]borne to Dane. He swallowed. Then nodded.

"Good." Osborne ripped the gag from h[is] mouth. "Who hired you to threaten Lord Dane[?]"

Larken spat on the floor. "I don't know."

"What's that supposed to mean?" Dane asked[.]

"Just what I said. It was all done anonymous[ly] through messages. I've never met the man th[at] paid me to blackmail your brother. You bruise[r] can beat me as much as you like, but I don't ha[ve] a name to cough up."

Warburton studied his face. "I think he's tellin[g] the truth."

"I don't even know what Rydell did that was s[o] bad. I was only told that he did something crim[i]nal and that was all I needed to know. And th[at] one"—he jerked his head in Dane's direction—"doesn't have anything more to worry about. [I] haven't been paid in weeks now, have I."

"That's why you haven't threatened me again[?]"

"Not going to do the dirty work if I don't get paid[.]"

"If the man who hired you contacts yo[u] again, you're to let me know, do you hear me[?]" Dane asked.

"What's in it for me?"

"You keep breathing another day," Osborn[e] said. "My brother compiled a lengthy list of you[r] petty crimes, and if you so much as look at Lor[d] Dane again, we'll have you arrested and you'[ll] be staring at the walls of Newgate if you aren[']t hanging by a noose."

"All right, all right, your lordships. I know when to keep my head down. Let me out of these ropes and I'll be on my merry way."

"One more question," Dane said. "Was it the man who hired you that fixed the prizefight?"

"That weren't him. It was a mate of mine. Like I said, we haven't been paid so that was something of my own initiative. Quite lucrative, what? Your friends were happy."

Osborne untied him and pulled him to his feet, none too gently. "Be on your way, Larken, before I change my mind and have you arrested."

Larken slunk from the room, accompanied by Osborne's manservant.

"One threat has been removed," Warburton said. "But we still don't know who was behind it and what he knew about your brother."

"I think my brother was stealing from the charities he purported to help. My investigating with Miss Oliver turned up a fictitious charity, and we have at least two reports of legitimate charitable concerns that were promised funds and received only a pittance or nothing."

"The person with the incriminating information on your brother could be affiliated with one of the charities that never received the funds," Osborne said. "Someone who found out what he was up to and decided to squeeze him for cash. Give Patrick that list of charities before you go."

"It's all in a pamphlet that will be distributed at the charity ball. I'll have one delivered to you today."

"It's possible that the person who hired the

blackmailers realizes that there's no more profi
to be made and has given up. Maybe they go
wind of my involvement," Osborne said. "
don't mean to brag, but I'm a strong deterrent."

Warburton shrugged. "Possible but unlikely."

"Thank you, Osborne." Dane collected his ha
and gloves. "It's good to know that I don't need to
worry about a knife held to my throat anymore."

"My pleasure. We'll find the person behind
this, don't worry."

"I think it's someone who hated my brother
enough to ruin him if it came down to it. And he
probably hates me as well."

"It's ME SHE hates not you," Ruby said later tha
afternoon when Sandrine visited her to tell he
about her mother's visit. "She shouldn't have
tried to force you to make a choice between us."

"She only loves me if I follow her rules."

"I don't think that's true." Ruby placed a can
vas over the painting she'd been working on and
rose from her stool. "She loves you dearly. Give
her time."

"I'm beginning to think that sometimes loving
someone isn't enough." Sandrine walked along
the gallery until she came to the portrait of Dane
"I love this man, but he's unwilling to admit the
same. He thinks that love displays weakness
That if he gives me his heart he's handing me
the power to hurt him. He only announced our
engagement to save me from Mr. Pilkington'
scorn."

"Lord Dane doesn't do anything he doesn'

want to do. I think deep down he loves you, but he's afraid to admit it. He might surprise you yet. And if you've been intimate, he'll do the honorable thing. Have you been . . . intimate?"

"I still have my virtue, if that's what you're asking."

"Excellent. If things do progress, I would urge you to make certain that he uses a protective sheath. Although that's not a foolproof method of preventing conception."

"He did mention to me that he always uses a sheath. I wasn't sure what he was talking about."

"A fitted sheath made of animal gut that is tied around his member before intercourse to protect against disease and unwanted conception. Girls are kept in the dark in our society. I've known too many young ladies who didn't even know why they were with child."

"You speak so frankly of such matters. My mother was never willing to speak of what she termed *indelicate topics*."

"Did she not explain to you about the act of intercourse?"

"She said that Mr. Pilkington would most likely leave his nightgown on and allow me to do so as well so that we were never naked in each other's presence. She said I would be expected to lie still beneath him, and that the pain would be brief and it would all be over in a matter of minutes."

Ruby rolled her eyes. "Good God. Doesn't make it sound very appealing, now, does it?"

"I've had some experiences with Lord Dane

that lead me to believe it might be far more pleasurable than I thought."

"If there's one thing a rake like Dane prides
himself on it's the giving of pleasure. I do hope
everything works out for the best. I've known
him for some time, and I believe him to have a
good heart."

"I believe that as well. But it doesn't matter
what we believe. He has to see it in himself before he can embrace a new way of being."

"Well said, my girl. How did you become so
wise at such a young age?"

"I was only allowed to observe life as a child,
not to really live it. I have many theories about
the workings of the heart but no practical experience until now."

"I am sorry that your childhood was so regi-
mented and lonely."

"Never mind. I've found you and so many new
friends now. Though, it pains me to think that
my mother is angry with me. Her mind is closed
to anything she doesn't want to hear or see. She's
so rigid in her beliefs, and she won't bend an
inch. I've shamed her in front of the vicar, and I
don't know if she'll ever forgive me. What if she
cuts me out of her life like she did you?"

"I can't imagine it would come to that. Give her
time. She'll come round when you're married to
a rich, handsome nobleman. Especially when he
admits to loving you and becomes the most devoted spouse in history."

"I told him that I wouldn't accept a proposal
that wasn't offered from the heart."

"Good for you. Now, I have another portrait to show you upstairs." She led her to her private chambers and gestured to a large canvas hung on the wall. "This is your Aunt Dawn and Cousin Sophia."

"Oh!" Sandrine stared rapturously at the painting of the mother and daughter standing on a cliff top, their laughing faces framed by sparkling blue ocean. "They're so beautiful. I can't wait to meet them."

"I wrote to them about you yesterday. Soon they'll receive my letter and know that their family has been expanded. I'm so very grateful we found each other." Ruby hugged her close. "No one can tell you how to live your life, Sandrine. Not me, not your mother, not Lord Dane. You must listen to your inner voice, your own heart, and find your own way."

WHEN DANE AND Warburton joined up with the Thunderbolt Club again, the lads were still celebrating, but Kenwick had gone home to sleep it off.

Somersby passed Dane the brandy bottle. "What made you decide to get shackled, Dane? Other than Miss Oliver's curvaceous figure—er, sparkling personality?"

"It's Sandrine's story to tell." She still hadn't revealed her connection to Madam Avalon to the group.

"She's lucky to have you," Dudley said.

"How can you say that? I don't have a way to erase the misdeeds of my past."

"But you could make her future bright and shiny," said Somersby.

"If you're a duke and a married man, we may have to kick you out of the Thunderbolt Club," Dudley groused. "You'll be far too respectable for the likes of us."

"I'm still praying that I won't be duke. And Miss Oliver hasn't yet said she'll marry me."

"She hasn't?" Somersby marveled. "What's wrong with her?"

"She thinks I only offered for her because I was trying to save her from that pompous vicar's scorn."

"You weren't romantic enough," Warburton said. "Young ladies like pretty proposals and flowers and sparkling diamonds. What did you give her? An ultimatum, that's what."

"Sandrine doesn't set stock in all that clap-trap. At least, I don't think she does." Maybe she did? Was he going to have to visit a jeweler's shop before she'd accept the inevitable and marry him?

"What would impress a lady like Miss Oliver?" Dudley asked.

"Charitable works," Dane replied without hesitation.

"Well, aren't you hosting a charity ball in a few days?"

"You know what—I am!"

"Then, there you go," Dudley said. "Easy as anything. Host the best damned charity ball London's ever seen, raise a barrow-full of money for starving orphans and destitute widows and whatnot, and she'll be hopelessly devoted to you for the rest of your life."

"I donated a curricle to be auctioned off at the ball," Warburton said smugly.

"Didn't know you were so socially minded under that tough-as-nails exterior," said Somersby.

"I help my friends. What have you lot done for the ball?"

"We'll do our part," Dudley said.

"You can auction me off to the young ladies," Somersby said. "Twenty-five quid a carriage ride."

Dudley kicked his shin. "They wouldn't pay twenty-five pence. We'd have to pay them to get in a carriage with you."

"Ha-ha," Somersby said.

"I haven't wanted to worry you," Dane said, "but my brother was being blackmailed by someone. We've stopped the immediate threat, but the man behind it all is still out there, and he may attend the ball. I want you to be vigilant. Keep a watch on the crowd. Let me or Warburton know if you see anything out of place, even the smallest little thing."

"You can always count on us," Dudley said. "We'll tell Kenwick when he's sober."

Dane could always count on his friends. He hadn't even put it together, but Dudley was right, damn his eyes. The charity event was the way to Sandrine's good graces.

Chapter Twenty-Five

So-called innocent diversions such as balls are a perfect cover for immorality and sin.
                    —Mrs. Oliver's Rules for Young Ladies

When Dane sent his carriage to Mrs. Mc-Govern's to collect Sandrine, she brought Miss Hodwell with her as chaperone. She didn't trust herself to be alone in the same house with him and stick to her goal of winning his heart before demanding more kisses.

She needn't have worried because every waking moment of the past few days had been spent preparing for the ball. She'd had to have the pamphlet reprinted to list only legitimate charities, and that had been quite the expensive last-minute undertaking.

Miss Hodwell had thrown herself into ensuring that the refreshments served would be talked about by the *ton* for years to come. For his part, Dane was being remarkably well-behaved and had overseen everything from the placement of the decorations to a dress rehearsal by the staff and orchestra.

They were working so hard that they hadn't had a chance to speak two words to one another.

The morning of the ball dawned fine and fair. The ballroom at Rydell House had been transformed into the duchess's vision of fairyland. The cavernous room, lit by five windows bordered by fluted ionic pillars and three grand glass chandeliers, glittering and dazzling the eye, was garlanded with hothouse flowers and greenery dotted with silk butterflies. There was even a grotto with a burbling fountain where it seemed that at any moment a woodland creature or fairy sprite might appear.

The weather held all day, which meant that guests would be able to enjoy the lantern-lit gardens as well.

"Everything is perfect," Sandrine pronounced when there was only a half hour before the guests were scheduled to begin arriving.

"I have personally sampled every refreshment, and I'm confident the guests will leave satisfied and satiated," said Miss Hodwell.

"Your work on the new pamphlet was inspired, Sandrine," Dane said. "We can now be certain that the funds we raise tonight will go to worthy, and legitimate, causes. Cleveland will record all donations and winning bids as they occur. My two most imposing footmen will guard the cash box."

It wasn't lost on Sandrine that he said *my* as if he were already the duke. They would soon find out. Truth be told, Sandrine was hoping Piety had a boy. Dane becoming the duke would mean more objections to their union. She wasn't meant to be a duchess. Though, she couldn't help thinking that she might do a better job than Piety, with her sharp words for her maidservants and thirst for diamond tiaras.

The orchestra began tuning, and Sandrine's heart hummed along with it. Perhaps everything could work. If Dane wasn't the duke, and if he stopped blaming himself for his mother's death, forgave his brother for being cruel, and realized that he had the capacity to love. If she could convince him to love Squalton Manor as she did . . . everything truly would be perfect.

She had her head in the clouds, per usual. But on a night like tonight, in this twinkling fairyland, it felt like anything was possible. She smiled at Dane. "It's going to be a wonderful night."

"Have I told you that you look ravishing tonight?" he asked.

Francesca had lent her yet another gown, this one made from soft white silk that caressed her limbs when she walked. She wore a pearl pendant around her throat, and her hair was dressed in a simple knot.

He caught her hand and kissed her knuckles. The admiration in his eyes started a warm glow in her belly. She couldn't help reaching out to touch the dimple in his chin. He stroked his thumb over her lower lip.

Miss Hodwell pointedly cleared her throat, and they jumped apart. "The guests are arriving."

Sandrine was surprised when Sir Somersby and Lord Dudley were the first to arrive. "I didn't expect to see you here so early, gentlemen. Aren't you usually doing rakish things this time of the evening?"

"I'm here for Miss Rowland, the famous soprano," Somersby said. "She's a pretty thing to dangle on my arm or sport in my curricle."

"The only thing dangling on your arm is going to be your walking cane when her protector, the Earl of Whitworth, shatters your kneecaps."

"My friends are here to help," Dane explained. "We still don't know who hired the blackmailers, and they'll keep a watch on the guests and tell me if they spy anything out of the ordinary."

A shiver traveled the length of Sandrine's spine. "I hope nothing happens to spoil the evening."

The first guests began to arrive, and Sandrine went to her post by the stage to make sure Miss Rowland wanted for nothing.

The room soon filled with well-dressed patrons eager to see and be seen. At least they were opening their purses. Sandrine watched as Cleveland recorded donation after donation.

"Sandrine, you're a vision," Francesca said, coming to join her near the stage.

"Thank you for lending me your ball gown."

"I did want you to wear the gold brocade."

"I would have felt too ostentatious. This simple white gown suits me."

"I agree, now that I see you in the room. These riotous decorations make you appear to be a glowing oasis of simplicity and taste."

"Your hair is amazing this evening. Is that a new wig?" Francesca loved to wear wigs of her own creation in pastel shades of pink and lavender, like the ones she'd made for them to wear to the Silver Palace. This one was pale pink and strewn with yellow silk butterflies.

"Do you like it?" she asked, patting the elaborate curls at her temple.

"It's simply stunning. And so are you, my dear friend." Sandrine hugged her. "I can't thank you enough for everything you've done for me while I've been here."

"You're speaking as if you're leaving on schedule. What are you going to do about that engagement Lord Dane announced?"

"I'm not sure yet. Francesca, I think he loves me."

"Of course he loves you. Everyone does."

"I mean I think that I could very well win his heart. The problem is that I've so thoroughly lost my heart to him that I don't know whether it's only my foolish optimism that tells me he feels the same."

"What happened to spurning him after he agrees to give you the manor house?" Roslyn asked, joining them. "What happened to making him grovel?"

"Sandrine's gone and fallen in love with him," Francesca said.

"Love's for the birds," Roslyn said. "I'll never catch that particular disease."

Marta sashayed over in a green satin gown that hugged every inch of her curves. "Ladies, what are we discussing?"

"Love and other diseases of the heart. I want a cheroot. Think I'll visit the gardens," Roslyn said, leaving abruptly.

"What's wrong with her?" Sandrine asked. "Oh, I remember my mother said something about a vicious rumor about Roslyn. Is it that? I forgot about it in the flurry of preparing for the ball."

A group of ladies stopped chattering to watch Roslyn walk by, then they all started whispering and gesticulating.

"It's not a rumor," Marta said. "She's with child."

"Oh no. I'll go and speak to her." But then the orchestra started playing, and Miss Rowland called for her.

"It's time to begin, is it not?" the soprano asked. She was a handsome woman with an ample bosom that Somersby couldn't stop staring at.

"It's time."

The crowd quieted and moved to the stage as Miss Rowland began to sing "From Rosy Bowers" by Purcell. *"Teach me in soft, melodious songs to move, with tender passion, my heart's darling joy."*

Dane caught Sandrine's gaze from across the room where he stood next to Cleveland. There was a promise of tender passion in his eyes.

Roslyn still hadn't returned from the gardens. As soon as the dancing began, Sandrine went to find her.

She was sitting on a secluded bench, smoking a cheroot.

"Mind if join you?" Sandrine asked.

"Go back to your guests."

"I saw those ladies whispering about you. People can be so cruel."

"I don't care. Who needs them? I have plenty of friends."

"I hope you consider me to be your friend?"

"A simple girl from the seaside? Hardly."

"You don't mean that. You've been nothing but kind to me."

"That's ridiculous. I'm not anything so ordinary as kind."

"Marta says the rumor is true?"

"Don't worry your sweet little head about me. My parents want to hide me away at an establishment where, as the brochure puts it, *Ladies whose circumstances require a temporary retirement meet with every attention due to the delicacy of their situations.* I say, damn their eyes and burn it to the ground!"

"Who is the father?"

"Kenwick."

"And are you engaged?"

"Ha." Roslyn stubbed out her cheroot against the marble bench. "He's not the marrying kind. And neither am I. Are you shocked? You don't want to be my friend anymore, do you?"

"Of course I do. I love you, Roslyn."

"Don't be ridiculous. You've only known me for a fortnight."

"And yet I know you to be one of the bravest and most extraordinary people I've ever met. You're so brave and so tough, but even you need love."

"Save that speech for Lord Dane."

"You pretend to be gruff and disagreeable, but I know better. You're soft and vulnerable on the side. That's why you need friends like me and ancesca and Marta to defend you and love you, matter what."

"I don't need love."

"I understand." Sandrine took her hand. "But en if you don't need it, I'm giving it to you."

Roslyn sighed and stared off into the distance, inking her eyes.

"You're not crying, are you, Roslyn? I meant to leer you by coming out here."

"I'm not crying. I never cry." She blinked her es harder. "Maybe I do need love. Maybe I am fter than I pretend to be. But don't you go and ll anyone, Sandrine Oliver. I might be forced to rm you if you did."

"Your secret is safe with me."

HESE EVENTS MAKE me sick," Cleveland said eeringly. "Rotten nobility who would never lift finger to help a starving family on the street but ho eagerly buy tickets to an event where they n display themselves in their finery and their lse generosity."

"Are you drunk, man?" Dane asked Cleveland, ondering why he would express such an incenary sentiment to the man who was paying his lary.

"I'm not."

"Have you forgotten that I'm your employer?"

"How could I? I'm only a lowly hired servant. u lot never allow me to forget it."

The look of pure hatred on Cleveland's face pped Dane cold.

"It was you." Why hadn't he seen it befor‹
"You hired those men to blackmail my brother.

Cleveland made a derisive noise. "Don't t
ridiculous. I have no idea what you're talkir
about."

"You know everything of my brother's finance
You knew that he was skimming from the cha
ity funds."

"If you're looking for someone to blame, hav
you thought about the duchess? Her lavish e
penses always exceeded her allowance, and th
duke refused to give her more."

Dane hadn't even thought of that. Could Pie
truly be behind this?

"Ladies and gentlemen, may I have your atte
tion please." Kenwick had climbed onstage ar
had told the orchestra to stop playing. What w.
he doing? This wasn't part of the scheduled ente
tainment. Perhaps Sandrine had added somethir
at the last moment? Where was she, anyway? Dar
searched the room with growing unease.

"SANDRINE, ROSLYN," MARTA called, rushing acro
the garden. "There's a commotion in the ballroor
Lord Dane is asking for Sandrine."

"Perhaps he'll do that public groveling aft
all." Roslyn jumped up from the bench and he
out her hand to Sandrine. "Come on, then, y‹
simple country girl. Go and get your duke."

All three ladies entered the ballroom togeth
and were soon joined by Francesca, but it w
Kenwick, not Dane, who'd taken the stage ar
was calling for silence.

"There she is, ladies and gentlemen," he called. The crowd parted as the four ladies walked toward the stage.

"Kenwick, what are you doing?" Roslyn hissed. "Get off the stage, you inebriated lout."

"I'm not inebriated, not in the slightest. I've never been more sober."

"What is he doing?" Marta asked.

"Can't you see?" Sandrine squeezed Roslyn's hand which she still held. "He's going to ask Roslyn to be his bride."

"He wouldn't . . ." Roslyn said.

"Oh yes, he would," called Kenwick.

Roslyn glanced wildly back at the balcony doors, as if she planned to make a run for it, but Sandrine pressed her hand again. "You can do this," she whispered. "Remember what we talked about."

"Lady Roslyn Stockard, we may not always get along, and you hate me more often than not, but I think we could be happy together if you gave me a chance to prove myself to you."

Sandrine held her breath. She knew Roslyn loved Kenwick, and he was madly in love with her, it was plain to see. But sometimes love wasn't enough.

"Lady Roslyn, you swear like a sailor, ride astride, and never laugh at my jokes, but I swear to you that it's not a lady I want, it's—"

"Get off that stage, Kenwick. I'll agree to marry you if only to shut you up!"

The crowd tittered, and Sandrine heard several people whispering about hasty proposals for scandalous reasons.

"You will?" Kenwick's expression was s
stunned that Sandrine had to laugh.

"I will, you big fool." Were those fresh tear
glittering in Roslyn's eyes?

Kenwick let out a triumphant whoop an
leaped down from the stage, grabbing Roslyn
hand and pulling her through the crowded room

Sandrine and the Pink Ladies cheered, an
there was scattered clapping in the audience. Th
orchestra played a romantic air and the dancin
resumed.

"That was unexpected," Dane said, appearin
beside her.

"Wasn't it romantic?"

"Not particularly. But I suppose it had the de
sired result. Where have you been? I've bee
searching for you."

"I was in the gardens with Roslyn."

"Please stay where I can see you. I was begin
ning to be concerned."

"Still no inkling of who was behind the ex
tortion?"

"I accused Cleveland of it, and he pointed th
finger at Piety."

"Cleveland. You know, that makes sense. H
was the keeper of your brother's secrets. Wher
is he, by the way?"

"What do mean? He's recording the donations

"No, he's not."

Dane whirled around. "Where did he run off to?

"Dane," Sandrine said, her heart dropping
"Where's the lockbox with tonight's collecte
donations?"

They both stared at the empty table. Cleveland, the footmen, and the lockbox were nowhere to be seen.

Dane set off at a run, weaving through the crowd, and Sandrine followed close behind. They burst out of the ballroom and onto the drive, only to see Cleveland grabbing the reins of Warburton's donated curricle and setting off at a breakneck pace, the donation box on the seat beside him.

"He's making a run for it, Dane. We can't allow him to abscond with everyone's money! Think of all the charities that will suffer."

Sandrine raced to Dane's curricle and a startled groom assisted her into the passenger seat. "What are you waiting for? We must go after him and retrieve that money!"

Chapter Twenty-Six

A lady moves sedately, always maintaining a calm and decorous demeanor.
        —Mrs. Oliver's Rules for Young Ladies

Cleveland had a lead on them and had Warbu ton's finest horses, but Dane was the more expe horseman. "He's heading for the docks."

"He might have a ship at the ready. If he make it aboard, we'll lose him."

"I should have questioned him before now."

"He's been with your family for a long time."

"But I could tell he resented me. I thought was for the same reasons Piety did, that I wa the usurper and never meant to become involve in the affairs of the dukedom. But he hates a nobility."

"There! He's stopped by the river."

Dane brought his curricle to a halt and jumpe down to tie the reins to a tree. "Stay in the ca riage, Sandrine."

"I will not." She opened the door and di mounted. "Remember what happened last tim you said that?"

"Stay close behind me, then, and don't mal any sudden moves. He might have a firearm."

"Do we have a firearm?"

"No," Dane said grimly.

"Don't come any closer," Cleveland warned. "I ave a pistol."

"That answers that question. Now will you go ack to the carriage and wait for me?" Her face as brave and determined in the moonlight.

"I won't. We'll risk this together."

"I'm serious," Cleveland said. "One more step nd I'll fire."

"Are you waiting for a ship?" Dane asked.

"They'll be here any moment."

"Turn yourself in, Cleveland. I'll be lenient if ou return the donations."

"That money belongs to charity," Sandrine said.

"I've been siphoning money from the dukedom or decades now," Cleveland said. "This is the final nstallment I'm owed. You'll never see me again."

"I thought it was my brother who was misman-ging our fortune."

"Oh, it was him. He was crooked as they come. nventing charities and keeping donations for is selfish purposes."

"Then, it was you who hired those men."

"I saw a chance for enrichment, and I took it. ıst like every nobleman does, not caring who ıey harm, who they ruin. Your father was the ne who taught him the racket. Once I discov-ed what was happening, I was disgusted. I ould have reported them to the authorities, but ho would believe me? The word of a scarred eward over a peer of the realm? I never stood a ıance. I had to stand up for myself. Create my wn opportunities."

"Why don't you put down the pistol, Mr. Cleve land," said Sandrine softly. "I don't think you re ally want to take that money from those who s desperately need it, more than you do."

"And risk a hangman's noose?" He waved th pistol, and Dane stiffened. "No, I'll be on m way. I was planning to leave late at night whe you were asleep, but when you confronted me had to make a run for it."

"Will you deprive the poor and the defenseles I appeal to your better nature, Mr. Cleveland."

"I have no conscience, and neither does Lor Dane. You think that he would deliver th money to charity? He's just like his brothe All he cares about is wealth, power, beddin beautiful women, and lording it over the re of us."

"You're wrong. Lord Dane is nothing like h brother. He's a good man. May I tell you a stor Mr. Cleveland?" She didn't stop to give him chance to respond. "It's about a little boy, fiv years of age, whose mother died in childbirth. boy whose older brother hated him because he caused his mother's death. This older broth was cruel to the little boy who worshipped hir His mind became warped by grief, and by h tred. He didn't deserve his brother's hatred, an he doesn't deserve yours."

"And I'd like to tell you a story as well Dane said. "It's about a little girl who grew u in a small seaside village. She had a moth who lived her life in fear of everything. Sh ouldn't allow her daughter to have friends, r go swimming in the sea, or even leave the ouse, sometimes for weeks at a time. And so iat little girl found a doorway that led from er yard into the secret garden of an ancient ianor house. And she spent days alone in that ouse, befriending ghosts. She felt a bit like a host herself, disembodied, haunting her own fe. That little girl stands before you, a grown oman who's learned to stand up for herself. o make new friends, real ones this time, and love fiercely. For some reason, she says that ie loves me. She has a heart big enough to ve the world. And if that girl says that I can hange, I must believe her."

"Very touching, you two," Cleveland snarled. You think by talking and stalling you'll come p with a daring plan to steal back the money. r perhaps you informed the authorities and iey're on their way? I didn't think so. Here's my iip now."

A small vessel arrived offshore, and a rowboat as launched to collect Cleveland.

"The only chance I have of surprising him is hen he climbs into that rowboat," Dane whis- ered to Sandrine. "I'm going to lunge for him. Vhen I do, I want you to run behind that rock nd stay covered in case there's gunfire."

She nodded. "Don't get shot, Dane."

"I don't think Cleveland is a good hand with a rearm. I saw him hunting once, and he couldn't rike a pheasant to save his life."

"Let's hope you're right. I want that money, but it's not worth risking your life."

"I know what I'm doing."

The rowboat approached the shore, and Cleveland hoisted the box onto his shoulder, keeping the pistol trained on them. "No sudden moves either of you."

Luckily the man rowing didn't appear to be armed.

"One, two," Dane muttered. When Cleveland turned to clamber into the rowboat, Dane launched himself at his back, catching him around the waist and knocking the pistol from his hand.

The cashbox flew free and landed with a thud on the ground. Cleveland dove for it, but Sandrine was suddenly there, throwing herself atop the box.

"Get off, you daft woman!" Cleveland shouted, grabbing the leather handle of the box. Sandrine grabbed the other handle, and the two of them labored back and forth in a tug-of-war.

Dane punched Cleveland's nose and he staggered backward, falling into the water and dragging Sandrine with him.

"Let go of the box, Sandrine," Dane shouted, but it was too late. She entered the water with a splash and a scream. Dane had no choice but to dive in after her.

Dimly, Dane was aware that Cleveland had made it to the rowboat, and it was moving toward the ship, but all he cared about was rescuing Sandrine.

He caught her by the waist and hauled her above water. She coughed and sputtered, flinging one arm around his neck. Where was the other arm?

And then he saw it. She was still clutching the cashbox, thrashing her legs to remain above water as its heavy weight threatened to drag her down.

He caught the box in one arm and lifted Sandrine with the other, throwing her over his shoulder and, with a mighty effort, climbing up the muddy bank to dry land.

"We did it, Dane." Sandrine laughed and kissed him full on the lips. "We have the money."

"Sandrine, I told you to hide behind that rock."

"And I knew that if you attacked Cleveland, the donation box would be ready for the grabbing. We make such an excellent team, do we not?"

Dane wiped river water and mud from his eyes. "You're mad, you know that?" He clasped her close to his chest, so relieved that she hadn't been injured. "Your teeth are chattering."

"A-are you going to r-rip off my gown like in my dream?"

"I think I'll leave the bodice-ripping for later." He set the box in the curricle and then lifted Sandrine into the seat. He found a dry wool blanket in the curricle and wrapped it around her. "You need a hot bath and some brandy. Let's get you home."

WHEN THEY ARRIVED back, all the guests had departed, but Warburton and Miss Hodwell were waiting by the door.

"Oh, your lordship, we were that worried,"

Miss Hodwell said when Dane carried Sandrine into the house.

"Dudley and Somersby went after you, but I told them you'd be home soon enough," Warburton said. "I had faith in you."

"The funds raised are in the curricle," Dane told Warburton. "Though, the notes will be waterlogged. And Sandrine's had a soaking as well. I don't want her to catch cold."

"I'm all right. Put me down," Sandrine said. But it did feel lovely to be held in his arms, to be the subject of so much concern and care.

"Come along," Miss Hodwell said. "Carry her to her room, and we'll soon have her warm."

"I still can't believe you lunged for that box, Sandrine," Dane said much later when they'd both had hot baths and Miss Hodwell had retired for the evening. "What were you thinking? You could have been shot. Or your gown could have become tangled with the box and you could have been dragged down into the water and drowned."

"But I wasn't."

"Don't ever do something like that again."

"Says the man who races flimsy curricles."

They faced each other across the bed. He had that dangerous look in his eyes, the one that made her fine ideals about talking instead of kissing disappear.

"That's what rakes do, Sandrine."

"And this is what young ladies who are claiming their freedom do, Dane." She marched around the bed and tangled her arms around him.

Chapter Twenty-Seven

A young lady, newly wed, must submit to her husband in all things.
        —Mrs. Oliver's Rules for Young Ladies

was afraid you would drown." Dane crushed er against his chest and wrapped his arms round her small body.

"And I was afraid you'd be thrown from your urricle," she replied, kissing him hard, scratch- ing her nails down his back. "I want to punish ou for making me so afraid."

This was no gentle exploration. This was ur- ent and raw.

"Maybe we're both addicted to danger," he said. He was addicted to her.

The rules of racing were that if the road threw ou a curve, you leaned into it. And that's all he anted to do, lean into her, embrace her curves. uide her to the finish line.

This hunger was a pounding, driving force. He idn't care if it was wrong anymore. It was too rong to fight. Her kiss demanded an answer. Ie turned her around, to face the wall.

He undid the hooks at the back of her gown and ipped it down her shoulders. She stepped free. Ie molded the shape of her buttocks, pulling

her shift tightly around the curves. "You hav
a luscious bottom." He knelt and bit one chee
playfully, and she gasped. He reached around t
touch her sex, and she melted back into him.

He rubbed his erection against the soft curve
of her backside, and she moaned softly.

"I'm going to make you come now, Sandrine."

HE WOULDN'T ALLOW her to turn around. H
was so hard and huge behind her, holding he
with one strong arm across her chest and th
other between her thighs. Her legs felt like jell
She wanted to collapse, but he held her up; h
wouldn't let her escape.

His hand moved to her throat, covering it, mov
ing her head. She was trapped, held so tightl
Her small throat clasped in his large hand.

He lifted the hem of her shift, and his finger
trailed up her thigh and then caressed her, e
actly where she needed it.

"Yes," she moaned.

He stroked her sensitive folds and flicked
finger over her core. The hand around her nec
tightened just enough that she was aware of he
pulse. She was completely in his control.

She could allow herself to let go and float.

Delicious, unpredictable freedom.

She was glad he couldn't see her face. She mu
be grimacing, searching for that elusive pleasur
It was so close now.

He stopped touching her sex, and she whim
pered. "Don't stop."

She felt him fumble with his breeches and then his hard length slid between her thighs, rubbing against her.

His hand left her neck, and he gripped her hips, sliding her along the ridge of his arousal. She fell forward, bracing herself against the wall, and he moved faster, pressing her thighs together around him, moving between her legs but not entering her, each stroke bringing her closer to her peak.

She pressed her bottom back against him and clenched her thighs together.

"That's right. That's my good girl."

She flew into a shimmering climax as he moaned her name.

"Sandrine." He kissed her neck, his hand circling it again, tilting her head around to kiss her lips and slide his tongue inside her mouth.

He lifted her into his strong arms, never breaking the kiss as he laid her on the bed and covered her with his body.

She broke the kiss, gasping for breath. "I said I want to punish you, and I'm going to. On your back and remove your clothing," she ordered.

His eyebrows rose, but he followed her order and rolled onto his back, throwing his clothing off with lightning speed.

She had no idea what she was doing. She wasn't following a script, only instinct.

She climbed on top of him, spreading her thighs wide and settling with her knees on either side of his hips.

She wrapped her hand around his erection "I'm going to ride you, Dane."

HE LOVED THIS side of Sandrine. And he desper ately wanted to be ridden. That's why saying th next words destroyed him. "Think about this Sandrine. You can't go back from this."

"You said you could use a sheath to guard against unintended consequences."

"That's not what I'm talking about. Losing you virginity to me is irreversible."

"I don't think I'll be losing anything. This i about winning. I'm making an educated choice Don't shut me out, turn me away, or tell me wha I want or how you're going to make me feel a some point in the future. Show me how you'r going to make me feel right now. In this momen Give me pleasure. Open your heart to me."

He wanted to open his heart, to forget the con sequences. Her words were seductive, and sh was even more so. A woman coming into he power, commanding him to pleasure her be cause she'd chosen him.

"Damn you, Sandrine. Why don't you just giv up on me like everyone else?"

"Because you're worth it. You're the freedon I've chosen, and you're worth the risk. You're nc a mistake. You were put on this earth to love me to do good, to be a good man. And a consum mate lover."

Her conviction, her trust, made him want t believe that it could be true.

"You won't use me to mask your pain, and I'm
ot using you to rebel against my strict upbring-
ng. In the garden after the masked ball, it was
asier to pretend that it was someone else who
vas breaking the rules, but it's me here in this
ed, Dane. I choose to be here, not for some sor-
id secret tryst but for a glorious, dangerous,
hrilling ride."

If she said *ride* one more time, he was going to
ose all self-control.

"Isn't your motto *Ride fast, ride hard, ride far*?"

Christ. That settled it. "I'll be right back."

He threw a blanket around his hips and ran for
is bedchamber. He fumbled in the nightstand
nd found the paper package containing one
f his sheaths. He was back in a flash, cock still
ard and ready.

He fit the sheath over his cock and tied the silk
bbon.

He lifted her and placed her back on top of
im. "You set the pace, Sandrine. Find what
els good."

He fondled her breasts as she fit her cleft over
he head of his cock, biting her lip as she bore
own.

"Does it hurt?"

"A little."

"Go slow, then." She accepted him into her
ody another inch. "Good. That's it."

Another inch. And another.

She tilted her head forward, her hair tumbling
round his face as she braced her arms on either

side of him and began to move, slowly at first, gentle rocking that drove him wild.

He was deep inside her. It had stretched and hur to put him there, but now it was beginning to fee more than good. It was glorious and sweaty an divine.

"I'm going to ruin you, Dane," she said trium phantly. "Ruin you for any other woman, be cause no one else will look into your eyes an truly see you."

Their gazes locked. His body jerked beneat her, urging her on.

She ran her hands over his chest, undula ing her hips, listening to his moans and feelin powerful. "No one else will touch you like this She laid one hand over his heart. "Will love yo like this."

She bent forward and kissed his lips. That wa a good angle. She stayed there, kissing him, as h took control, cupping her bottom with his hug hands and guiding her.

"Fuck, Sandrine. It feels so good."

"You crave this, Dane," she whispered in his ea "You crave love. That five-year-old boy chasin after his brother. He wanted to be loved. I'm giv ing it to you so fully, so well, that you will neve have to look for it again, never have to deny your self again, never have to hide your heart again."

Seated deep inside her. Racing to the finish lin Their sweat mingling. Her hand over his heart a

he rode him, destroyed him, as she ruined him
or any other lover.

Staring into each other's eyes, tangled together.
"In this moment, in this bed, we can heal the
rift. The feud between our families, generations
of bitterness and enmity here tonight, you and I,
with our touch, our words, our bodies, we are a
symbol of love and healing," she said.

He'd never understood why people called it
lovemaking. The act of sex wasn't about love. It
was about the giving and receiving of gratifi-
cation. There was a goal in mind. A summit to
reach. It was exertion, and skill. He was good at
, and he was proud of that.

But this was different. Her soft touch, her husky
demands, her eloquent words, pierced his heart
in a thousand places.

She made him want to believe that he could
be something better, something more. She made
him feel strong and powerful in a new way.
Not physical prowess, not how long he could
last, how many times he could make her come,
though there was power and pride in that. No,
the strength was in letting go.

Letting go of the expectation that he would fail
her. That he would hurt her.

Believing that maybe they had a chance of making a life together. Coming together as equals.

She clutched his shoulders, fierce concentration
on her face as she rode him, her back arched, the
column of her neck exposed.

That cynical part of him started to whisper *Yes*,

she loves you while you're inside her, but what abou *later?* but he refused to listen.

He thrust up to meet her as she rode harde now, her breasts bouncing, jaw slack. He wa nearly there. Using his thumb, he stroked her cl toris. "Now, sweetheart. Now."

As her inner muscles clenched around his coc and she moaned above him, he stopped holdin back and pulled her hips down, thrusting insid her roughly, losing himself to the rush and run ble of pleasure.

She collapsed against his chest, and he hel her there, rocking her in his arms. Whisperin promises into her hair. That he wanted to ho her forever.

That she was made for him.

That he'd never let her go.

He pulled out and discarded the sheath, re turning quickly to hold her close again. She fe like redemption. She felt like peace.

She lifted her head. "As a young girl I was alway writing lists of unpredictable and thrilling occu rences, longing for adventure. And then it ha pened. You arrived in Squalton-on-Sea and I'v never been the same. You don't see yourself as giving person, but you have given me a gift. You'v shown me that I can be my own person and decic for myself who I want to be and who deserves m love. I know that deep down you care about me."

"I do, Sandrine. This is all new for me. I don have the words yet."

"That's all right. I can wait." She kissed h chin. "I love this dimple in your chin."

"And I love your breasts." He fondled them, filling his hands with her curves.

"Typical rake."

He chuckled. "What can I say? The first moment I met you I fell madly in love with the sight of you in that transparent shift."

"It's a start," she said with a smile. "You know it's simply not true that the world would be a better place without you in it. The way you threw yourself into organizing the charity ball showed me that you care about the same things that I do."

His plan had worked, then. The charity ball had been the key. Part of him realized that he'd enjoyed working so hard on a worthy goal. By the end he hadn't been pretending at all.

"Your reaction to being threatened in an alley by three men with knives was to go after them and turn the tables. Treat your fear of not being able to love in the same way. Face it. Chase after it. Learn its dark secrets. Have a conversation with it, invite it into your heart on your own terms. Find a way to live with it, instead of allowing it to stop you from living. You can choose a different path in your mind, in your life, Dane."

Perhaps he could. She made him want to try.

He held her against his chest, breathing in her scent of sun-warmed lavender.

Her contented smile lit a gentle, warm light inside him.

She'd taken up permanent residence inside his heart, and there was a stubborn little flame of hope that he couldn't extinguish, no matter how hard he tried.

He was cold when she wasn't nearby, and the thought of spending the rest of his life without her would be consigning himself to a barren wasteland.

He was weary of fighting it, weary of living in this prison of his own design.

"Sandrine?"

"Yes, Dane?" she murmured sleepily.

A distant, piercing shriek rent the air. And then another. Animal noises, a woman screaming and the sound of doors slamming, footsteps.

Dane sat up, bringing Sandrine with him. "Piety. She's giving birth."

"It sounds dreadful."

Another scream and the sound of sobbing. "She can't die like my mother did." Dane left the bed, searching for his clothing.

"We'll go to her, Dane. We'll be there for her."

Chapter Twenty-Eight

Lead a blameless life and you will never need to beg forgiveness.
         —Mrs. Oliver's Rules for Young Ladies

Is she going to live, Sneath?" Dane asked the harried-looking doctor outside of Piety's bed-chamber.

"She's perfectly healthy," the doctor replied.

"Thank God!"

"That's such good news, Doctor." Sandrine smiled. "We heard the screaming and feared the worst."

"It was a difficult delivery, but the duchess is strong, and a healthy child was delivered. The piercing screams you heard were uttered when her grace discovered that the babe was a girl."

Damn. He was the duke.

"May we visit her and meet the baby?" Sandrine asked.

"Only briefly."

They knocked on the door, and a maidservant answered. "Oh, your grace," she said, dropping a curtsy.

And so it began.

"Is that Lord Dane?" Piety called. "Come to gloat, have you?"

Dane and Sandrine entered the room. "Not at all," Dane said. "We were concerned about you."

"It's a girl," she said bitterly. "I failed. I don't want it."

"You don't mean that," Sandrine said. "Oh there she is." The nursemaid held the red-faced babe near Sandrine as she cooed and fussed.

"You didn't fail, Piety," Dane said. "She's a healthy, beautiful baby girl."

"She'll never be a duke."

"I wish that weren't the way of the world. She'd probably make a more fitting duke than I will."

Sandrine lifted her head. "Don't say that, Dane because it's not even remotely true."

She turned to Piety. "The ball was a success Everyone loved your decorations."

Piety collapsed back against the pillows "You're going to cast me out without a penny."

"I've already told you that you have nothing to worry about. There may need to be a few economies."

"*Economies?* The very word makes me shudder."

"So I gather from reading the account books. I was Cleveland, Piety. He was blackmailing Roman. That's why you said what you did on his deathbed. You told him that he couldn't die without telling you who was to blame and what you should do. Cleveland is gone for good, and the blackmailers have been dealt with. It's all been resolved. You don't need to worry anymore We'll speak of this more when you have your strength back."

"And no one knows what Roman was doing?"

"No one will ever know. We'll replace the funds. I swear to you, Piety, I swear on Roman's grave that I will provide for you and your family, and I will strive to be a good and fair duke."

"Humph. I'll believe that when I see it."

"Look at her. She's absolutely gorgeous," Sandrine said, still gazing at the babe. "She's going to be a great beauty, like you."

"Do you think so?" Piety asked, her voice trembling.

"I'm certain of it."

"Perhaps I could hold her . . ."

The nursemaid brought her the babe, and Piety gingerly accepted the small bundle. "What shall I call you, then? I was going to name you Roman, of course, but that won't do anymore."

"How about Rowena?" Sandrine suggested.

"Hmm. Are you a Rowena?"

"We'll leave you to have your rest now, Piety." Dane took Sandrine's hand as they left the room.

"I'm proud of you, Dane. You handled that very well."

"Maybe she'll come round yet."

"We can only hope. And perhaps my mother, with time, will also be able to forgive me."

"Sandrine." Dane stopped walking. "I'm the bloody damned Duke of Rydell."

She giggled. "May you damned well rot in hell."

"Insolent girl!"

"Damned duke!"

It was too late, or too early, to go to bed. Morning had already broken, and the household staff was preparing for the day ahead.

"In which room did your brother die?" Sandrine asked.

He glanced at her. "This one." He gestured to the door in front of them. She opened it and walked inside, looking back over her shoulder. "Maybe it's time you told him a few truths."

"He's gone."

"Humor me."

He could do that. She'd just given him the best night of his life, after all.

Dane stared at the bed, seeing the ghost of his brother. "He lay in this bed all pale and mute. He didn't even look like my brother."

"Pretend you're introducing me to him."

"Roman, this is Miss Sandrine Oliver, my fiancée. Sandrine, this is my brother, Roman, the Duke of Rydell."

"Very pleased to meet you, your grace." Sandrine curtsied. "It's going to be a beautiful day today. The sun will shine so brightly that every leaf on the oak tree outside your window will look like it's been dipped in gold."

Dane cleared his throat. "This is silly, Sandrine."

"It's not. I think it's necessary. Will you do this for me?"

"We've had a long night and no sleep to speak of. Which was entirely your fault, I'll have you know."

"Tell your brother how you felt about him."

"I can't. He's dead."

"You've kept yourself so tightly closed away from pain. You told me that to love someone is to give them the power to hurt you. I've given you that power over me, Dane. I know you could hurt me. I'm willing to take that risk because love is worth it. Breaking free of the patterns that drag us down, the people that seek to keep us down, is worth it. You can't ever hide your fear deep enough or outrun it. It will always be there. It's a part of you, but if you keep trying to outrun it, you allow it to rule you. Face your brother, face your dark memories, one last time." She moved to stand beside him. "You can do this."

Dane stared at the empty bed. "Roman, Sandrine says I need to face you, to forgive you. And forgive myself. But I don't think I can. You did your job too well. You made me hate myself. I know it's because you loved our mother so much and you missed her dreadfully. It was a hatred born from love, wrought by the pain of loss. And that's the most vicious kind, I think."

Sandrine lifted his hand to her lips and kissed his knuckles. "Go on," she whispered.

Her touch calmed him. Gave him the strength to continue.

"Our mother's death wasn't my fault, Roman. I wish I could have known her as you did. I wish I had the memories, however painful. I've always envied you for having those ten years with her. I loved you, Roman. I worshipped you."

He closed his eyes. "I don't think I can do this. I'm talking to a pillow. And if I had ever said such words to him, he would have laughed in my face."

"You're doing so well." The approval in her eyes wrapped him in warmth.

"Roman." He clenched his jaw. Released it. Sandrine squeezed his hand tightly until he could feel her fingernails digging into his palm. "I . . . loved you."

Christ. Tears behind his eyes, demanding to be shed. He hadn't cried since he was a boy. He wasn't going to do it now.

Too late. A tear escaped his tightly clenched eyes and fell on the bed. Sandrine squeezed his hand even tighter, and when he looked at her, she was crying.

Damn it. Another tear fell. "I forgive you, Roman," he blurted out, needing to be done with this.

Sandrine nestled into his arms, and he buried his face in her neck and held on to her, allowing the emotion to come for the first time since he was a boy.

"I need a brandy," he finally said.

"I think I need one, too," she replied.

Dane informed the maid that they were not to be disturbed. He didn't care who knew he and Sandrine were sharing a room. All he knew was that he would sleep next to her for the rest of his life.

They had their brandy, and then they fell asleep together.

When he awoke, Dane was momentarily disoriented. Then he remembered what had happened. All of it. Chasing after Cleveland. Thinking that Sandrine might die. A night of unparalleled passion, followed by becoming the duke.

Forgiving Roman.

He kissed Sandrine on the lips. She stirred, and her eyes fluttered open.

"I can't believe you love me, Sandrine. What did I do to deserve this?"

"You gave me carnal cravings, listened to all my stories, led me far, far away from the path of righteousness, and now you're going to renovate Squalton Manor."

"I am, am I?"

"In grand fashion. Lucidora and Coraline will be so happy to have their home restored."

"Brazen minx."

"Oh yes. I'm insatiable now. Where were we on the wicked list . . . ? I think you said something about taking me, facedown, from behind?"

"Christ, did I really say that?"

"You thoroughly corrupted me, Dane."

"And I'll keep corrupting you, over and over again. Now drape yourself over that sofa, head down, bottom up," he growled.

Desire, swift and bright, flared in her body as she obeyed his command.

She laid her head on the sofa cushion. He slid her nightgown up, pushing it over her waist. "You deserve a spanking, young lady."

"What for?"

"For asking me to corrupt you."

"That doesn't make any sense."

"Then, you deserve a spanking for contradicting me, young lady." He smacked her bum, and she gasped. "That will teach you," he said sternly. He smacked her again, playfully, the smart of his palm on her naked bottom bringing heat to that area and warmth and wetness between her thighs.

"I don't think I learned my lesson."

He smacked her a little harder. "That's for telling me about the dream where I sprouted horns and cloven hooves and defiled you. Come to think of it, I think *you* might have corrupted *me*."

She giggled. He smacked her again.

"Spread your legs," he growled.

She waited, breathless and aching with need as he shed his robe. He rubbed his erection against her backside and slid it between her thighs. The friction felt so good, she wanted more.

She pushed back against him, matching his strokes.

"Please," she begged.

"Yes?"

"I want you . . ."

"Is this what you want?" He rocked against her, sliding between her thighs.

"Yes."

"Yes, what?"

"Yes, please."

"Sandrine. God, I want you."

"Then, have me. I'm yours, Dane." The words were heartfelt, and they were true.

She was his, now and forever.

Afterward, as they lay panting and breathless, Dane lifted her chin and stared soulfully into her eyes. "Are you going to marry me? And don't say I'm only asking you to marry me because I'm in a hazy state of postcoital bliss. I know what I'm doing."

"I'll think about it."

"What's that supposed to mean? There's nothing to think about. We consummated our love, and you're marrying me."

"Don't be such an arrogant damned duke."

"And don't be so stubborn. It's the only course of action."

"The Pink Ladies helped me devise a campaign to disarm you, flirt with you, and make you fall madly in love with me so that you would grant the leasehold to the historical society. And after you'd signed it over, I was supposed to spurn you publicly. Show you how it felt to be the humiliated one."

"And is that what you're going to do?"

"The plan has changed. I'm the one who's fallen madly in love with you, but that doesn't mean that I'm not still making my own choices, following my own path."

He still hadn't told her he loved her, and she'd given him so many opportunities to do so. She still hadn't brought him to his knees. He hadn't groveled yet.

The campaign wasn't over.

Chapter Twenty-Nine

The sight of young ladies riding horses gives gentlemen licentious ideas.
  —Mrs. Oliver's Rules for Young Ladies

And then he asked me to marry him. Again," Sandrine said.

Marta sighed dreamily. "And you said, 'Of course I'll marry you and become your duchess, you big handsome brute!'"

"I said I'd think about it."

"You didn't," Francesca said with a giggle.

"I did. Because you know what? He hasn't groveled sufficiently yet."

"Well, my goodness, Miss Pristine Sandrine has outpinked us, ladies. She refused a duke's proposal," Roslyn drawled.

"The first evening you spent here, Sandrine, we talked about a make-a-rake-grovel gown." Francesca's eyes lit up. "I went the very next day to my modiste and gave her an order with your measurements. It's finally ready."

"Let have a look, then," Marta said.

Francesca left the room and returned with a black riding habit made from buttery soft leather. The ladies helped Sandrine into the habit, which was no small feat given how tightly it fit.

"Ooh," breathed Marta. "It's perfect."

Sandrine spun in front of the looking glass. It's extremely close about the bodice. I may not be able to breathe."

"But you're definitely going to make a rake grovel," Francesca said.

"You're brilliant, Francesca," said Roslyn. "A riding habit is far more superior than a gown. It will put him in a mood to ride."

Sandrine knew precisely what she meant by that. And she heartily approved.

The skirts were long with a train, to cover her legs as she rode sidesaddle, and there was a loop inside that she could grasp to hold them up as she walked.

"You do know how to sit on a horse?" Francesca asked. "I forgot to ask you before I ordered the habit."

"I don't. My mother said it gives gentlemen licentious ideas."

"Exactly!" Marta cried.

"You should practice in the habit," Francesca said. "We wouldn't want you falling off your horse."

"I'll lend you my curricle," Roslyn said. "I think that will be easier than teaching you how to ride."

"Let's rehearse what you'll do when you approach Lord Dane," Roslyn said. "I think you should be holding a cheroot. It will give you an air of daring and sophistication."

"And you should wear my heeled red leather calf boots," Francesca said. "They'll look perfect with the habit."

Marta sighed happily. "He doesn't stand
chance!"

DANE WAS OILING the fittings on his curricle in
the yard when a commotion sounded nearby.

"Women," shouted Somersby, running toward
him. "Women at the gate!"

Dane and Kenwick exchanged amused glances.

"Well, go and see what they want," Dane said.

"They want to join the Thunderbolt Club."

"I did say we'd allow ladies if they possessed
suitable equipages and were excellent horse
women," said Dane.

"Come and judge for yourself," Dudley said
with a wide grin.

Dane and Kenwick followed Dudley and Somersby into the club.

"Roslyn, what are you doing here?" Kenwick
asked. "It's gents only."

"I don't see any gentlemen, do you? I see rakes,
rogues, and rapscallions."

"Who are you calling a rapscallion?" Somersby
wanted to know.

"You're right. You're more of a reptile, Somersby."

Dudley guffawed.

"Roslyn, you have to leave. That's an order from
your future husband."

"I don't take orders. You should know that by
now. And I brought reinforcements." She pulled
several bottles of brandy out of her cloak. "And
pretty women. Come in, ladies."

Francesca and Marta waltzed into the room followed by . . . followed by a vision in tight black
leather.

"Sandrine?" Dane's jaw dropped. The black riding habit she wore lovingly hugged her curves,
leaving nothing to the imagination. Her hair was
a halo of sunshiny curls.

"That's my name," she said in a husky, seductive voice. She threw down the cheroot she held
and ground it under heeled red leather boots.

Chills chased up and down Dane's spine. He
dropped to both knees before her, filled with an
uncontrollable urge to grovel. "Marry me, Sandrine."

"What was that? I didn't hear you."

"Miss Sandrine Oliver, I don't deserve you, but
I'll die if you don't marry me."

"I'll think about," she said, spinning around
and sashaying out the door.

His friends hooted and laughed as Dane rose
and ran after her. "Sandrine, wait."

He caught up with her beside a spirited horse
in a red leather harness. "Let me try that again."

"Well? I don't have all day." There was laughter in her blue eyes, but Dane was determined to
truly win her heart this time.

"Sandrine Oliver, you make me want to listen,
to be still, to wake with the sun of your smile, and
plunge into the sea of your eyes, get lost there, be
happy. Be content." He brushed his thumb over
the curve of her lower lip. "I've always had darkness in my mind, blame and shame. I thought I

wasn't worthy of happiness, but now I want t
prove myself worthy of you every single day fo
the rest of my life."

"You already have, Dane. I hope you see that."

"Those men at the Squalton Squire on my firs
day at the seashore said that you thought yo
could melt my cold, cold heart. And they wer
right." He clasped both her hands in his an
brought them to his chest. "Can you feel it bea
ing wildly?"

She nodded, her eyes shimmering with tears.

"I love you, Sandrine. I've loved you since th
moment I hauled you out of the sea. You weren
drowning, but I was. Drowning in dark thought
in perilous living. You rescued me on that beac
You showed me the man I wanted to be. Yo
saved me, sweet Sandrine."

"I love you, Dane." She lifted onto her toes an
kissed him, pressing those breathtaking, leathe
encased curves against him and causing quite
stir. "How could I not fall in love with you?" sh
asked when he allowed her a moment to breath
"You're the most unpredictable and thrillin
thing that ever happened to me."

"Is this your curricle?" he asked, eyeing th
elegant chariot with red-painted wheels tha
matched her boots.

"Roslyn lent it to me."

"How fast does it go?"

She traced the line of his jaw with one fir
ger, her gaze hungry for more kisses. "Shall w
find out?"

He lifted her by the waist and set her on th

arriage seat. Then he climbed in beside her nd took the reins. "This might be slightly dan- erous."

"I certainly hope so," she replied with a smile hat was pure seduction, both innocent and vicked, and sent his heartbeat racing. "And it's nly the beginning, Dane."

Epilogue

"Shh. Dane, did you hear that?"

"I didn't hear anything."

"A faint thumping sound. It's Lucidora an[d] Coraline. Listen. You can hear them walking o[n] the floorboards above us."

The workmen had gone for the day. The ren[ov]ovation of Squalton Manor was proceedin[g] apace.

Ruby had painted delightful portraits of th[e] ghostly sisters to hang in the entrance hall. Sar[n]drine's mother still wasn't speaking to her, bu[t] they'd both attended the wedding, seated on op[p]posite sides of the chapel, which had been a sma[ll] step toward reconciliation. Sandrine hoped tha[t] with time her mother might learn to forgive, an[d] they could all be one happy family.

Roslyn wasn't with child. It had been a fals[e] alarm. She and Kenwick had married, whic[h] hadn't stopped them from arguing like cat[s] and dogs.

Marta had collected several new beaux, an[d] Francesca had decided she loved creating wig[s] for fancy masquerade balls and was doing [a] brisk business.

Warburton had moved to the countrysid[e,] claiming he was tired of London life, but Dan[e] suspected he was tired of people staring at his scars. And Dudley and Somersby, well, they were probably up to no good, racing carriages, swigging brandy, and trading insults.

Dane and Sandrine split their time between London and Squalton and planned to accompany Ruby abroad to visit Sandrine's aunt and cousin. Mrs. McGovern and Miss Hodwell were back in Squalton and very involved with the restoration of the manor house.

Dane rolled over and pinned Sandrine's arms above her head, pressing her into the mattress. "Do you hear that, Sandrine? A great thumping, coming from the master bedroom!"

He pounded the headboard against the wall.

She giggled, and then she moaned, because he transferred both of her wrists to one hand and used his other hand to push her nightgown over her hips.

"Ghostly moaning," he said in an eerie voice. She couldn't laugh because she was too busy writhing beneath his talented fingers.

When they were exhausted and twined together, breathing heavily, Sandrine lifted her head and kissed the dimple in the middle of his chin. "Dane?"

"Yes, my love?"

"You don't really believe in ghosts, do you?"

"No, my love."

"Lucidora didn't think so."

"Sandrine. Seriously?"

"She told me that you were a skeptic, and cynical and arrogant to boot. I told her that you had your

good qualities, at which she sniffed and faded
into the air and became a shimmering mist."

Dane hugged her closer. "You have real friends
now, Sandrine. You don't need Lucidora."

"But she needs me. She's very excited about the
historical pamphlet detailing their lives, and she
and Coraline are planning to inhabit their portraits and use the eyes to follow visitors about the
room and give them a delicious thrill."

"You're all the thrill I need, Sandrine Oliver."
Dane had stopped racing flimsy curricles around
hairpin bends, although he did sometimes ride
Gladiator fast and furiously along the beach.
"And you're delicious too. Sweet as honey on my
tongue."

"Show me what you mean," she said breathily.
And he obliged.

THEY SAY THAT on a moonless night you can
see shimmering apparitions in the windows of
Squalton Manor. Hear strange thumpings, rus-
tlings, and moanings over the sound of the surf
pounding the shore below.

It could be the ghosts of Lucidora and Coraline
Oliver, two beautiful sisters who never married
and perished in a tragic fire.

Or it could be the lord and lady of the manor
ripping off each other's clothing and testing out
each one of the fourteen bedchambers in turn.

Acknowledgments

All my gratitude to my wonderful agent, Alexandra Machinist, and to my fantastic editors, Carrie Feron and Asanté Simons. I would never finish books without the love and support of my partner, family, and friends. Big thanks to Rachel, Neile, Esme, Charis, Zoe, Janna, KL, and Choul for the inspiration, critiques, and writing sprints. Thank you to the readers, reviewers, librarians, and booksellers who champion the romance genre. A special thank you to the members of the Backlist Book Club for all the laughs, story ideas, and friendship. Hope we can meet in person soon! I hope you enjoy this lighthearted homage to one of my favorite musicals, *Grease*!

Read more by
Lenora Bell

Wallflowers vs. Rogues

School for Dukes Series

The Disgraceful Dukes

You're the

DUKE

That I Want

For Brian. I'm hopelessly devoted to you.

You're the

DUKE

That I Want

The Thunderbolt Club

LENORA
BELL

AVON

An Imprint of HarperCollinsPublishers

YOU'RE THE DUKE THAT I WANT. Copyright © 2023 by Lenora Bell. All rights reserved. Printed in the United States of America. No part of this book may be used or reproduced in any manner whatsoever without written permission except in the case of brief quotations embodied in critical articles and reviews. For information, address HarperCollins Publishers, 195 Broadway, New York, NY 10007.

First Avon Books mass market printing: December 2023

Print Edition ISBN: 978-0-06-331688-1
Digital Edition ISBN: 978-0-06-331689-8

Cover design by Amy Halperin
Cover art by Paul Stinson
Cover image © LilKar/Shutterstock (flowers)

Avon, Avon & logo, and Avon Books & logo are registered trademarks of HarperCollins Publishers in the United States of America and other countries.

HarperCollins is a registered trademark of HarperCollins Publishers in the United States of America and other countries.

FIRST EDITION

23 24 25 26 27 BVGM 10 9 8 7 6 5 4 3 2 1